loud
awake
and
lost

loud awake

and lost

ADELE GRIFFIN

Alfred A. Knopf
NEW YORK

THIS IS A BORZOI BOOK PUBLISHED BY ALFRED A. KNOPF

All rights reserved. Published in the United States by Alfred A. Knopf,
an imprint of Random House Children's Books, a division of Random House LLC,
a Penguin Random House Company, New York.
Knopf, Borzoi Books, and the colophon are registered trademarks of Random House LLC.

Visit us on the Web! randomhouse.com/teens
Educators and librarians, for a variety of teaching tools, visit us at RHTeachersLibrarians.com

Library of Congress Cataloging-in-Publication Data
Griffin, Adele.
Loud awake and lost / Adele Griffin. — First edition.
p. cm.
Summary: Eight months after a debilitating car accident leaves her with brain trauma and a back injury, amnesiac teen Ember tries to piece together the six weeks of her life leading up to the accident—and determine why none of her friends or family are willing to talk about it.
ISBN 978-0-385-75272-5 (trade) — ISBN 978-0-385-75273-2 (lib. bdg.) —
ISBN 978-0-385-75274-9 (ebook) — ISBN 978-0-385-75275-6 (tr. pbk.)
[1. Memory—Fiction. 2. Amnesia—Fiction. 3. Love—Fiction. 4. Traffic accidents—Fiction.
5. Brooklyn (New York, N.Y.)—Fiction.] I. Title.
PZ7.G881325Lo 2013
[Fic]—dc23 2012049042

The text of this book is set in 11-point Goudy.

Printed in the United States of America

November 2013
10 9 8 7 6 5 4 3 2 1
First Edition

for Courtney Sheinmel

In pitch dark I go walking in your landscape.
—Radiohead

1

The Time of Your Life

I got back from lunch to find they'd cleaned out my room. They'd even taken my nameplate off the door. According to Addington Hospital, EMBER LEFERRIER had already left the building.

And I would be on my way, in just a few minutes. Strange that I'd slept in this narrow metal bed for eight months. Looking around, I could already feel my time here losing shape. I'd never felt real at Addington. I'd never been me here. I'd been a restoration project, and now I was done.

Earlier this morning, I'd jammed eight months into two brown cardboard boxes that were now in the lobby, ready to load into my parents' car. I'd rechecked under the bed, in the cupboard, inside each desk drawer.

Yep. I was finished. I was gone.

Maybe I needed a final gesture. A secret note for the next broken person. Should I use a file to scrape my initials *E.G.L.* into the windowsill? Or I could carve out some vintage Green Day: "I hope you had the time of your life."

Or . . . was that just mean?

Skip it. Mean was the last thing I felt.

Fragile. Freezing. Lonely. I felt crudely refashioned, like a Frankenstein monster. Barely on this earth, like a ghost.

2

You're Always Embie

But the terror didn't hit me until I buckled in. My parents had driven up in their new Prius—a different car, of course, from the family Volvo that I'd totaled. They'd leased it some months ago, but I'd never seen it.

Now they were taking me home in it.

On the hospital's front steps, I hugged Summer and Gab, my two favorite nurses. Even Dr. P had braved the cloudless glare of October sunlight. He fit his arm around my shoulders—"okay, and you've got my email, my cell"—shook hands with Dad, and kissed my mother on the cheek.

Then he whispered something in Mom's ear, something kind and supportive, probably. I couldn't hear what, but I saw her eyes fill. I wanted to do something, too. Squeeze her hand, tell her I was okay. But it felt more important to be still, to show calm. I'd had so many meltdowns, there had been so many tears. If I could stay on the verge, then I wouldn't tip over.

And now we were off.

It might have been my father's harmonizing to the radio. Or my mom's twist-arounds to check that all of my needs had been met.

"Are you cold, honey? Or maybe it's stuffy, a teeny bit hot in here? Would you like some water? Hang on, I have a bottle." Mom always had deep concerns about hydration.

Or it could have been that final turn out of Addington's harp-shaped iron gates.

Whatever it was, being confronted with the fact that right now, the thing I'd wanted most for eight months was actually happening, I felt the fear begin to take hold of me. I wasn't ready. I'd been put in a dunk tank, only instead of water, I'd plunged into a bottomless panic. I bit the insides of my cheeks. What was scaring me? This didn't make sense. There were no surprises where I was going. Just nice, boring home with my nice, boring parents and my nice, boring life before the accident.

The accident, the recovery. What had happened in February sometimes sounded like another person's dream, endlessly retold to me. Even yesterday, Dr. Pipini was still warning me about case studies where brain-trauma victims are forever attacked by headaches and auras or episodes of vertigo. That we're susceptible to night sweats, tremors, and ringing in the ears. Sometimes we regain memory—a smidgen, or about half, or sometimes even all of it.

But sometimes everything is lost.

Studies had proved so much. In fact, every single thing I'd experienced in connection with my accident seemed to have another person's case study already stapled to it. Dr. P said I was lucky to have lost only six weeks of memory before the night of February 14th. According to Dr. P, this wasn't a lot.

Studies had proved the normalcy of my ordeal.

As the car E-ZPassed over the Verrazano Narrows Bridge and then hooked up with the Brooklyn-Queens Expressway to Atlantic Avenue, I breathed through the kink in my stomach. For weeks, the urge to get back to Brooklyn had been strong as a riptide inside me. So why did every mile that went by between me and Addington increase my desire to return to the safety of the hospital?

I felt light-headed, empty-handed. Like I'd forgotten to pack things. Big things. Things I needed. No, no, no, I wasn't ready, I wasn't complete, I couldn't face down the real world.

Because Addington hadn't been the real world. It had been a space to rebuild myself from parts. To practice being human again.

Dad drove impossibly slowly and smoothly, as if the car were filled with crates of eggs and bowls of goldfish. Onto Atlantic, left on Hicks, and another left.

Same thin brownstone. Same balding olive carpet, same rummage of catalogs and flyers on the front hall table. My parents were a tag team of worry.

"Ember, why don't you leave your suitcase for us to take up with the boxes?"

"Some tea, sweetie? You look tired."

"No, I can handle it. I'm not thirsty. I feel fine."

I left them downstairs. Would it always be like this? Then

again, it had always been something like this. Mom was a math professor and Dad up till his retirement last year had taught music, and their personalities played out along those roles. Right down to my mother's logical list-making and Dad's inability to exist in a room without layering a harmony into it. But when it came to me, my parents wore their worry in a matched set. Batting at me like catnip with the nervous paws of their excess fears.

On the landing, I felt faint. I caught the railing and my breath. I waited a moment, gathering myself, before I opened the door into my past. Hello, bedroom of slanted pine floors and wild-flower wallpaper. Hello, faded friendship quilt. Hello, braided rug, ballet bar; hello, farmhouse door that Dad refinished three years ago, the summer I turned fourteen. All that July, I'd watched him sand and finish it, then paint it my specially-picked-at-Sherwin-Williams color, periwinkle, and mount it on blocks for me to use as a desk.

The room had that same walnut-gingerbread smell, but it was also musty and unused—despite the ferny bloom of marigolds Mom had placed on my windowsill. Almost everything in this room was as natural as my own voice.

Almost.

The back of my neck prickled hotly. My room wasn't quite as I'd left it. Something was wrong here. Something was off.

Deep breath. I was just in shock to be home.

And maybe I was overreacting to tiny things, like these fancy arty pens, fanned out in the lopsided glazed pot I'd made in fourth grade. When had I bought them? Slowly, I picked up a silver pen, popped its cap, sniffed the ink, and then marked my hand with a funny-looking sideways A.

Huh, why had I done that? So automatic, almost thoughtless.

Now I was teetering on the verge of being on the edge; I went as still as the room as my eyes roved around for the next oddity. What was this, wedged in the upper corner of my door mirror? A ticket stub for a movie I'd never seen. I darted to it. I didn't remember anything about that movie—the title was in German, I couldn't even pronounce it.

And here, what was this? A black business card for a dance club called Areacode out in Bushwick. Areacode? I must have gone to that club, right? And it had been memorable enough that I had a souvenir.

The poster tacked to my wall corkboard startled me most.

Whoa, how had I not seen that, first thing? When'd I put that up? I didn't know any group called Weregirl. I stared. Against a rusted sunburst posed three guys and one girl, all dressed in old-fashioned military jackets.

My heart was pounding. But I hadn't heard this band's music. I hadn't tacked up this poster. Or bought those. Or seen that. Okay, okay, *calm down*. This must have happened inside the memory sinkhole. The missing weeks. Dr. P and I had shared multiple discussions about this.

Weregirl: The Reconnaissance Tour

It was lettered in retro-typewriter ink along the bottom of the poster, with a list of dates from last winter. WEST TWENTY-FIRST AND SURF AVENUE was circled in blue, for a March 12th concert. Of course, I'd never made it to the show. By March 12th I was at Addington, relearning how to walk and chew food.

Five minutes home and I was unraveling. My armpits damp, my breath shallow. And I hadn't even left my room.

"Remember your PBR." I could hear Dr. Pipini's voice in my ear.

Positioning, Breathing, Relaxation.

Slowly, I unclenched my hands. My back was pinching—I dropped to a hinge, tried to touch my toes. Forced my mouth into a smile—"smiling helps when you feel worst," Summer always said—and then rolled up.

Okay. I would finish excavating my room later. Now I unzipped my suitcase, which spilled out the time capsule of my convalescence. It was strangely comforting. All the familiar paperbacks that had been lined up on my hospital shelf, along with my textbooks and progress notebooks. Sweatpants and T-shirts, scrubs and Crocs. Get-well cards and stuffed animals and even my temporary teeth—a bridge they'd created for me to use for a couple of months before I got my permanent veneer implants.

The temp teeth had been too fascinatingly ugly not to keep. After a moment's thought, I placed them on my bureau between my sandalwood jewelry box and the photo I'd framed of my parents from a few Thanksgivings ago.

God, my parents had aged drastically. Because of me. My fault, all my fault.

Downstairs, the doorbell chimed and Mom got it. But I could have guessed who it was. Not ten minutes home, and here was Smarty. I listened to their hushed voices—*"Can I see her?"* *"Yes, of course. Go on up; she's in her room."* Followed by the soft bound of Rachel Smart's mismatched—one pink, one red—Converse

All Stars on the stairs, before she burst through the door and swept me up into her signature crushing hug.

"Smarty, I can't breathe! Put me down!" But I was laughing. It felt so good not to be treated like glass, like a patient.

Rachel's gray wolf eyes swept over me for information as she let me drop. "Ooh. The Hollywood smile. Are they *all* capped now?"

"Jealous?"

"Maybe. They're so *white*. And with the short hair—you definitely look . . . Okay, let me see how the battle wounds are healing."

Rachel and I hadn't known a modest moment between us since the night we both peed my bed during a sleepover playdate back in pre-K. Rachel, just under six feet with a rock star's hips and a swimmer's shoulders, was as easy with her own sharp angles as I—seven inches shorter and about the same weight—was usually okay with my curves. And anyway, I was happy to lose my cotton shirtdress. Mom had brought it to Addington because it was one of my faves, bought with my own money at an end-of-summer pop-up-shop sale in the East Village. Happy yellow gerbera daisies printed on thin green cotton.

Except it was a dorky dress. Mom loved it, but I'd been self-conscious in it all day. In the back of my mind was a sticky wriggle of lost memory—I'd been meaning to donate it to Goodwill. Hadn't I?

The thought, like the pens, like the Weregirl poster, was an itch that I couldn't find to scratch at.

I stripped to my tank and boy shorts and let Rachel circle me as if I were a used car she wasn't sure about buying. "Can I touch them?"

"Sure. If you want to."

I shivered reflexively as Rachel's index finger traced the six-inch herringbone scar where broken glass had split the skin of my forearm down to my elbow like a hot dog bun to the meat inside. Then around back to the base of my spine, where her fingers found the buried bolt. It was about the size of a couple of D batteries, a result of fusion surgery for traumatic spondylolisthesis. Also known as a fracture-dislocation of the fifth lumbar vertebra.

An injury that, had it occurred one inch higher up my spinal column, would have left me paralyzed.

Her finger next came to the stippled graft along my arm to my elbow. Then moved up and across my forehead. Her face went politely blank as I lifted my overgrown thicket of bangs to reveal my scar. Almost grotesque, I knew. But I also knew Smarty would knee-jerk joke it off. When the going got tense, Smarty got jokey.

"Hear about the dude who lost his left arm *and* his left leg in the car crash?" The flat of Smarty's hand pressed against my forehead. As if pushing back the fact of the scar, like the fossil imprint of a lizard that extended from my temple to the arc of my brow.

"Waiting for it."

"He's all right now."

"Ugh. Terrible."

"Not the worst." She grinned.

Rachel. Raye-Raye. Smarty. My bestie since before I knew the word *bestie*. Who'd made the trip to Addington more than a dozen times, and always with treats from the outside world—copies of *Elle,* smuggled boxes of Little Debbies and Mike and Ikes, new music downloads. Which reminded me.

"Who's this group Weregirl? You never downloaded me any of that."

Rachel's lips thinned as she glanced at the poster. "Sorry. I'm not big on Weregirl. Sorta forgot that you went very fangirl right before the accident."

"There's still a lot I don't remember from right before the accident."

"Yeah, yeah, I know. But I didn't feel like it was my job to make you remember the stuff that I personally think should have stayed forgotten. Weregirl sucks." She smirked, joking, but we both knew that my lost memory was a sensitive topic.

"Ha-ha—I'm glad you think it's funny, to lose a chunk of my mind."

"Hey, come on. I thought your doctor said—"

"He said it *might* come back. He can't write me a prescription. 'Here ya go—take this pill and get your six, seven weeks of memory returned, presto.'"

"Yeah, yeah, yeah. Okay, I'm sorry. But look. Maybe it's for the best. It's not like you forgot that you got elected president or you can't remember how to play concert piano." Kidding all the way, so was it my imagination that Rachel had gone tense? Averting her eyes, cracking her knuckles down the line. As if waiting for me to admit something.

"What?"

"What . . . ?" Rachel repeated. Then she blew through her cheeks, her eyes scanning the room. "What the yuck is that?"

"Oh." I reached and picked it up. "It's plasticized teeth. I had them for a couple of months before I got my veneers."

"Ew! What's it doing here?"

"I guess I wanted to keep it. Sentimental, maybe. I thought I could hold pennies in it or something."

"Ember, that's vomit-worthy. But lucky you, because I'm making an executive decision." Rachel grabbed my teeth and made a show of dangling them between her thumb and forefinger. Then she dropped them, used-Kleenex-style, into my jewelry box.

"Were you always this bossy?"

"I'm not as bossy as you are gross."

"Gross hurts nobody. Bossy has the power to annoy. Bottom line, poor me."

"Gross offends everyone. Bossy can be helpful. Bottom line, poor *me*."

Our "bottom line, poor me" routine was an old joke, worn thin as a favorite T-shirt. Pretty dumb, but it had been such a long time since we'd done it that I had to smile.

"I'm so glad you're back," said Rachel. "And the best part is I can tell it's the real you."

My smile lost heart. "What do you mean, the *real* me?"

"No, I didn't mean— Nothing." She flinched, barely. "I mean, you're always Embie. But you're more Emberish to me when you're actually here. And here you are. That's all I meant."

"Ookay."

Suddenly Rachel jumped at me and hugged me again, hard. "Forget it. Don't listen to me. I'm overly happy. I missed you like crazy and now everything's back to normal and that's a good thing. And that's all there is to it."

"I missed you, too." The time for questions wasn't now. But Rachel had lodged the thought, and now it was stuck. If there had been a real and a not-real me before the accident, then . . . which one of us had come home?

3

Good as New

"What? You're cold? How?" Dad got noisy when he felt doubtful. He didn't mean to be. Mom liked to say that Sam Leferrier's voice was the loudspeaker to his soul.

"Not so much," I lied as I accepted the platter of wild rice. Frozen, more like. I'd pulled on my ugly-comfy pajama-jeans and a baggy cable crewneck right before we'd come downstairs for dinner. Rachel hadn't noticed, and I didn't want to tell her, but my body temperature had suddenly plummeted.

I'd had similar moments at Addington, and they still spooked me. It was as if my veins were getting pumped with an injection of ice water. My still-healing body was a mystery to me. I randomly seemed to switch on and off, on and off, in jets of heat and frost, tears and laughter, sleep and sleeplessness, dreams and nightmares.

Of course, Dr. P's case studies had already proven that this was normal.

"But it's sixty-eight degrees!" Dad reproached, following me into the dining room with a platter of roast chicken. Mom and Smarty were finishing setting places.

"I know." I set down the rice and the mat for the chicken. Dad's face was rosy from cooking. I'd inherited his love of it. "Dr. P calls them 'abreactions,'" I told him, aware that Mom was listening in. "It's like an energy purge. There are physical and psychological kinds. They'll get better."

"But he never told us about that," said Mom. She looked upset—she never liked to be caught by surprise when it came to any detail of my recovery.

"Yes, yes he did, Natalie. He did once, to me. It's a post-traumatic symptom—yes, yes he did," Dad overly assured her. They were always in a back-and-forth, making sure the other knew everything. Full shared custody of their broken treasure.

"Just be sure you keep regular contact with Dr. Pipini," Dad reminded. "You've been under rigorous medical surveillance for eight months. And now you're almost totally unmonitored."

"Except by you and Mom, my twenty-four/seven EMT monitor team."

"Hmm, funny." Dad's tone said that I wasn't, not really. But I wasn't exactly joking, either. Appeasing my parents' concerns had become as routine as breathing.

14

Sunset fell through the dining room windows as we all seated ourselves around the table. The light dappled the herbed roast chicken, the wild rice and string beans, the blackberry cobbler in sundae glasses. Across the table, Rachel was happily inhaling all the potato salad like it had been a week and not a year since she'd last dropped by our house for supper.

"I can taste the rosemary, Dad," I mentioned. Conversations about Dad's window-box herbs were a better choice than conversations about medical surveillance. Taste, my best sense, hadn't been exactly spotlighted by the Addington cafeteria experience.

"All summer I watched it grow, thinking about you coming home to us, Emb," said Dad.

"It feels like proof I'm really here." I yawned.

"You're overtired. Maybe you shouldn't go to school tomorrow." Mom spoke quickly, as if she'd been waiting for the right way to work this in. "Honey, I was thinking. You might need a few more days at home to get your bearings. And we could use the free time to go into the city and neaten your bangs, maybe get you a new winter coat."

"I kind of like my bangs looking a little wild," I said.

Not the right answer. Mom pretended she hadn't heard. "School will seem awfully intense, probably, with all the academic demands."

But now Dad was restless, folding his dinner napkin into small triangles. He didn't agree with Mom; I could sense it before he spoke. "Come on, Nat. Ember starting back at school is the smarter, more proactive move. She's got a net, with all her same friends and teachers there to support her. And it's a gentle transition, no matter what happens. We've all been over it."

All been over what? The smarter move? Was there a dumber move? What did my parents think might happen to me at school? "Dad, what do you mean, no matter what happens?" I asked. "That sounds so dire."

"No, I just meant, because we need to gauge your recovery. That's all. Take it day by day."

"Right." Though I wasn't sure that Dad was saying all that he meant.

"Hey, Chef." Rachel waved a spud-speared fork across my line of vision. "When are you whipping up a dinner here? We've gone too long without a Leferrier Friday Folly. Might be fun—a chance to bring the whole gang together."

"Oh." I hadn't hosted a Folly in . . . a year? Over a year?

"You didn't forget how to cook, did you?" Rachel gave me a look of mock inspection. "I can handle the lost memory. I can handle the Frankenbolt in your spine, but you've been a kitchen genie since fourth grade."

"I didn't forget. Actually, I've been saving recipes like always. I was making files at Addington." What I couldn't say was that every time I'd started reading one of my floppy, dog-eared cookbooks or visited some of my favorite gourmet websites, it had been like the language of a country I'd studied but had never visited. Except for now—boom!—here was some taste back. Homegrown rosemary. Bright buds of whole-grain mustard in the potato salad. The blackberries baked soft and sweet under their biscuity cobbler blanket. "We'll do something this Friday," I said impulsively. "Let's invite the crew. Why not?"

"Done! Deal!" Across the table, Rachel leaned forward and high-fived me. "I'll come over early and chop stuff."

"Sweet." But this Friday felt close. Could I? For real? I glanced down at my hands, soft and pink, the only part of my body that was less marked up than eight months ago. Hardly any evidence of my chef's nicks, scars, or blisters on them.

"And maybe we'll ask Holden?" Rachel's voice gave away how much she was pretending that this was a casual question.

Holden Wilde. My ex and Rachel's other bestie—plus Holden and Rachel were first cousins, a thicker skin of closeness. Rachel had been shocked at our breakup, almost a year ago now. So had my parents. Everyone adored Holden.

Obviously I had, too. I'd adored him most.

Holden had visited me at the hospital right after it happened. Then, a few weeks after, when I'd transferred to Addington, he'd come to see me again. I could hardly remember the first visit. I'd been on drips, feeds, the IV. In pain, out of it.

But when I saw him in the doorway at Addington, my eyes had stung with gratitude. He'd brought me a teddy bear and a six-pack of cozy socks, and he stayed with me past the soup and custard lunch. He'd looked cute that day, too, in his preppy Mount Gay Rum insignia hoodie and with his hair swooped over one eye. His casual put-togetherness had made me feel even more mortified about my scars, my straggly hair, and my stubbly legs. Holden being sweetly Holden, he'd seemed to understand this. He'd let me grip his hand, he'd let me cry, he'd let me lash out in rage—it had been so hard, in those first weeks, to hold on to any one emotion for longer than a minute. Every feeling had been an imperative, and they'd all needed to be exorcised like demons.

"You'll get through it, Ember," he'd said, cupping my face in his hands and pressing a kiss to my chapped mouth and my chin, just before he'd left. "I know you're feeling pretty beat up, but never forget it's what's inside that counts."

Which had confused me. As bruised and damaged as I knew I looked, it was me-on-the-inside that felt the most in need of repair.

After that visit, Holden had called a few times—conversations filled with more clumsy brakes-and-goes than a driver's ed test. Eventually, the calls stopped. And I didn't call him, either. We were broken up, after all. Besides, it was his senior year. I owed him the kindness of not dragging him down into my mess.

And then one late-in-August weekend, Mom had arrived at Addington with some family albums—Mom preferred the old-fashioned process of cutting and pasting and hand-note captions to anything digital. I opened the most recent album, not quite knowing what I'd find. What I found was Holden. Through the months and holidays, Holden kept staring back at me. Navy eyes, walnut-brown hair. His signature smile that was almost fierce, even though he was one of the gentlest, most unassuming people I'd ever known.

I'd unpeeled my favorite shot—Holden and me last fall, at Clarence Pumpkin Patch on Long Island—and hid it under my flat-foam Addington pillow. For company. For privacy. For memories—although, truth be told, by the time that picture had been memorialized in the scrapbook, we'd been walking the plank toward breakup.

But still I didn't contact him. Not until a month ago, when it looked like I'd be released. I sent the first text. He answered in thirty seconds. The texts turned into Gchats that lasted for hours. Suddenly we had so much to say.

And so we'd gotten close again. On laptops at least.

"Not sure you've heard, but Holden's started NYU. He's on campus, but he's home some weekends." Rachel's voice broke my reverie. "I'll invite him from you? Super casual?"

"Yeah, that'd be cool. We've been texting a little bit, actually. So maybe I'll invite him myself." Obviously I knew about NYU. I'd helped Holden pick out his classes, and I'd heard about his sweaty, clarinet-playing roommate and his brilliant Intro to Psych professor. Holden had even let me in on some details of his crush, Cassandra Atwater from Toronto, who lived down the hall and was on the diving team.

"Oh! Well! That's great!" Rachel couldn't hide her surprise. Holden plainly had kept Rachel in the dark about us being in touch. I was relieved and grateful for his discretion, but not surprised. Holden wasn't exactly Mr. Overshare.

"Friday Folly. Oh my goodness. There were times I thought I'd never . . ." Mom's voice broke. She cleared her throat and lifted her glass of water. "To Ember. Good as new."

And now everyone raised a glass to knock mine in loving bumps. The thanks for my second chance beaming in their faces. After all, I, Ember Grace Leferrier, beloved only child of Sam and Natalie Leferrier, had survived a car accident that should have ended my life. Instead, February 14th had cost me a broken jaw, two major spinal fusion surgeries, a shattered right kneecap, and nine teeth.

Not exactly my happiest Valentine's Day.

I'd been rescued from the wreck of my parents' car, pulled from the ice and filth of Bowditch River, and medevaced to NYU's ICU. Where my first back operation had been followed by emergency neurosurgery four days later, after my blood pressure had mysteriously plummeted and CT scans revealed that my frontal lobe was red-imaged with brain bleeds from what they'd first thought to be a minor concussion. I'd been on the ventilator for a week and a half and at NYU for five more weeks before transferring to Addington in April.

Where I'd spent the past eight months relearning how to use myself.

I'd been repaired by the very best that science could do for me. Tonight, I was home for roast chicken. I was as good as new. Except that I was too cold, and my head was thumping, and my stomach had knotted up with a harsh, inexplicable fear, as if only hours ago I'd been dragged up from that winter water like a ghoul. With a taste of blood and brine in my mouth, and a heart pumping wild for all that I'd lost and couldn't even begin to remember.

4

Survivor's Guilt

"Whaddaya call a deer with no eyes?" I watched Rachel slip her messenger bag over her chair arm and then let her body fall into a yoga butterfly pose, knees pitched over the edge of her seat.

"I give up. What?" I dropped my lunch tray of grilled cheese, salad, Sprite—and braced for her bad joke.

"No eye deer." Rachel scrutinized me. "Sooo? How was your very first morning back to the grind? Would you rather be doing arm curls and therapy at Addington? Or did you miss Mr. Altoona playing air guitar in the courtyard?"

"Ha." Mr. Altoona was our school's manic IT guy. I cracked

the soda tab. It wasn't until I'd sat down that I could feel my muscles ease. Like I'd gone a few rounds in a boxing ring, instead of just shown up six weeks late for my first day of senior year. "I'll be playing a lot of catch-up. I'm just patting myself on the back that I got through it."

"What's your schedule?"

I ticked it off. "Concepts in Math, AP English, Theory of Knowledge, and a meeting for yearbook staff."

"And? So far, tolerable?"

"My adrenaline's on overdrive, my brain's fried, and I probably could use a couple of Advil. But otherwise, yeah." I nodded. "I'll survive."

"Truth is, I always knew where you were today," said Rachel, "by the trail of *Oh my God there's Embers*."

I smiled. "Everyone's been amazing." I'd been pretty embarrassed by it. I'd walked in to find my locker festooned with foil balloons. There was a fruit-and-cookie basket for me at the yearbook meeting, and a box of chocolates personally delivered to me by Mr. Singh, our school principal. I'd been bombarded with hugs from kids I hardly knew. It had been a veritable outpouring.

What I didn't trust myself to tell Rachel was how it had all seemed . . . *off*. Lafayette was a huge high school, nearly thirteen hundred kids strong, and in my time here I hadn't exactly distinguished myself with my unique brand of fabulous. I'd been a good dancer, I knew I was cute, I had friends—but I wasn't some physics genius or *Vogue* beauty or star athlete or the Campus-Hot-Guy's girlfriend.

Even my standout identifying feature—my long, coppery hair—was gone. Mermaid hair, Holden had called it, though I'd usually kept it pinned up in a heavy dancer's bun. After the accident they'd cut it short, and now it was chin length, with my bangs shaggy to hide my scar and with short, raggedy patches behind each ear where squares had been shaved for all my EEG scans.

My hair hadn't made me famous. But my accident had.

Crazy as it was, it was kind of like I really *had* died last February. All day, I'd been treated almost as if I were a hologram. All day I'd had this jittery sense that kids were waiting for my Tales from the Other Side. I'd wanted to find Rachel, to cling to her a little, to explain my fear of being this spectacle—a freak-show apparition at my own homecoming.

Instead I'd hid in a bathroom stall, letting the panic rip through my body in short jagged breaths. It was too much. It was too much to rejoin this slipstream of kids and classes and after-school pep rallies, caught in a dazed half-smiling, half-pretend state that just because I hadn't died, I was all the way here.

Maybe Mom was right. Maybe I wasn't ready to handle it just yet.

Emotion was a rush and roar, and I let it sweep over me. Splashed water on my face. Pulled the Shetland lock of bangs over my scar. Made it to the cafeteria in a basic state of okay.

But Rachel had her eyes on me. She always did. "*You're* amazing," she told me now. "Go, Embie! You are strong like bull." Another old joke, because I was a Taurus, a sign that I'd never felt kinship with. Rachel was always trying to make it better for me, probably acting on her instinct as a fair, justice-seeking Libra.

Soon enough, like clockwork, like I'd never been gone, the roundtable began to gather with all my best school friends. Kids

I'd been sharing lunch with since middle school. It stunned me to see them. My eyes and cheeks were hot. Junior year seemed like both a week and a decade ago.

Sadie Anderson, Perrin Seymour, Tom Haas, and Keiji Takana. We were eight in all, including Claude McKechnie and his new Italian girlfriend, Lucia, an exchange student who even made sentences like "pass the salt" sound cranked-up sexy.

Lucia kept stealing covert glances at me. Sadie, Keiji, and Perrin were hyper-smiley, but whenever Tom met my eyes, his were careful with concern. Nobody was sure how to act.

"I'm a phone call away, Ember," Mom had advised last night, slipping into my room with a mug of tea. "If you need me tomorrow, for any reason. Any reason at all." Her good-night kiss was deeply familiar as always, but there'd been something strange in her tone. Something that kept me up, tossing in bed for another hour. She hadn't said anything strange. Not really. But there was something hidden in the cracks, the weight of what she'd left unspoken, that worried me.

And now here it was again. That squiggle of a question mark. That itchiness just outside my reach.

I sipped my Sprite and attempted to listen to the lunch conversations zipping past. Everyone seemed to be talking so fast, with an overspill of energy. I felt like no matter how hard I tried, I was a couple of beats behind real time. Seniors had the second-shift lunch—I was glad the school day was essentially over. Afternoon was one study session, and then I'd be heading downtown for physical therapy.

This would be my first afternoon since seventh grade without dance class. No scooting across the street to the Fine Arts building, no boomerang gossip, no yoga warm-ups in mirror-banked dance studio J, no Birdie Tallmadge stepping behind the dance line, the flat of her hand adjusting a spine or realigning a pelvis, or changing her Pandora on a vote. No more rehearsals, no more fleeting exhalant moments of landing a perfect step or mastering a sticky sequence.

I missed Birdie. Could I handle a visit? In my imagination, I saw myself opening the door of studio J, clumsy and leaden, my presence interrupting the dance line. Birdie turning, her heart-shaped face splitting with her surprised smile—"Oh, Ember! Stay awhile!"—as the other dancers broke file, shifting to murmur with one another. Some familiar faces. Others not. All in a whisper . . . *She's done, she can't dance . . . wrecked . . . if you actually saw her body . . . ruined for life.*

No, I wouldn't go see Birdie. Not yet. I could handle my new scarred, warped self, but only in increments. I tuned in Claude. Crazy Claude. At least he was just the same. Slurping up pasta and spewing his opinions in a million different directions, though most of today's lunchroom topic was pretty tame: homecoming and college applications. Not that I was dealing with the second. Part of my handshake agreement with Dr. P had been not to rush the whole get-into-college thing.

"You guys want the truth? The admissions process is a scam," Claude decreed between his fork attacks on Mount Tortellini. "You gotta save the dodo bird with one hand and invent a flu vaccine with the other. And that's just to get in to your safety school." His eyes fixed on me. "But your college applications are cake, Ember. Survived the jaws of death. Got some cool stories out of it, huh? Frickin' good read."

"Shut up, Claude. Don't even go there." Rachel aimed at Claude's blandly handsome face with a carrot disk, then pegged one neatly off his nose.

"Leferrier knows what I'm talking about."

"The dodo bird's been extinct for three hundred years." I stared down at my grilled cheese. Greasy margarine and Kraft singles. I used to flip great ones at home, on thin rye bread with Gruyère cheese and apple slices. "Anyway, I'm not applying this semester—or maybe even this year." I looked up. "The plan is to take everything slow."

Claude nodded. "Nice. Although, I'd apply and then defer. You better strike while the iron's hot, Emb. While you can work the pity angle. You got pictures of the car? Before and after?"

Bing. Another carrot bounced, this one off the tip of Claude's chin.

"Cut it out, Smarty. I'm just saying." He shrugged. "A sympathy vote can make the difference."

Typical Claude. Cold, right on point. That was why his bookshelves were crowded with a gold-plated plunder of Lafayette's debate-team victories. He could be dickish, but we all loved him anyway. Either that or we just loved to hate him.

"Thanks for the advice," I said. "I'll file it."

"Under Useless Crap," muttered Rachel.

Claude pointed a finger at me. "Don't listen to Smart-Ass. I'm giving you good advice. You shouldn't play down what you went through, or your injuries, or the whole survivor's-guilt thing. That's one powerful essay, if you've got a handle on not overdoing the self-pity tone."

I was staring at him as he said this, and yet at first Claude's words didn't make any sense, outside an excruciating feeling that the entire table had gone silent. My brain gnawed at it, working to peel back layers of memory—what guilt? What had I survived, that someone else had not? What—who—was Claude talking about?

Survivor. Survivor's guilt. Because I . . . . Because there was someone . . .

Brutal as a nail gun to my brain, I remembered. But I couldn't rip my gaze away from Claude's. I must have looked a touch intense, because now he was faltering.

"Easy, girl," he mumbled. "You can stop with the evil eye anytime you want. I haven't said anything you don't already know."

"I . . ." I might be sick. My vision blurred. I hadn't known. Or maybe I had known on some level, but somehow it had slipped . . . somewhere . . . I . . . The table was waiting for me to say something. Anything. "I should pay *you* to write the pity angle for my application, Claude," I said. "What's your rate? Don't pretend you don't have one."

"Is it more money than what you pay Lucia to hang out with you?" deadpanned Sadie.

I felt the too-quick thrust of laughter. They all wanted to get off this subject. Talk moved back to homecoming. Claude bowed his head to focus on his pasta. I could sense the table's relief that the moment had passed, along with a lingering over-awareness that it had happened at all.

"'Scuse me." Holding my tray, I stood up, dazed and unsteady— my low blood pressure, Dr. Pipini had warned, would kick back if I did anything too quickly.

Rachel stood, too. "You need me?"

"No. I'm fine, thanks. Stay put, finish lunch. I'm . . . just . . ."
My vision blurred again, my legs were clay, propelling me in a
crude, choppy animation from the lunch table, toward the tray
drop, and then toward the exit doors.

Upstairs, in a quiet hall of the pre-renovated science wing, I
sank down to sit beside a row of chunky metal lockers, and with
trembling fingers I stuck in my earbuds. Weregirl. I'd searched
them last night—they were a newish band out of Cork, Ireland,
with only one studio album, *Half-Life*, to their name. I'd finally
dropped deep into one of my bottom-of-the-sea sleeps before
the download had finished. And then I'd completely forgotten
about it.

Now I pressed play on the title track. The effect was instant,
stunning. The grace and clarity of a simple vocal melody skated
the surface of deep-rumbling bass drum strength. The music spun
me out of the moment and washed me onto calmer shores, burying me for its duration in a safer place that my conscious mind
couldn't dredge. Caught on the hook of this song, I was holding
it, and it was holding me, and I was still here.

I listened once, then twice, and then I let go of the song, and
I was left with the hard fact of him. I could even feel his name,
even if I couldn't have said it.

Finally I stood, and somehow, like some wandering nomad
who'd never been inside this school, I got to the front lobby, past
security, and through the doors. Outside, the air was almost warm,
one of those fall afternoons that was just a touch too muggy to
be pleasant. My body matched it, a dull thudding, and my head
ached. My hands didn't speak the same language as my brain; it
took four tries of my fingers to key up Mom's cell phone number.

She answered on the first ring. She'd been waiting; I knew it to my core.

"I need to come home. I've got a headache."

"Of course. I'll pick you up."

"I think I remembered, sort of, about him."

"Yes, yes, yes, all right—that's what I was . . . okay."

"Come get me."

"Ten minutes. Just wait right there."

I ended the call and plugged back into the music. Sat on the steps with my fingers gripped around my knees. The locked muscles of my body held me like a robot. I jabbed the play button. *Half-Life,* track two. A brisk, more upbeat song. It pumped a blood-beat rhythm inside me, the catchy snap of verse and lyrics dancing its ring around me, blocking out my bucking, kicking thoughts.

Hadn't I heard it before? It didn't matter. What mattered was that this music had the power to transport me somewhere better, temporarily.

But it couldn't hide me from the truth.

The truth that I'd killed somebody.

5

That Young Man

Anthony Travolo. In the safety of the car, I heard Mom speak the name. As soon as she said it, I wondered how I ever could have forgotten it.

Anthony Travolo. Dr. P had said his name, too, in those early sessions. I'd had the information all along. I'd been "working through it," Mom told me in the car. That I'd been "dealing with it the best way you knew how."

Which apparently entailed that at some point, my brain had shoved him, his name, his death, my guilt, deep into the void.

"And that's neither uncommon nor surprising." Dr. P spoke

slowly into the phone while Mom sat upright in a kitchen chair, as if she were at church. Hands folded, listening. "You had no data chain with this person."

"Data chain," I repeated. I pictured a daisy chain made out of twisted, severed steel, a body mangled up inside it.

"The night of the accident, you were going to visit your aunt Gail, upstate. Apparently that young man was along for the ride. You might have been planning to drop him off somewhere. But there's no indication that you knew him well. You both were seen out at some dance clubs. The clubs, we think, are the single point of intersection."

"Right." Club friends. Because I was such a club girl? That wasn't me. Sure, I'd been to some clubs—anyone in Lafayette's A-squad dance liked the odd night out dancing. But I didn't have a special set of club friends. And Holden wasn't into that scene. Neither was Rachel.

But I'd heard all of this before, and now I remembered that I had. Right down to Dr. P's refusal to speak his given name. Never "Anthony." Always "him" or "the person" or sometimes "that young man." As if by my not knowing him, I was less culpable. Maybe this was why the name had slipped away from me so easily—along with the crime.

The visit-to-Aunt-Gail part wasn't a mystery. I'd made the trip to Mount Kisco with my parents plenty of times. My dad's only sister's country home was one of those rustic, kick-back Adirondack-style cabins. It was a perfect place to unplug, and Aunt Gail was mellow, an easygoing host.

"Ember?" Dr. P's voice snapped me to. "Are you there?"

"Yes." I refocused. "But I don't understand. I killed someone.

31

A person is dead because of me." My voice was more breath than sound. "It's a major thing to forget."

"The trauma surrounding selective recall is usually congruent with a memory disorder," said Dr. P. "There have been many similar cases."

"You always say that." My voice was warning me that I was close to crying.

On the line, Dr. P suddenly seemed to remember that I was a person, not a file of case studies. "Think of it this way, Ember. Your body has taken hits that you can't even feel in your day-to-day. For example, do you realize that you won't have fully regenerated all of your lung tissue for seven years?"

Yes, I realized. Dr. P had only mentioned it a hundred times before. But so what? In seven years, I've got all-new lung tissue. In seven years, Anthony Travolo will still be dead. What kind of monster was I to have forgotten this person?

"So you need to give yourself a break. Your brain creates the shield while your body works on the repairs. And memory loss can be a natural defense mechanism to protect us from psychological damage. We never thought you'd forgotten it. Only blocked it. We were expecting this, and now you need to listen to me, Ember." I imagined Dr. P hunkering forward in his office chair, shuffling papers, his wide shoulders up over his neck. "In recent weeks at Addington, we talked about your depression, and how much you wanted to return home. I trusted your instinct. With your parents' concession—and several conversations about it—we thought it might be best for that particular memory, of the young man, to reawaken naturally. In an atmosphere where you felt most comfortable."

"What happened to me at school today did not feel natural," I told him. "No offense," I added. I was annoyed by my shrill voice, my sarcasm. I really didn't like to be disrespectful to Dr. P, who'd done so much for me. "I guess what I mean is my instinct was not for Claude McKechnie to give me that news." I closed my eyes. "He's not exactly anybody's first pick for the circle of trust."

"Claude might not have been the best trigger, but it seems that you transitioned smoothly. You were in complete control of the memory."

In control? Carrying the death of Anthony Travolo around for months like an invisible skeleton wrapped around my body— this was me being smooth and in control?

Dr. P was just not helping. I told him I'd call him back later.

"Tea, sweetie?"

"No, thanks." Ah, liquids—my mom's cure-all for everything, including accidental homicide. I drifted into the living room, Mom softly padding behind.

"So this is why everyone's been on eggshells around me," I said, flopping onto the couch and curling up into a ball. "It must have been in all the papers, right? That there were two of us, and one survived?" For the first time, I wished I were back at Addington. The familiar unfamiliar of it. Home made everything too real.

"Your name was withheld because you're a minor. Ember, you have to understand. It was an—"

"An accident, right. It doesn't matter. I'm like Bethanne, aren't I?" Bethanne Hill was a former neighbor who'd survived a house fire she'd started by accident, which had killed her toddler sister, Violet. It had happened over ten years ago.

That first day Bethanne returned to my elementary school, I hadn't been able to take my eyes off her. She looked just the same, and yet her sister was dead because of her. What would it mean, I'd thought, to be *that* girl—guilty and left over?

Now I knew.

"Maybe you can meet Dr. Pipini tomorrow. He'd clear his day for you."

"Sure, whatever." I curled up into a tighter bundle, pulled up the afghan, and watched twilight drag off the sunset. Accepted the cup of tea Mom was compelled to prepare, but then I let it go cold.

Mom settled in and took out some knitting. Softly clicking needles filled the silence until I broke it.

"Mom." I spoke through closed eyes. "Do the Travolos want to see me?"

The needles picked up speed. "I have the family's email."

I could feel the cold, heat, cold in my skin. Thin jets of panic rose up through the floorboards of my consciousness. "Just an email? What does that mean? Do they blame me?"

"Ember, there's no lawsuit here, there's no finger-pointing and litigating."

It wasn't really the answer to my question. I tried another way in. "Does the family want to be in contact with me? Do you think I should email? Is that what they want from me? Have you met any of them?"

"Oh, Ember, I don't have all the answers for you. I wish I did." *Tic-tic-tic.* "What I can tell you is that they're private people. Same as us, in their own way." *In their own way.* What did that mean? Poor? Religious? Foreign? "You just tell me when you want their information, and then you and your father and I can talk about how to approach it. Let's go carefully, Ember. I don't want you to feel alone in this."

As if my parents' company, as I hauled them out with me to any meeting with the Travolos, would purge my guilt. Of course, it was how Mom and Dad always handled my problems—by absorbing them. Not this time. There was only one person behind the wheel that night.

Anthony Travolo. I rolled it around in my brain. Forcing myself to reaccept it. He was a stranger, or so they all said. Some kid who'd needed a lift out of the city.

"What else do you know about Anthony Travolo? Personally, I mean."

Tic-tic-tic-tic. The clicking of the needles was steady, exact. Mom brought her math to her knitting. "Very little. From Bensonhurst. No criminal record. They showed me a photograph. I'd never seen him before in my life. You might have met him at a party. You'd fallen in with some different people, after you and Holden broke up."

And now what did *that* mean? My mother's voice was not a window to her soul; it was all bricked up in neutral.

The grandfather clock in the hall was antique and never kept the right time. Now it chimed six courteous bells, although it was only half past five. I'd spent hundreds of peaceful, happy versions of this afternoon. My mother knitting, me doing homework or reading or dozing, the muted sounds of passing cars making a soft quilt of noise.

Would I ever know a truly peaceful sleep again?

"Dr. P tried; he really did." Mom broke the silence abruptly.

"But the death was so hard on you. Unbearable—you couldn't even speak about it. So Dr. P decided to take his cues from you. Which meant, ultimately, not speaking of it at all. It just seemed to be the best way to solve it temporarily. So much of you was broken, and needed mending. Inside and out."

"Solve it?" I snorted. "Anthony's death isn't a calculus problem. It's not like we solved anything. In fact, I'd call it pretty regressive—as Dr. P would say—to have blocked the whole thing out." My voice was just way too horribly, childishly snappish. I wanted to control it, I wanted to sound stable, but it was as if I couldn't hold on to my center.

And I'd got Mom uptight, too. I could tell by the way she set down and gripped her knitting on her lap. "You're right. It's not solved. But you can't go back and undo it, either. Young people die in car accidents. The fatalities are staggering. It's horrible, it's unspeakably tragic, but it happens, and not just to you, Embie. There are hundreds of thousands of brand-new drivers on the road every year."

"So it *was* my fault!" I sprang up. "You think Anthony died because I didn't know what I was doing! If I'd been thirty years old, a seasoned driver, then none—"

"No, no—stop it, Ember!" Mom dropped her needles to clap her hands to her ears. "That's not what I meant. I wasn't thinking—I was speaking statistically. I wasn't referring specifically to you. Not at all."

But of course she was. The silence stretched accusingly, a distance between us.

"And I really don't want to watch you lying on that couch," Mom continued in a bare, thin voice, "with senior year and everything you worked so hard to get just passing you by, while you obsess on the past."

"Whatever. On this couch, right in your sight, is where you like me best," I mumbled. Hating myself, hating that I knew how to hurt her so easily.

"Maybe I'm protective. Fine. That's just a mom's job. But I don't want you trapped here, beating yourself up endlessly about this. And *nobody* can tell me it wasn't a mistake that you went back to school so early." Mom spoke with force. "I warned Dr. Pipini. I warned him more than once. You need the comfort of your home."

Did I? Because home didn't feel very comforting right now.

I walked back into the kitchen, where I picked up the newspaper clipping that Mom had laid out for me to see when I got home from school. Rereading it, scouring it for anything I might have missed, anything that hadn't appeared in my Google search—which had brought up the same clip, along with a brief notation of Anthony Travolo's funeral services, which had been held out on Long Island.

The accident had occurred in Croton-on-Hudson, New York. February 14th at approximately 9:30 p.m. Anthony Travolo of Bensonhurst, aged nineteen. My name was withheld. Both of us had been taken to Weill Cornell with grave injuries.

"He never regained consciousness." Mom spoke wearily from the kitchen door, where she'd been watching me. "So he went peacefully. He wasn't from our neighborhood or school district."

"Nobody knew him?"

"You'd have to ask around. But he didn't have any overlap with your close Lafayette friends. No drugs, no alcohol. No indication of foul play."

"Why were we going to Aunt Gail's?"

"She said you'd called about a week before, and you hadn't mentioned a guest. That's why we think you were giving him a lift, dropping him off somewhere before Gail's. You hadn't told me you were going to visit her, either—I'd never have let you drive in that storm. Never. I suspect your plan was to call us once you'd gotten there. That bridge was a sheet of ice. The car skidded, you lost control, and that, unfortunately, is the whole story."

A story with a lifetime of consequences. I dropped the clipping. I was sleepy. Addington-nap sleepy, as if my body yearned to spend a few hours in the dark, healing.

Mom went to the fridge and began to take out options for dinner. Ordinarily I would have helped. Not tonight. I didn't have the energy to lift a loaf of bread. I wandered back to the living room, to the couch. I wrapped up in the afghan and listened to dinner being prepared. Through closed eyes, I could feel the room gradually turn to night.

Did it matter that I didn't know Anthony Travolo? Probably not.

It's not as if knowing him would have changed anything.

One night, one car, one bridge, one survivor. I was here and he wasn't. The poison of this knowledge was inside me. Now and forever.

6

Because. You Glow.

"Your journey to full rehabilitation is complicated," Dr. P had told me at our last session, the afternoon before I left Addington. "And not every day will be perfect."

Perfect was a funny word, when I thought about it later. No way could a whole, entire day be perfect. With or without a car wreck in your past. There were only perfect moments, and those moments were precious. But most moments were flat, or hazy, or sleepy, or boring, or baffling, or just okay.

I got through the rest of the week with no more hope than for "okay," trying to function in an approximation of normal.

But there weren't many moments when the shadow of Anthony Travolo didn't claim me. Memory had also cleared a path to those early weeks at Addington, when all I'd felt was the horror of it.

The horror and the guilt. My knowledge was like a vine that had sprung up and tangled around me, clingy and resilient as if I'd learned about Anthony's death just yesterday.

And now, finally, it was Friday. The last school day of my first week back home. Friday wasn't perfect, either. But it seemed better. Possibly because I allowed myself a feeling of quiet achievement that I'd crossed the finish line. Or because the day itself was such a bright, shiny apple. Blue sky, newly turned orange leaves, October crispness.

A perfect day? Sure. Was I perfect, spinning inside it? Not a chance.

Friday also meant that the weekend was on its way.

And even if the shock of Anthony Travolo hadn't receded, at least I was dealing with it consciously again, and his death was mine to drag around with me, along with my own recovery. But I'd bailed on my physical therapy classes. Just couldn't handle it. Dr. P had sort of conceded Mom's point—that I needed to take it low-key. Today, though, on his urging before my long weekend rest, I was scheduled to show up for an hour of PT.

"You're not ready," Mom had judged as she watched me walk out the door that morning. But at least she didn't stop me.

After school, I walked to the subway station on Dekalb Avenue, breathing deep, and descended gingerly. It was my first public transit trip in nearly a year.

The moment the L train roared into the station, I felt the familiar cold-hot-cold panic—*turn around, turn around!* Instead I inhaled like a scuba diver, ready for the plunge. I waited right to the last moment before leaping into the car, its motion detectors bouncing the doors apart at the shove of my shoulder. I found a seat and sank heavily into it. My breath and body were shaking. I plugged in my earbuds and let Weregirl transport me. Okay. For real.

After another minute, when I realized I wasn't going to implode—that I was, in fact, fine—I reached into my backpack and withdrew some note cards for my Theory of Knowledge course paper, "Individual and Society," which was due Monday. Might as well get a leg up. I used to love doing my homework on the subway—something about the motion, the quiet, the knowledge that I couldn't get online . . . it had been better than the library.

Course work was all a little bit loopy for me, since I'd started the year almost six weeks later than the rest of my class. I knew my teachers were grading me with a softer touch—so maybe that was why I'd been enjoying school more than I'd anticipated.

I uncapped a pen and got cracking on my theory statement.

Creating a high-functioning society does not mean we should become robotic drones that serve only to aid productivity. It is every bit as important to be a thinking member of the majority while learning what makes group dynamics . . .

The paper was so white. My concentration was melting into sleepiness. Lulled by my iPod and the motion, my eyes unfocused, I yawned and looked around at the colorful blur of Tupperware seats and tired faces. I relaxed, letting my muscles soften and the back of my head come to rest against the window. Slowly but surely, trancing out so deep that I woke with a jolt.

Where was I?

Panic set in. I couldn't breathe. Because I'd waaaaay missed it—I was out in . . . Bushwick?

That arty black business card stuck up in my bedroom mirror had a Bushwick address. Earlier this week I'd looked up Area-code online and found a site for some sceney club dance space. Obviously, I hadn't been planning to come see it today. But if I doubled back on my route, I'd be at least twenty minutes late for therapy class.

Skipping another class was not exactly the way to Dr. P's—or my brand-new therapist's—heart. But what if I just got out in Bushwick? What if, instead of therapy, I went to check out Area-code? Maybe something would click. After all, I'd grown up hitting dance performances and concerts all over the city. From Manhattan to the Bronx, from Alvin Ailey to Symphony Space and all the halls and theaters in between. Last year I'd even dragged Rachel out to a couple of clubs, too—not exactly her best environment.

I'd been to Bushwick. I knew it. It was inside the memory pocket. What if I'd met Anthony Travolo out here? What if I started walking the streets and suddenly discovered all those days like easy treasure, a scattering of shells washed up on the beach?

Yes. Do it. I ran up the subway stairs, my backpack knocking my side. There must have been a hundred steps. My breath petered out pretty quickly. Through the exit, I found my cell and made the call to Jenn Stoller, my new therapist, in a whisper.

"Jenn? I'm really sorry, but I missed my stop on Lorimer and now I'm far out and I think it'll take me—"

"Ember, it's fine, calm down," Jenn interrupted. "No damage done. If you feel like this is too much activity in your weekday, let's think about changing to Saturdays and Sundays, okay?"

"Totally," I wheezed. "That's a good idea."

"Because the thing is, I'm only as committed as you."

"Right. I know. I'm sorry." My chest was burning. I stopped and leaned against a building. My lungs were creaking for oxygen.

"You were a dancer, right? So you know about scheduled practice."

Were. That past tense made me feel strange—even if it was true. Of course I wasn't a dancer anymore. Not in this body. "Yes. See you tomorrow, thanks, and I promise it won't happen again."

"Cool. Okay, see you then."

I shut off my phone against Mom's pinging texts (are you there safe? / how do you feel?) and slipped it into my backpack. Then let myself take stock of where I was. Did I really know this place? Had I been here? It wasn't completely unfamiliar.

Walking along Myrtle Avenue, I turned left and left again. Grimy industrial space. The sun was losing to dusk. My nerves flicked alert as I approached the building, a prewar in an ugly checkerboard brick the color of liver, peaches, and salmon. There was hardly any sign of life. A newsstand on the corner with a blinking Lotto banner, but the rest of the block was warehouses and garages, a gas station, a closed Laundromat, a line of narrow row houses. I felt under-armored and overexposed, as if I were being watched. The woman wheeling her baby stroller around the corner didn't look scared—but she looked tough.

I squeezed my eyes shut to visualize the card in my room.

Between Myrtle and Evergreen. As in, right around the corner.

The building was nothing to see, but as I drew nearer, I could feel a twinge of something. Yes, I'd seen this before, I'd been here before. Only it had been different. Night, maybe . . . My sense of it was like a mist, like a dream. . . .

I stepped across the street, my body zinging with urgency to possess the memory. Though there was no sign, nothing on the building's cheap door intercom system that gave me an indication that this was the "right" place. It looked vacant, too, with a roll-down grill over the front door and a padlock on the side door. The fire escape was the only means up.

I rubbed my hands together, grabbed the ladder's rungs, dug a breath, and almost instantly let go.

What was I doing? I stood stone-still, staring at my open hands, the ladder rust streaked across my palms like dried blood. Was this like me? Not like me?

Just do it. A slip-slide of memory, of being outside, night, kids, joking and whispers. We'd been up to something mischievous. Maybe illegal. But what? With who? Not the Lafayette crowd . . .

It was killing me. Now I *had* to do it. Had to prove that the adventure still lived in me. Quickly, I began to haul myself up.

Why five floors? If my brain didn't know, my legs did.

When I arrived, I was sick with exhaustion. My lungs felt as thin as plastic wrap. I leaned against the rails and let myself catch my breath.

The window was a dry film of orange dust. I rubbed a patch clean so I could look in.

44

Huge, empty. A vaulted crossbeam ceiling and sloppy mortared walls. Was this right? Was this the place? I turned, stepping to the farthest corner of the fire escape, scoping it out.

The sun was setting in harvest colors, outlining the water towers and flat-top warehouses. I was far from home, I was alone, and suddenly I was wiped out. As if I'd depleted my entire reserve of strength. I sat down and wrapped myself into a ball. I felt slow, and yet I was tingling, it reminded me of those first conscious weeks after my accident, and all of those sleep-inducing drugs.

My eyes grew heavy.

At Addington, I'd taken a nap nearly every day, right about this time. Lying quiet as a mouse in my narrow bed, watching the sunset draw away over the smooth fields. Sometimes my sleep would be so deep that I'd wake into blackness, and find out that I'd missed dinner. . . .

Scrrrritccccch! I jumped up at the sound, nearly losing my balance as I knocked backward slightly and caught myself against the rails.

"Sorry, sorry!"

"You scared me!"

"You scared me, too." He laughed as he pushed the window up and then swung a leg out, then another, so that he was sitting on the ledge. I could tell he wasn't nearly as startled as I was as we stared each other down.

"But you *really* scared me. I'm serious." My hands flew to my flushed cheeks.

"Sorry," he repeated. "Once I saw you, I didn't want to lose you. That's all, Red. I'm harmless." He smiled. "I'm Kai."

I paused. "Ember." I knew that I'd surrendered my name only

because he'd said his. And because he was cute. A different cute than Holden—which I'd always considered to be my type. This guy was nothing like Holden, nothing at all. Kai was caramel skin and prickly dark haircut, with eyes the brown of a stone you'd want to pick up on a beach. He was also thinner—less varsity-athletic than Holden, who'd never met a racquet, stick, or ball that he couldn't master.

"Ember?" he repeated. "Perfect."

"Perfect how?"

"Because. You glow."

"You were watching me?"

"Yeah, for a while. I was sure you'd seen me."

"Right, okay, look . . ." I crossed my arms over my chest. This guy had such a slow-motion ease in his speech and movements, it was hard to be on full alert. But easygoing didn't mean harmless. "There's a stalker element to you following me onto a fire escape. And believe me, I can scream a lot louder than I just did."

"Have some faith." Kai's smile opened his face as he joined me out on the fire escape. He looked cold—he was shivering. I fought the urge to button his jacket, an olive-drab whipcord, thick but shabby. His clothes were beat-up jeans and lug-heeled boots that were big with the Bowery kids. His T-shirt, visible beneath his jacket, was printed with a graphic of a tree that had been photographed in black light.

"Anyway, I wasn't looking at the view," I told him. "I was kind of more trying to figure out where I am."

"For me, the best view is out here." He meant his view of me? His tone was casual, but my face burned up again.

"I like it out here," I said. "It's a little urban decay, sure, but it's also got . . ." I didn't have the right word for what I saw.

"Breathing room," he finished.

"Yeah. That's it, I guess."

"If you want to know, I've already officially declared this an unspoiled fringe area." He stepped back and raised his voice. "So watch it, gentrifiers—this area is cupcake-shop-protected." I smiled; but when he reached behind into his back pocket, I was suddenly frightened.

"What've you got, a knife?"

"Almost." Casually, Kai withdrew a flat silver flask.

"Ah." I watched as he unscrewed the top and took a swig. "Hot coffee?" I guessed. Not hard, since the scent of dark roast wafted in the air.

"Yep. Why else would a person carry a flask?" He leaned forward to hand it to me. As I took it, I saw the initials *R.G.O.* inscribed.

"Who's R.G.O.?"

"Roberto Guillermo Ortiz." But he didn't offer more, so I sipped and handed back the flask. I thought it seemed cool and un-nosy not to ask. Though I really wanted to know.

"What's your deal, outside of being the unauthorized protector of industrial Bushwick?" I asked instead. "You go to school around here?"

"Sorta. I'm enrolled in pickup and night classes so far, but it looks like I'll head to Pratt next semester," he answered. "With a concentration in silk screen. That is, when I'm concentrating. Check this out." He pulled a small notebook from his back pocket. "My new inspirational five-by-seven. And"—from his jacket pocket—"a bottle of Parker Super Quink Ink."

He tossed them both to me.

"You're a human pack rat," I joked. But the notebook was tiny, a black marble composition. The ink was contained in a sealed glass bottle, like an exotic indigo perfume.

"I start a new one each year. It's sort of a datebook, sketchbook, journal type of thing."

I turned the book over in my hands. "The spine isn't cracked."

"The first mark's the hardest."

"Or maybe you just don't know what to write."

"Maybe now I've got something."

My cheeks went red. Again. He meant me.

"Lately I've gotten really into T-shirts," Kai said, easily switching subjects. "Me and Hatch. We want to start a business: 'Tao of T.' We've got the name and we know what we want to do with our massive profits, but so far that's it. No business model."

"So can you skip to the end? And tell me the post-massive-profits part of the plan?"

The right question. He smiled. "We want to start an after-school arts center, with our T-shirt empire funding it. Underserved youth, some people call them. I just call it kids from where I'm from. I want to give them more than what I had." He looked embarrassed, even as he laughed. "That's my dream. You're up."

"I don't think I have one right now," I told him.

"Not dancing?"

"What?"

"You move like a dancer," Kai explained. He had a way of staring at me that was so curious and unflinching, I wanted to look away.

"You're right, actually. I was dancing for so long—I loved it.

All of it. Being part of a troupe, running from classes to rehearsals, auditioning, seeing my name on the list."

"What changed?"

"It stopped being fun," I said, surprising myself with my honesty. "I got sick of stressing out about my weight. Standing in a leotard between two matchsticks and feeling like I was the crazy one. Or spending two hours making a chocolate silk pie, and not letting myself have one single bite because I needed to be exactly this or that many pounds. My parents lived for my recitals. I'm an only child and I hate disappointing them—but what was I supposed to do? Dance my whole life away for my parents?" I stopped. Shocked that I'd just admitted such excruciating, almost surprising, things to this guy.

And was it true? Was I always planning my exit from the dance world—and the car accident simply forced a perfect path out?

"You can dance whenever you want," said Kai. "Recreationally, I mean. Like any sport."

"Sure." I didn't have any desire to tell him about the accident, either. My scars, Addington, the therapy I was missing this afternoon. There was no reason to confess everything and burden the moment.

"Anyway, you seem like you know yourself by instinct, more than by analysis," he remarked. "So it was probably the right call. Some people use up their whole lives trying to stop caring about their parents' approval. That's not you, am I right?"

"That's . . . yeah." I felt shy. Who was this guy, who seemed to have me figured out cold? And yet who wasn't trying to figure me out as one of the walking wounded? Under his gaze, I felt springy, newly sprouted.

"Anyway," said Kai with a wry smile, "I wouldn't want to be denied chocolate silk pie. Unless it was a choice between that and a slice of pizza at Grimaldi's."

"Or a slab of Junior's cheesecake, with strawberries."

"A hot dog with everything from Nathan's."

"Arancini from Spumoni Gardens."

"Cheesesteaks at Yankee Stadium, followed by baba ghanoush at Fez." At my puzzled look, Kai explained. "It's good, promise. Eggplant and onion. Fez is up by 161st Street, the Yankee Stadium stop. How about we go there sometime? They've got speakers in the windows and this crap, concrete dance floor—and come to think of it, everyone dances pretty crappy there, too. It's stupid fun."

"Sure." Was he asking me out? Or just being nice?

"We'll get you the dancing back. It should be an impulse. Like art." And then Kai jumped up and began to move in the tiny square of the fire escape. He was a good dancer, even without music and even as he started to pull out some self-consciously joking moves.

And then it was so gentle, it was just a continuation of his dance and his fun, the way he rolled my hand into his and pulled me up to meet him so that we were standing together, facing each other.

Ice and heat pounded my temples. I closed my eyes. Opened them again.

He was still staring at me. His eyes seemed to find me at my center.

"Funny thing is, I came out here for no real reason," I told him. "And I met you instead. It's so . . ." I couldn't betray myself with something corny, some "past lives" idiocy. Kai's eyes didn't break our connection, so I made myself say it. "Do you believe in coincidences?" *Fate*, I'd wanted to say. Except that *fate* was such a loaded word.

Kai checked his watch, and then he seemed to decide something. He pulled me down so that we were sitting together. He smelled so good, it was driving me crazy. "Ember, I want to answer this. I do. But I've got a new priority. I just made a promise to myself that in the next fifteen seconds, I'd either get your phone number or kiss you, or both."

My heart was a piston. "I never give out my cell."

"What if I give you mine? Not that this is some big deal— I hardly ever turn it on. But I do check my messages. Besides, I was watching you before you saw me. So I've known you a few minutes longer than you've known me, right? I feel like I've known you a long time." He seemed suddenly shy. "Anyway . . ."

"Anyway what?"

"Anyway I think you want to kiss a stranger."

"Ha! I'm not sure you know as much about me as you wish you did," I challenged. Or flirted. Probably both.

"Five seconds."

And then I decided to take hold of the moment. Quickly leaning over to kiss him before he could kiss me—and why not? I wanted it just as much—even if the nerve of acting on this sudden urge turned my face hot.

Kai's lips were warm on mine, and so I kissed him again. A real kiss. Slow enough that he could push against my mouth before I parted my lips for the pressure of his teeth against mine.

The catch of his fingers on my neck, the thrill of his hands

51

cupping the back of my head to draw me close, and the newness of it all, the stranger's hands mouth lips tongue click *bite* shot sparkling pinwheels through my body.

"Fireworks," he said softly. "Do you see them? They're everywhere."

"I do; I see them everywhere."

"Because there are no coincidences."

And as I opened my eyes, I recalled the honey-menthol cough drops I'd take whenever I had a sore throat. How the menthol was a balm after the sweetness had been sucked away to nothing.

Kai's kiss was the same—a balm.

Mine and mine and still mine, even after it had ended.

7

Two Cats in the Washer

It wasn't until I'd jumped off the J train, my mind still in a sand-storm of him—*Kai, Kai, Kai, who are you, Kai?*—that I remembered.

Friday Folly. My house. Holden and Rachel.

The moon was a visible sliver when I turned on my phone. Five voice mails. Two were from Rachel and three were from an increasingly tense Mom—the last with the bass-note rumbling of Dad in the background as Mom pleaded with me to please call them back.

Where had the time gone? I couldn't make sense of it. It was past seven—two hours snuffed out. My muscles were kinked and knotted. I tried to piece it together. I'd watched the sun sink into a warm rainbow sky while I was out on the fire escape. Then I'd left Kai—was it dusk by then?—with twenty more minutes on the subway.

Time had buckled and flexed and swirled down the drain.

Had my phone been off the whole time? Yes, I must have shut it off right after I called Jenn.

"It's me again," began Mom's final message. "It's gotten so late, Ember. Much too late. Will you call, please?" Then Dad's grumbling: "As soon as she gets this." And Mom again: "As soon as you get this message. We need to hear from you. Okay?" There was no hiding the tremble in her voice.

When I saw them—Mom, Dad, Rachel, and Holden, all gathered in the kitchen—Mom started to cry in earnest.

"Oh, Mom." I hugged her and she clung to me in a damp clamp of relief. "I'm really sorry. I lost track of time." Which sounded so lame, even if that was the truth.

"We sent the others home," piped up Rachel. "There was some party they wanted to hit. But Sadie left those brownies." She indicated the wrapped pan on the counter.

"I feel terrible."

"We're just glad you're safe." Rachel gave my arm a squeeze. "Not that we were all worried." Rachel's reproach was gentle but it was there. Because yes, my mom was overreacting, but—Rachel's eyes seemed to entreat—how else did anyone expect her to act? "We ordered takeout from Mumbai Dream. It just came. I was betting hard that you'd show up hungry."

"I *am* hungry." The takeout was lined up buffet-style, lids off, but nobody had touched a thing.

Holden came around from the other side of the kitchen island. I'd been over-aware of him from the moment I'd walked in the door, and now I let myself observe him. He looked great.

"Emb." He reached for me, a quick, firm hug.

"Loving the five o'clock." I let my fingers brush the scruff of his chin.

"Thanks." He rubbed at it sheepishly. There was something else about him, too, something new—an elegance. Maybe it was simply the fact that he was out of his parents' house, living at the NYU dorm. Or maybe it was just that I hadn't seen him in a while, and I missed him.

"I'm really sor—"

"No worries." Then he tweaked my ear, something he used to do back when we were going out. It seemed natural—but I could feel Rachel absorbing the intimacy of it.

"Kids, I'm starved," said Dad. "Let's eat."

That's when I spied tonight's Folly ingredients—brown rice, cans of chickpeas, red and yellow bell peppers, scallions—heaped on the counter. Waiting for me. I felt horrible thinking of my parents pacing up and down the aisles of the grocery store with my list of items, fussing over brands of long-grain rice, accepting and rejecting onions and peppers, all for a dinner I hadn't bothered to make. "Wow, I really screwed up. I didn't mean to—"

"We know you didn't mean to." Dad looped his arm around my shoulders. "We're just glad you're safe."

"Where were you again?" Rachel cut in.

"Just walking around." My racing heart would have betrayed me, if anyone had heard it, as I began to heap my plate with garlic naan bread, basmati, tamarind sauce, palak paneer, and then the korma glopped like the world's most delicious baby food on top—with a glass of mango lassi so it all went down sweet.

It was inexplicable that I'd lost that time. I thought it had been an hour or so. It would upset everyone if I told them that. It frightened me. "I missed my stop on the way to therapy. So I got out at Bushwick. There was a club . . . something I wanted to check out." It was then that I remembered—I'd gone looking for memories of Anthony Travolo.

Strikeout on that front. There had to be an easier way.

Nobody spoke as plates were filled and everyone sat around the kitchen table. Rachel seemed to be taking extra time ladling out her precise portion of tikka masala. "I haven't been to Bushwick since we played PS 480 the first weekend in February. You weren't there." Her voice seemed clenched. Had Rachel asked me to come see her play basketball, and I hadn't? And early February landed smack in the black hole of memory.

"What about a dance space near Myrtle Avenue?"

"If you went clubbing in Bushwick, it wasn't with me." Yep. Clenched.

Holden saved it. Yes, there was definitely a new elegance to him, as he deftly switched topics and began telling a story about his NYU dorm's resident advisor, Raphael, who slept every night rolled up naked in his oversized raccoon coat. Which was fine till the night of the fire drill.

The story even got Mom laughing.

I sensed the whole table breathing easier. Holden had brought some star power, for sure. He'd really changed. Usually more of a listener and question-asker, Holden worked the room smoothly tonight, flirting just enough with Mom and jousting over politics with Dad—but then backing off, whew, before Dad got what Mom called "stentorian." It had been so long since I'd seen Holden and Rachel together, and I loved watching their old cousin routines, especially how Holden stood up to her in all the right ways, teasing her about her "Executive Decisions" and her general bossiness, but never taking it too far—the way Claude often did, so that she got sensitive and masked it by being prickly.

And when it came to me, Holden was careful. He made a point of not discussing our reconnection while I was at Addington. Nobody had a clue that we'd been in such close touch. When Holden answered Smarty's tossed-off question "So, Hold, are ya seeing anyone?" with an equally casual and joking "Do Canadians count?"—a direct reference to Cassandra Atwater that only I got—I attempted to strike a mood between curious and relaxed.

Inwardly, though, I crimped up with resentment. Why had Holden even acknowledged Cassandra? Why did he want to prove to everyone that he'd left me behind? Why did I care? Did I care? I was so confused. Kai's golden-brown eyes were like lanterns, beaming me back to earlier this evening.

"You should bring Cassandra by for the next Friday Folly," I said instead, trying to sound like the chilled-out ex-girlfriend I wasn't sure that I was, as I stood up to pick through the near-empty container of korma. "And this time I won't space out. This time, amazingly, I will actually be here."

"Mmm," said Holden. "Could be fun." But I couldn't tell if he really thought so.

It wasn't until after my parents had gone up to bed and Rachel had slipped away to the kitchen to polish off the saffron rice pudding and not-so-secretly check the Facebook status of her brand-new-big-fat-crush-who-she'd-actually-known-since-sixth-grade, Jake Weinstock, that I let myself drop the cool-ex mask a little. Downstairs and tucked into the sectional while Holden scrolled the On Demand menu, I caught the wave of a hundred other Friday nights, back when we were a couple.

"So where *is* Cassandra hiding out tonight? Did you ask her to Oktoberfest already?"

Holden kept his eyes on the television screen as he reached back, grabbed my knee, and squeezed—a horse bite, my gramps used to call those.

"Cut it out! It was a friendly question!" I gasped.

"Not yet. I'll ask her when I'm ready."

"Does she know you're at my house?"

"So what if she does? Or doesn't? It's not like something's going on with you and me. Right?" As Holden looked at me, I felt chastened, like a puppy in need of a tap on the nose.

"So you're saying it's serious with Cassandra?"

"Enough—you're worse than Rachel. There's nothing holding it back, I guess." He paused. "Now watch me change topics—what made you go all the way to Bushwick this afternoon?"

"I missed my stop. But I'd been there last year for some dance thing or party that I didn't remember. And so I got out, thinking I'd catch some kind of déjà vu." But instead I'd met Kai. Which was more private, even, than my quest for the past—and a lot more difficult to explain.

"Listen, I don't want to sound obnoxious. But just for the next coupla months, I think your folks'll be two cats in the washer every time they can't find you. You know they were at the theater when your car went over the bridge? Their cell phones off. By the time the play ended, you were already in the OR."

"Right, I know." But I hadn't known. Or I'd forgotten.

"It sucked, Ember. To see them going through all that anxiety tonight of wondering where you were—especially when you had no real reason to be out late. I just feel like I had to say something to you."

"You're right." Except it had started with a reason—I'd wanted to chase down Anthony Travolo. The ghost of Anthony Travolo. But obviously I didn't want to confess that part of it. Not to Holden, anyway. I took a breath. "I'm glad you said something. I am." I grabbed the remote. "Also, you never change channels when it's *The Notebook*. This is no joke the best movie ever."

"You're such a girl." Holden made a face, but then sat back, regarding me as if I were an odd and interesting puzzle to solve. Which maybe I was for him now. He was scratching at his beard scruff as if attempting to get it off. "I can see your folks are different now," he said. "I don't think parents ever totally recover from conversations about who should receive their daughter's eyes and kidneys."

"No. That job went to another set of parents."

Holden looked a little startled. I could feel my face getting warm. Did I sound too detached, or "emotionally miscalibrated"—the way Dr. Pipini had said I might, when dealing with personal issues? But I made myself keep talking. "I've decided to start pointing to the elephant in the room. I re-remembered what happened. Anthony Travolo."

"Yeah. I found that out from your doctor, back when I visited you at Addington. That you'd sort of . . . lost . . . that information." Holden spoke carefully. "How do you feel about it now?"

"Outside of crushed by guilt? I don't know. It goes back to that same thing, trying to remember who I was then. Or who he was." I knew I had to say it, though it pained me. "Holden, what if I'd been doing drugs that night or something else that I can't remember? Messing around, driving too fast, or talking on my phone? What if the whole tragic thing was just completely because of me being stupid or reckless?"

"No." He shook his head. "No way."

"How are you so sure?"

"Emb, just because we weren't together doesn't mean you were unknown to me. You weren't taking drugs or acting crazy. Actually, you were doing kind of okay after our breakup—I was in a darker place, probably. You were hanging out with your dance friends, Lissa Mandrup and those people."

"Lissa . . ." Lissa had been in Holden's class, and had graduated last year. She'd been captain of our dance troupe. I could see her clearly in the dance studio, those red lips, those long black braids spinning with her as she executed a perfect pirouette. She'd always been a bit of a free spirit, fun and quirky. I hadn't known her well. At least, I hadn't thought I had.

Wow, that was something—friends with Lissa. She was studying dance full-time now, over at ABT. Maybe I could get her new email. No doubt Birdie had it. Though that would mean emailing Birdie . . . and I wasn't sure I was ready yet.

Holden's arm was around my shoulders. I'd missed that weight. It wasn't until Kai had kissed me this afternoon that I realized how much I'd missed boys in general. Holden's clean, cotton T-shirt smell could be intoxicating. But when he shifted his arm to pull me in, I winced.

Immediately, he let go. "You hurting still?"

"I'm achy tonight. Like maybe I slept weird on myself."

"Want me to get you some aspirin? Anything?" Holden peered at me, and his good looks struck me fresh—he could have modeled for one of those preppy catalogs. With the golden retriever at his side and a Martha's Vineyard breeze at his back. Except Holden wasn't vain. The furthest thing from. He'd never tried to be anything other than his own sweet self.

"No, thanks. I'm good." I stretched out. Just like old times. "It's only . . . after a day like today, I can't stand not knowing myself at that time," I confided. "It's so frustrating, that this sliver of me has been spirited away. And I think I was changing. Really changing."

"Changing how? Talk to me."

"It's little things. Hints and whispers. But I came back from Addington to find this poster in my room. You know that group Weregirl? I listen to their music all the time now. And when I was in Bushwick, I went to check out this dance club I'd been to. And I didn't remember it exactly, but I could swear I'd been there before. The thing is, I'll follow any clue because I keep thinking I'm missing something. Something big. Some, I don't know, elemental piece of myself."

I could sense Holden working through his words. "I wish I could help you with this. You know how much I'd want to. We broke up last Thanksgiving, and in January we weren't hanging out. We were really trying to give each other space."

"Right, I know. Dr. P says it's natural, almost normal, that

I've blocked those weeks before my accident. He promises I'll get it back. I've looked at calendars. My last memory sputters off around the end of December. And January, forget it—it's gone. Like it never happened. Bits and pieces start creeping in in late February. After I'd been at the hospital for about a week."

Holden stretched, extending his arms along the back of the couch as he tipped back his head. "First time they let me visit you had to be the end of February. Do you remember that?"

"When I was still drinking meals through a straw." And peeing through a catheter, and barely tolerating the pain that hammered down my spine, through the backs of my legs, into my feet, even through the wall of painkillers.

"But we broke up three months before the accident," said Holden. "The plain fact of it is we weren't together. And you weren't spending much time with Rachel."

"I don't remember. I don't remember about Lissa, either. January is just so not there for me."

"Well, in terms of the whole Rachel thing, neither of us wanted to involve her to the extent that she wanted to be involved. Rachel can be really bossy—"

"No way! Rachel?" I snorted.

Holden grinned. "Exactly. And it was a private thing."

Yes, private. Like that night, back in October, when Holden and I had been fooling around, nearly naked under the duvet, a nest of warmth against the autumn cold snap. Holden's parents had been away that weekend. He'd bought an apple votive from Yankee Candle. Docked "our" playlist. Made everything perfect. Except it wasn't perfect. I'd used the moment to confess that I thought we were getting too serious. The pre-breakup breakup. I remembered it perfectly.

He'd been crushed. So had I. A year ago. Did he still think about that night?

"Lissa's uptown, doing the full ballet press. I think you should get in touch."

"Did I really know her that well?"

He nodded. "Yeah, she was with you a lot, you know, after you and Rachel had a falling-out."

"Wait—now you're saying I had a *falling-out* with Rachel? Why?"

"It sounds mildly ridiculous to say our breakup was major drama for Rachel, but there it is." Holden shrugged. "She was like this kid that we both had custody over. And we wanted to be good parents, but sometimes we couldn't because that would have meant getting back together. Which was the only thing she wanted."

"I can't imagine not being friends with Rachel."

When he looked at me, eyes narrowed, I could feel it. Something Holden could have said right then, in the intimacy of the moment.

Could have said, but wouldn't. And I didn't even know how to ask for it.

"What'd I miss?" Rachel bounded like a gazelle into the room, hurtling over the back of the couch to land between us, then taking charge of the remote control.

"Nothing," we answered in unison.

8

Moments of Departure

Dear Ember,

Of course you're not "bugging" me. I'm glad to hear from you, and to learn that you're handling a full school-day workload. You've come a long way. And I promise to explain my answers to your questions in "regular" (I'm guessing by that you meant not too technical?) words. Send me a follow-up if there's anything you don't get. Or call me directly. Or, better yet, stop in—I can always make time for you!

1. Numbness/disembodiment. A common problem. We've spoken about miscalibration. People who sustain frontal lobe injuries often find it hard to emotionally communicate in response to a personal/charged situation, even if they are connecting with it. In response, they check out—the med-slang term is "to dishrag"— rather than react "correctly" to sudden noises, lights, loud music. Dishrag responses should mitigate with time. Ember, at vehicular impact, your brain was subjected to massive depolarization from acceleration/deceleration. It is the cause of most neurological fatalities. And even when the victim survives, it can take years for brain tissue to fully regenerate. You are probably far more sensitive to these "moments of departure," however, than those around you. Accept them; do not let them shock you.

2. Paranoia/terror. I appreciate your bravery in coming forward with this. I'm sure it is a disturbing sensation, to feel that you're being discussed or that secrets are being kept from you. I agree that you are grappling with a lot of stresses as a result of returning home and resuming your life. Nevertheless, if this persists or worsens, I can contact a clinical mentor at Long Island City Psychiatric Hospital. Let me know if you would like me to pursue this.

3. Missing memories. We have discussed this a bit, yes? And don't forget the good news: in over 70% of cases such as yours, a head-trauma patient will get partial-to-full memory restored. Given what you have told me about the preceding weeks (a breakup

with your boyfriend and a fight with your best friend), your amnesiac brain merely might want to bury unpleasantness. It is a bit as if Brain is telling you, "Ember, why do you need to hold on to that disturbing file? Let us delete it! We certainly have got enough on our plate right now!"

4. Tingling/sensations of cold & heat. Your last EMG (8 Sept.) was consistent with the radial nerve damage that was a direct result of spinal trauma. Your best treatment: plenty of sleep, a balanced diet, and scheduled, rigorous physical therapy. Your body wants to regulate and reestablish normalcy. When you come in next month for your cortisone shots, let's do another EMG.

Finally, just to restate what you already know, please keep up your work with Jenn. She was a visiting practitioner here, and she is extremely competent. A mature commitment to therapy will bridge the difference, in terms of restoring your body's flexibility and easing residual pain, as you return to a full schedule of physical activities.

> Best regards,
> "Dr. P"
> Vassilis Pipini, MD
> Department of Neurosurgery
> Weill Cornell Medical Center

9

Twenty Bucks Says

Just before I'd left, I'd given Kai my number. So he had mine, and I had his. But I figured he'd be the one to call me. Not the next day or even the next. But he'd be in touch. No doubt he would. So when I hadn't heard from him by the middle of the following week, I started to check my messages compulsively—a few times even phoning my cell phone from the landline. Just to make sure the ringer was on and working.

Full-on doubts began to replace my anticipation. I'd just assumed we'd made a connection. Had my battered brain missed some basic social cue? Maybe Kai hadn't felt the same entrancement, the same intrigue to know more about me.

He sure hadn't felt the same urgency.

Or, or—maybe he'd been playing me. Maybe I'd been the victim of one of those cruel best-friend bets. Maybe there'd been some second guy in the shadows across the street, egging him on: "Kai, twenty bucks says you can walk over and hook up with that lonely girl hanging out on the fire escape."

And then Kai took the dare and strolled across the street and stepped into the building while his pal—maybe that guy Hatch, his T-shirt business friend—stood smirking from across the street.

I could just imagine Hatch, the wingman. That semi-Neanderthal guy's guy with the greasy skin who looks like he'd barely know his own address.

Before we'd parted, Kai had torn the first page from his precious notebook, ripping a scrap for me to scribble my number, then printing his own above the quick sketch he'd drawn of me. The lines were loose but the likeness was spot-on. He'd even given me more hair, not that I'd asked for it. But it was as if he'd guessed how I felt about the raggedy chop I'd gotten in the hospital, and wanted to help me out.

Forget him, I decided, when it seemed the call was not happening. But I couldn't. Kai was stuck in the grooves of my thoughts. It scared me to think that I'd bungled the situation. Like I was too damaged and "miscalibrated," imagining there'd been an electric connection between us when there hadn't been anything.

I felt duped, and in other moments I felt like an idiot.

On Wednesday evening, almost a week later and still no call,

I decided to do it. Just one brave, quick "Hi, how are you?" and then I'd know exactly where I was with him. I wouldn't even ask Rachel's advice—if it went badly, I'd bury it, and force myself never to think about Kai again. But somehow I'd misplaced the scrap of paper. Which just didn't make sense. I tore through my room like a CIA agent, searching everywhere—pockets, drawers—before I sat down and attempted Kai's number from memory.

When I punched the numbers in, I was pretty sure I had it right. But the voice mail message was impersonal, a droidbot informing me that if I wanted to leave a message, please wait for the tone.

I didn't. I clicked off, my cheeks hot. Maybe Kai had given me a wrong number? Or I'd memorized it wrong. How could I have lost the paper?

I sank to the edge of my bed.

Okay, *think*, Ember. I wouldn't have thrown it out. And now I was going to turn my room upside down to find it. Again, I ransacked my backpack, my desk drawers, my closet, my bureau, searching, flinging items, cursing—where the hell, what the— *aha!*

There it was. Inside my jewelry box. Folded into a tight square, in the corner. Next to my teeth.

My heart beat hard as I smoothed the stiff creases and stared at the sketch of perfected, prettier Ember. The sequence of digits above, in Kai's elegant, artist's lettering. And yes, it was the same phone number that I'd memorized. How could I have forgotten that I'd placed it here? My temples were beginning to throb with the threat of one of my headaches—a pain I'd never suffered until the accident, but which now frequently plagued me.

I called the number again. Again, voice mail. My voice was the worst kind of girl-speak, too high, quavering.

"Hey. It's me. Ember. Just wanted to see what you're up to. We talked about maybe getting together, sometime? Chocolate silk pie or pizza pie, or whatever. So if you want, or, you know, maybe . . ." And then I recited my own phone number. Hurried, nervous, not casual enough.

My whole body was thudding with my head as I ended the call.

It was a total desperation move. I should have waited for him to call me. Eager, vulnerable, pathetic me.

If Kai didn't call me back by the end of the week, I'd chalk it up to a Small, Humiliating Failure, with a touch of Learning Experience. The problem with a guy like Kai was that he was too "fringy"—a term Smarty used for city kids we couldn't cross-check through other friends or schools or anyone. He was too many degrees of separation, and I had no character references; nobody I knew would know this kid Kai, not in Lafayette or the neighborhood. Nothing.

And if I really thought about it, the whole thing was too clumsy. To kiss a total stranger on a fire escape? Of course he wasn't calling back. Served me right. No matter how exotic it had seemed at the time.

I'd always been too ready to believe in the fairy tale. But it wasn't good to keep rolling around in the memories of this first chapter, when that was obviously all the story there was.

10

Blood Perfume Shoes

"Presenting! My famous! Roasted fig and goat cheese with rosemary in a Stilton crust pastry pizza!" I slid it out of the oven onto the counter. It looked pretty damn gorgeous, if I did say so myself. Bubbling and crisping in all the right places.

But right from Rachel's first bite, I knew the truth. "What?" I demanded. "What's with that face?"

"I've told you how I feel about goat cheese. Tastes like goat butt."

"Oh, so sorry. I didn't realize that my making you this special homemade gourmet lunch was so bottom line, poor you."

"I'm just saying."

"Try a corner."

"Eh. I don't know, Emb." After a third bite, Rachel set down her slice. "Give me a stuffed-crust Little Caesars pepperoni any day over this."

"It's not that bad." Except that when I wheel-sliced out my own triangle, I had to admit it wasn't great, either. It wasn't anything. It had no soul. I flipped back to the recipe. "What the hell. You saw me follow this to a T." Did it need more honey? Were the figs watery? You couldn't do anything about the mustiness of goat cheese—you were either into it or it tasted dirty, or as Rachel had more bluntly put it, like butt. "The ingredients looked so fresh at the farmers' market."

But none of the elements had added up.

"The main thing about your cooking," said Rachel, "is that it used to be . . ."

"Used to be what?"

Her teeth found her bottom lip. "I dunno."

"No, seriously. Used. To. Be. What?" I could feel myself all flamed up in agitation. I didn't want to be. I wished that Rachel's answer didn't matter so much to me.

"Ember, not everything about you needs to be remade into a Nancy Drew mystery. And it's the weekend. I thought weekends meant time off from playing 'The Clue to Your Old Self' or 'The Secret of the Rehabbed Psyche' with you, right?"

"Don't joke, Smarty. Just tell me—for two seconds indulge me and explain what you meant. How was I different?"

"Okay. Fine." Rachel sat up straight, like a pupil ready to recite the correct answer in front of the whole class. "Here's the thing. Your cooking used to be a hobby that you enjoyed. You did it for fun and games. A pinch here, a dash of that, oops, forgot to preheat in time, but who cares? That kind of thing. But now you do it like homework. Like something you're studying for—a physics test. And the whole process . . . well, I hate to see how it upsets you, okay?" She put up her hands. "I come in peace."

I nodded. I knew Rachel was right. My attitude was off. I couldn't find the joy of the experiment. The measuring, tasting, seasoning, wondering. In the past couple of weeks, I'd challenged myself to multiple dishes—comfort food like lasagna, plus more complicated recipes using egg whites and double boilers. Not a single dish had turned out to be anything special.

I had to face it: I was just an okay cook.

My friends used to love dropping in for Friday Follies because those Fridays had been a party, with the menu made up of their own special requests: blackened skillet chicken for Perrin, butternut squash tart for Rachel, ginger-chocolate ice cream for Keiji. They'd come over, hang out, and inhale my feasts, then gear up for a later night of parties or clubs or the movies—or sometimes they'd just thump downstairs, lazy and overfed, to the den to watch random television.

I'd daydreamed of those Follies while I'd been at Addington. It had been yet another reason to get well and come home. Dr. P had even encouraged it.

"Find your safety zone," he'd told me. "Find your comfort."

Once upon a time, I'd loved being in the kitchen. And I'd been good at it, too. Was the love still there? Or was the new me just flying blind in a wobbly parody of my old self?

I refocused. The sheet of figs and cheese, no longer bubbling, now looked curdled and sad. I picked at my slice. "It's like somewhere down recipe lane, I just dishrag and then—"

"Will you please, *please* stop describing yourself as a *dishrag?*" Rachel asked exasperatedly. "I don't need a smelly hand towel for a best friend."

"Easy for you. You're not the one who's lost—"

"You haven't lost a single—"

"Don't tell me what I haven't lost," I snapped. "Or what I was. Or who I am." I foil-wrapped the pizza—maybe my parents would want it—and then began tearing the extra pastry apart with my bare hands, shoving it through the garbage disposal's rubber shield to the teeth below and flipping on the switch for the motorized grind.

Had Anthony Travolo liked to cook?

These kinds of questions had begun to circle me like vultures lately, especially since my Google searches hadn't pulled up anything more breakthrough than names and addresses of various random Travolos in Carroll Gardens and Bensonhurst. His name was Italian—had he been a pasta guy? A steak eater? What had his last meal been, before he got in the car with me? What had we been talking about, that moment before I lost control of the wheel? What were the last words in his last conscious breath? My eyes brimmed at the thought, my throat went thick. Another side effect of head trauma—laryngeal reflux. Also known as occasional mucus overload.

Pretty gross. Plus it made me hate to cry.

Rachel was at my side, her hand steady on my shoulder. "Relax, Ember. It's only food."

"It's not. It's me. It's a part of me that's missing. Where did I go?"

"You're right here. Come on. You have to stop being so hard on yourself. It's going to come back just the way you want, Embie. I know it." She began to crack her knuckles, her usual sign of nervousness. "Okay, here's my worst, but I really feel like you asked for it. What did the cannibal order for takeout?"

"What?"

"Pizza, with everyone on it."

"Ugh." But I could feel myself smiling. "Are all your jokes from the How to Be an Annoying Fourth Grader's operating manual?"

"Hey, I got a smile out of you. I'd way rather see you be exasperated than sad. And listen—you've got your whole life to be a French chef. Truth is, the average high school class runs on Pop-Tarts, Corn Pops, and Red Bull. So how about you just sit back and enjoy something that crunches while we talk Halloween." With one long arm, Rachel easily plucked two bowls from the top shelf and then shook the box of cereal on the counter.

"Yes, Halloween. No, Corn Pops."

"Cereal snob." Rachel replaced one bowl with a sigh, then dumped her own bowl straight to the rim. "So here's our dilemma, as I see it. Are we going to Lucia's Halloween party? Even though it's in Tribeca and we have no idea if superrich Italian beauty queens know how to throw a party?"

"I think so," I answered. "If we don't drop by, Claude will feel snubbed. And then we'll never hear the end of it."

Rachel made a face. "Annoying but true. Agreed."

"So, wedding zombies," I said. "Are we definitely decided on that?"

"Yes, but not gross-out. Fashionable zombies, all dressed up.

With the blood daubed on like perfume. A couple of tasteful splotches at the neck and wrists."

"Mmm. Let me write this down." I found a notebook by the phone and wrote, *blood—perfume*. "What about shoes?"

"Dunno, but it sounds like a joke, doesn't it? Where do zombies buy their shoes?"

"A bad joke. A Rachel Smart joke." I wrote, *shoes?* Then I stared at the paper. The words *blood perfume shoes* seemed to blur and break apart into fragments before my eyes. It was as if a winter wind had slivered through the room. Shivering, I looked down. I saw my bare feet and I saw black biker boots with thick silver metal grommets at the ankle. I saw a kitchen floor and I also saw a concrete pavement. Wet leaves blown by the chill of a first freeze. I could hear a rhythmic thud of footfalls. I was on a bridge, a gray chop of water stretched all around me, and I was singing, from faraway I could hear an echo of my own voice, the tune was Weregirl, I was singing with someone, and now he stopped and I could feel his mouth on my neck, nipping it, his lips soft and cool against me, but somebody was watching, somebody I disliked, my body tensed, I turned my head—

"Ember!" Rachel had zoomed in close, flapping a hand in front of my face. I jumped. "Dishrag girl! Where'd you go?"

"What?" I blinked.

"You just completely freaked me out! Talk about zombies! You weren't here!"

My heart was pounding. On the notebook, I'd doodled that funny-looking A, that same character that I'd written on my hand my first day home. I stared at it hard, as if it were capable of giving me more. Was the A for *Anthony*?

"Smarty," I whispered. "I think I went back."

"Back where?"

"To January. In the memory pocket. In my head."

"Aaaand?" Rachel raised a stagy eyebrow. "Whatever did you see there, time traveler?"

She was joking, but I was right. I'd been back. I closed my eyes to find it again. Pressed the heels of my hands into the hollows of my eye sockets. "Nothing really. It was winter, and I was walking, singing. I was with someone." I didn't mention my neck, his mouth. "It was ice-cold, but the images were etched so clear. Like a dream."

When I glanced at Rachel, she had her arms crossed. Skeptical.

"Sorry." I flushed. "Forget it. I'm back! Zombie costumes. Shoes—to be decided." I picked up the pen and scribbled loop-de-loops through the mark. "Let's see if we can find hospital gauze instead of toilet paper. I bet that the gauze will be more durable. Especially if it's raining on Halloween, our costumes will dissolve."

"Ember."

I looked up. "What?"

"Are you okay to be a zombie?"

"What do you mean? Why not?"

"Maybe you'd rather be something less morbid. Maybe zombies are putting you in the wrong head space."

"God, Smarty. I'm not that sensitive, am I?"

Rachel began popping her knuckles, from thumb to pinkie. "Sometimes it's hard to tell what you want, minute by minute."

"The bandages will hide my scars." I touched my forehead. "Unless . . . I went as the lead singer of Weregirl. Now *that's* an easy costume—ripped tights and an army jacket and patrol boots."

"And then you can enjoy all the blank stares since nobody knows that band."

"Smarty, when did I start liking Weregirl? I listen to them all the time now."

"Ugh, Ember. I don't know. I wasn't keeping babysitting tabs on you after you deep-sixed Holden," said Rachel—her voice had gone flat in that way I'd come to recognize when she spoke about last year. "You turned distant. Holden was in a terrible place, and I had cousin custody of him. Plus you didn't want me." Then it was as if she were making a conscious effort to lighten up, as she stuck out her tongue, then dug back into her Pops. "So bottom line, poor me."

"I don't remember Holden being in bad shape."

"Well, he's proud, you know. Not pitiful."

"The breakup was hard on us both."

"Hard on us *all*. You checked out, Emb. Even when I tried to find a way back to being friends."

"Right. I know."

"Hey, I think I want to be the groom zombie," she said. "I'm taller with no boobs. You wear—used to wear—dresses all the time. You should be the one to go bridal."

Used to. I used to wear dresses all the time. But I don't anymore. Ever. I fobbed off the suggestion with a shrug. "Except it's the one night I can put on Dad's eighties tux jacket. So how about let's be two groom zombies?"

"Oh, you're so *difficult* sometimes." But then Rachel begrudged a smile. "Okay, fine." And then, as if daring herself, she wolfed down the rest of the pizza slice. "Not bad, actually."

"Liar." I smiled. She was trying, I knew. Trying to understand this girl I'd become, after the breakup, the accident, the year away from her. She wanted to preserve and maybe even reinvent our friendship, to be here for me—whatever parts of me she could find. And I knew I wanted her back, too. It wasn't her fault I was partly hidden from her. In many ways, I was hidden from everyone. Myself included.

11

Get Sweaty, Look Sexy, Dance Freaky

"Eeeeee!" Perrin squeaked and hopped for warmth, battling the sudden temperature drop and sounding a lot like the mouse she'd dressed up as tonight. "Let us in already!"

I pressed my finger three seconds longer on the bell of Lucia's chrome-and-glass Tribeca apartment. It was rude, but we were freezing.

"Fancy-schmance building," murmured Sadie, huddling deeper inside her fake-fur cat coat. "Doesn't Robert De Niro live here?"

"People think De Niro lives in every single building in Tribeca," said Tom.

Sadie giggled. "Maybe he does."

"Well, I don't see him up there." Rachel had stepped back to squint up in the window. "But I am seeing a vast parent conspiracy. Yeesh. What if it's *that* kind of party?"

"Then we all drop the cyanide tablets together," murmured Keiji-the-Hulk. "After we eat, of course. I bet there's good 'derves."

"Parents?" Sadie pursed her lips side to side to make her wire whiskers twitch. "What is she thinking?"

"Who knows? Of all the guys at Lafayette, Lucia picked *Claude*," reminded Rachel. "So who knows what further secret insanity she's capable of?"

Perrin had started a round of jumping jacks. "It's the freezingest night of the year tonight. Why'd I only wear a hoodie?"

I'd underdressed, too, in a bubble-gum-pink overcoat that I couldn't believe I'd ever picked out for myself, let alone wanted to wear in public—but it beat the electric-pink ski jacket that I'd left hanging in my closet. Except the ski jacket would have been warmer, and the left pocket in my overcoat had torn so that its bottom hem was weighted with at least a pound of loose change. My cold fingers dug for a handful of coins stuck in the hem, but then I couldn't manage to pull everything back up through the lining.

At Addington, there was always a nurse or a therapist with a blanket or a warming pad, making sure I was retaining my body heat. Tonight was the first time in months that I was in genuine discomfort—and there was nobody looking to rescue me from it. Which was kind of awful and wonderful at the same time.

"JAY-sus." Tom grimaced, flashing his Day-Glo vampire fangs. "Answer the door already, Lucia. I can practically taste my mug of cider."

I've been here before. The thought knocked the air from my lungs just as the door swung open to reveal Claude in a gold silk shirt and black pants paired with a velvet blazer that gave off a hint of vintage porn star.

"Claude! Is that a costume—or are you merely acknowledging that you're the creepiest person we know?" Perrin made a face as we all stumbled like a flock of badly herded sheep into the warmth of the foyer. I laughed along with the others, but my thoughts raced in a private blizzard.

Yes, I'd been inside this apartment! I'd been here to see something—*what?*

Claude gave Perrin the finger. He was overly excited and way too full of himself as he led us through the sumptuous foyer. "Let that dude take your coats. He's their butler, a pretty cool guy," Claude explained as a uniformed man began to whisk away our coats and stack them under his arm.

"There's a lot of beautiful art here," I said to Rachel as it struck me. A painting. Yes. That's why I'd been here. To look at a painting.

"Yeah?" Rachel gave me a look. "How do you know? Did Lucia tell you that?"

"Um, I think so." I'd been here, but not with Rachel. But it was familiar enough that I could have predicted the art deco furniture, the black-lacquered wood polish and gilded mirrors. Blood rushed to my head as I stepped in deeper.

Where was the painting? Someone had told me things about

it, *whispered them in my ear*, when I'd seen it hanging here for the very first time.

We were all following Claude, who was still insisting on playing host. "It's a duplex with the roof deck. It belongs to Lucia's uncle," he explained, "and he's a big-deal art collector. They're in a house swap. Right now he's living in Bologna with his family, and that's why Lucia's family's here."

"Was Lucia's family depressed to find out you came with the place, Claude? Kind of like their own pet weasel?" Perrin teased. She and Claude had dated briefly freshman year, and they had a way of dealing with each other that was rude and yet affectionate—the secret language of exes.

"Yeah, yeah, keep on me, Perrin. Like you wouldn't do the exact same thing. Best views in the city. Check out the gold-leaf detail in the doorway. Eighteen-karat."

I didn't care about gold leaf. Which was the room that held the painting? This party was strange, too crowded and too formal, too many blank faces staring me down into social quicksand. But when I closed my eyes, I could feel myself back here, only in a less-stressed zone, wandering again through these vast, extravagant rooms as if lost in a lovely dream. With him—I'd been with him. The boy who kissed me on the bridge was the same one who'd whispered in my ear.

"We're screwed." Now it was Rachel whispering in my ear. "This scene is totally old people. Worse than church. *Not* how I saw my Halloween."

"Give it a few more minutes." I spied Lucia's kid sister—she couldn't have been more than eight—handling a tray like she was running the party. Cute, but obnoxious. It was definitely that kind of party. But I wanted to explore. The living room was enormous and yet secretive, with long, dark corridors and closed doors in all directions.

The painting wasn't down those halls. It was in a darker room . . . the dining room. Yes, that felt right.

"Hey, where's the dining room, Claude?"

"I'll show you. By the way, Lucia's parents are totally *prego* about drinking. Italians aren't hung up on stupid legality," said Claude over his shoulder as we followed him to the far end of the living room, then through an open archway and into the velvet cocoon of the dining room—*yes, this was it*—where the table was a king's feast of runny cheeses, glowing pink sushi, and oysters on their iced, tiered platters. "Try the oysters; they're like fifty bucks a pound. You have to use those tiny forks."

Right over there.

Goose bumps sprouted over my arms.

Near the corner. You'd miss it unless you were looking for it. The tucked-away, wood-framed square was overshadowed by a pair of old-fashioned portraits hanging above the sideboard. I sidled closer, leaving Rachel to maneuver a cup of punch from the crystal bowl, while Tom clattered up his plate with oysters and Claude bragged about the caviar like he'd harvested it himself.

I moved to the painting as if pulled in by a magnet.

It was a portrait in oil and gouache—okay, and how'd I know this word *gouache* anyway, but I did, both spelling and pronunciation (gwash)—of a young woman. Her fingers were splayed over her face, her skin was dappled in light, her eyes were outlined with feathery, exaggerated lashes. She was lush and unreal, but not artificial. She was like a dream girl, possibly hallucinatory.

But it was the signature that really startled me. The insecty lettering on the bottom right: A. *Travolo*.

No. Impossible. But yes, he'd painted this. I yearned to reach out my finger and touch the surface. To trace the shape of the mark. Had it been Anthony's whisper in my ear, then? Had it been his kiss on the bridge? Was it at his invitation that I'd been at this apartment before?

Of course it was. We'd known each other, somehow. But I was too nervous, too uncollected in my head to point out the signature to Rachel. Not that she was particularly preoccupied with my mental state.

"No DJ, no music," she murmured. "This is worse than my cousin Marva's wedding reception in Palm Springs. What are we gonna do next?"

"I don't know." I couldn't take my eyes off Anthony's signature. I wished I could be here alone to stare at this painting in silence. But that wouldn't work tonight. Rachel's disappointment was making her clingy.

"And it looks like we lost Sadie and Perrin to a couple of weird Euro-yuppies." Rachel frowned out into the living room, where I saw that Perrin and Sadie were drinking champagne and madly flirting with two past-college-age guys. "It'll be hard to motivate them. Meantime, Tom's going to eat oysters till he pukes if we don't spring him. Don't you think we should take off?"

"Um . . ." I did want to go, but I was reluctant to leave the memory. My mind reached back into this new, glowing warmth. The secret brush of an arm against mine. The hush of that whisper in my ear again. Had it been Anthony, or someone else?

"I could call some people," Rachel continued. "Would it be

too awkward to call Holden?" She was fiddling with her phone, dying to use it.

That luminous bath of light and color. Who was that girl in the painting? I had to look away and I couldn't.

"Okay, fine, Holden's a bad idea," she answered into my silence. "But look over there. I bet Keiji won't leave, either. Check him out, mingling, being charming. Traitor. What is *wrong* with us that we didn't make a Halloween plan B?" Rachel was staring at her phone as if hoping it would beam her a new plan. She glanced up. "And why do you keep looking at that picture?"

"Don't know." I stepped away, physically removing myself from it. Suddenly the banquet table made me realize how hungry I was. "I think I need to eat."

"Go nuts; you're in the right place. But what I need is a bathroom. Don't you dare sneak off anywhere. Be right back." As Rachel slipped away, I reached for a bread wheel and spooned up some tapas. Tahini, black olive, plum tomato—was that fennel? There was a time when I could reel off every ingredient on a first taste. I'd been a champ at that. Had I lost it? Didn't seem so. I could even taste pink peppercorn. I smiled quietly to myself. Cool.

Then I stole another look at the painting, scouring it for answers. It wasn't unfamiliar. What else did I know about it? About Anthony?

"Ember!"

I turned. The girl was boyishly elfin, with pale, silky hair sliptucked behind her ears. She was staring at me from the way other side of the room, wearing a latex yellow superhero mask that hid half her face. Her eyes were big as drain stoppers beneath it. Immediately I knew that like this apartment, she was someone from the *then*. The blackout pocket. I'd known her once, absolutely. Even if I didn't quite exactly know her now.

"Hey!" I gave a weak wave as I swallowed my last bite of bread. Could she see through my smile, my cheerful "recognition"? Not a single name buzzed my brain.

The girl stared at me another second and then decided to approach, sidestepping bodies down the length of the table to come around and meet me.

"Did you know me?" The way she asked it assumed that I did. "With the costume, I mean?"

"I mean, I'm like ninety percent . . ." My laugh was an apology, that she wouldn't take it too personally.

"Oh. It's me. Maisie." Her eyes drank me in. "Wow. I heard you were home. I guess I heard right. You don't look—you don't look as bad as how I'd heard."

"You might not have said that six months ago." My mind was flying through the mental filing cabinets. Who was she?

Luckily, Maisie didn't appear to sense my confusion. "The whole thing. Oh my God, Ember. So horrible. And then to think how long you've been away. I'm just so sorry. I can't really." She paused. "But, just to say, you look great. From what I can tell. Under the zombie-costume situation."

How do I know you? I couldn't make myself ask her a single question. I just couldn't. It shamed me. I didn't want to admit that the accident had stolen every memory of the elf girl, too, when it had already taken so much.

"Look, I'm about to go," she said. "This party's a little bit, um." We smiled. On that point, there was no need to elaborate.

"But first I'm gonna go pick up Alice—she's in the studio till last minute as usual. We're heading over together. It's supposed to be incredible tonight. Hey, idea." Her smile was shy. "Wanna join up?"

She seemed to think I understood what she was talking about. I faltered, then confessed. "The thing is, I don't know where you're going."

"Areacode." But now something clicked in Maisie. She stared at me like I'd failed an easy quiz. "You can still get sweaty, look sexy, and dance freaky, right?"

I smiled in nonanswer. *Areacode*. Now the word just reminded me of Kai. Beautiful Kai. Stupid jerk who disappeared, who never called me—wrong number Kai.

But Areacode must have been a place I went to before, a routine from before Kai. And Maisie's name was familiar—Facebook, right? I had over one thousand friends on Facebook, and most of them weren't friends. And who was Alice?

"The other thing is," I told her, "I'm here with other people."

Maisie nodded, put her hands on her hips, and lifted one leg to stand like a sultry flamingo. She was a girl who wanted to be looked at. She was almost defiant about it. Now I saw her shoes— Doc Martens, covered with a rainbow of spray paint. She'd obviously done it herself. Now she was looking at the painting. Her gaze flicked back to me, as if she was deciding whether to ask me something. "Have you been in touch?" she asked. "With anyone else in his crew, anything like that?"

My throat closed up. Anthony. "Um, not so much," I managed.

"Are you tight with any of them?"

"Actually, no. I mean, it's not like I knew Anthony that well, either." It had to be true, right? How does someone know anyone that well, in a space of six weeks?

"Okay, sure." Maisie's mask made it harder for me to tell what she was thinking. She glanced again at the painting. "At least they didn't take it down. Anyway, it's good to see you, Ember. Come by if you can. But I understand if . . . that's too hard." And then she was gone, floating out through the archway, her superhero cape paunched out behind her, just as Rachel cruised up on my side.

"Who was that?"

"Some girl I used to know. A dancer." The heat in my skin seemed uncomfortably constricted under all my wrapped gauze.

Anthony must have been a regular at Areacode, too. There were reasons I'd been drawn to it. I shouldn't have let Maisie slip away so quickly. "She gave me a tip. There's a good party tonight, over at this club called Areacode."

"Where's that?"

"I've been there. It's just a warehouse out in Bushwick." I stared Rachel in the eye. "Might be better than here. We should go."

"Go where?" asked Tom, joining up with us from behind, his cocktail napkin full of toothpicked shrimp.

"The good news is Ember sniffed out a party. The bad news is it's way the hell out in Bushwick," said Rachel. "Probably some crappy mosh pit."

Tom rolled his eyes at me. "The day has come. I knew it was a matter of time before you'd go all club rat on us again. With the breakup boots and the attitude."

"Shut up, Tom," Rachel snapped. "This is a social emergency. Stay here and it's your funeral." But Tom was annoyed. I'd struck a nerve with him. *Club rat.* And what were breakup boots? I tingled with embarrassment, but I stood my ground.

"Even a mosh pit beats this party," I said.

"Count me out," Tom said. "I'll freeze my nuts off outside. Meantime they're letting us drink in here, and it's not watered-down tap beer. And Lucia's got some cute cousins. So, no, I'm not changing anything. I'll tell Keiji and the others you're both taking off." And with a neutral shrug, he loped off.

"Buzzkill! Who needs him chaperoning us, anyway?" Rachel wriggled her eyebrows. "The painful truth is that Tom knows it's too hard for high school guys to get into clubs. He'd have held us back. The night's in our hands now."

12

Manic Edge

It could be heard from the street, a tribal drumbeat that became a buzz saw of sound once we'd stumbled out of the freight elevator and into Areacode's black-cave dance space. Five minutes later, I was pretty sure I'd gone half deaf from it.

"Now *this* is what I call a haunted house! Am I right?" a female voice blasted in my ear. Was she talking to me? I whipped around to stare into the face of a phantom. Her face was caked in white paint, her eyes were raccoon-smudged in eyeliner, and a black hag wig was perched like an actual raccoon on her head.

"What?" I asked. *Do I know you?*

The girl blinked and reared back. "Oops! Sorry! I *totally* thought you were someone else!"

"No problem." A true stranger. Not a semi-stranger, like Maisie. It could make me crazy wondering who I knew, who I sort of knew. At least I had Rachel. Her lanky, poised presence was a buffer.

"You sure we never came here together?" I asked.

Rachel made a face. "No way. But since we *are* here, want to drop coats?"

We'd been holding on to them. But I gratefully tossed my pink-bubble-gum coat in with the others, in a huge corner pile. The nerdy LANDS' END tag painfully visible. Obviously this had been another Mom purchase, for the version of me who hadn't minded dressing like a Hello Kitty doll. I'd need to find a weekend job soon if I wanted to start saving for a cool winter coat.

"You see anyone you know?" shouted Rachel. "That friend of Anthony's?"

I'd been squinting for Maisie since we'd come up. My body was on alert, waiting to be recognized. Wondering if any of Travolo's people might approach. Their tentative smiles, my name spoken shyly—"*Ember? Is that you?*"

"I never, ever met that guy," Rachel attested, though she'd told me this before. "It makes sense he was a club-scene kid. And I don't know what kind of conversation you need about all this, Emb, but I'm not sure a nightclub Halloween party is the best time to go looking for it."

She was probably right. But I hadn't told her about the painting, and I couldn't let Maisie glide off, either. On the freight elevator, I'd felt a spark of déjà vu. Something about the way the car had lurched and groaned, how the traction cables had stuck above the fourth floor, then bounced to the fifth, shuddering a moment before it fell plumb and was safe to manually unlock.

It was more of a sensation than full recall—and yet it stopped me from being scared. If I'd been here, it was because I'd wanted to be here.

"Be honest. Was I really a club rat last year?" I asked Rachel. "And what are breakup boots?"

"They were just motorcycle boots. Breakup boots is what Claude starting calling them. As in post-Holden. Hey, *I* thought they were badass, but you know guys like Claude. They always prefer girls in camis and ballet flats." Like the prow of a thin ship, Rachel was guiding us into the overcrowded main space.

Two weeks ago, when I'd been on the outside peering in, Area-code had been an empty cave. But now it was painted in black-light and Day-Glo from floor to ceiling, with dry-ice machines puffing fake fog to make it look like a Halloween graveyard. The corners were tangled with "webs," dummy bodies dangled from the rafters, and rubber heads stared in anguish from their spikes along the bar. In the booth, a DJ in a grim reaper hood was spinning mash-ups.

Suddenly, for the first time in months, *I wanted to dance*. And yet I hung back, unsure. Ever since my kindergarten ballet class, my body had identified with dancing. Even after that uneasy blooming summer between sixth and seventh grades, when I'd gone from being tiny and twiggy to the weighted, curvy shape I lived in now.

It had been almost a year since I'd tried so much as a spin in place.

"This scene is on," I commented softly.

"You think?" Rachel was coughing, waving at the air. "I say it's too much!"

"At least we got in." There'd been a huge line outside. Our zombie costumes, combined with the fact that we hadn't arrived with guys, had definitely helped us past the ropes.

"Listen, Embie, if you can't find those other people, I don't want to be here forever." Rachel pulled a face. "It's all fun and games till my eardrums burst like crystal." But she didn't stop me when I moved in deeper.

"We'll leave as soon as we find out it sucks," I promised. The thumping bass line ricocheted off the walls through the marrow of my body. The dance floor was dark and writhing. The combination of mood and music excited me—even if I didn't dance, I wanted to stay.

"Ooh, Lafayette alum sighting." Rachel pointed. "I spy with my little eye Lissa Mandrup. Of course. This party was *invented* for Lissa Mandrup."

I glanced over. Lissa had seen me first. Eyes shining, she threw out her arms wide, beckoning me to come join her.

Rachel tensed. "I'm not sure I want to dance right now. Do you?"

"Kind of I do, kind of I don't know."

"I should have had a nice drink at Lucia's when I had the chance." Rachel was turning, scanning the crowd. Suddenly she latched her fingers to my wrist. "Don't look, don't look. I've got a Jake Weinstock sighting!" She spun to face me; her eyes were huge and unblinking. "Okay, I've got to talk to him. I need to go pretend to read those fake tombstones, and see if he says something to me."

"I think Lissa just saw me," I said. "You go. Jake won't want me third-wheeling."

Rachel appeared doubtful. She stole another look across the room. "Okay. But keep a watch on me. And don't get too into it with Lissa. She looks like she's on drugs tonight."

I mostly doubted that. Lissa Mandrup could find her natural dance high better than anyone. But Rachel's warning niggled at me. Had I been friends with a druggie? It tapped my deepest fear, that I hadn't been chemically myself that night that Anthony Travolo and I went over the bridge. No matter how clean Dr. P had promised the report had been, or how purely accidental my loss of control on the wheel, it couldn't tell me about my general trending behavior, my influences, whatever darkness I might have been going through that dragged us to the deep Below.

But I let Rachel go find Jake, with assurances that I wouldn't leave the club without her.

As if.

Lissa was still waving, beckoning me to join.

I checked around just one more time for Maisie. Nothing. Damn.

Okay. Breathing through it.

Lissa's dance style was polished and pretty, with a manic edge. She was a magnet on the floor, pulling everyone's attention toward her. Last year she'd been captain of Lafayette's A-squad dance, and she'd been a lead dancer every year. I'd taken ballet, jazz, tap, and modern dance with her—both in and out of school—since sixth grade. And I'd been in awe of her in each and every class.

Tonight, Lissa looked like a fractured fairy tale in her shredded tutu and ripped tights, her raven braids pinned up in a messy,

Swiss-doll style. Like Holden, she seemed older and more remote, now that she'd graduated from Lafayette.

I couldn't dance yet. I wasn't ready. But as soon as I'd crossed into her space, Lissa whooped and stopped, her planky arms hugging me long and damply.

"You're back, finally!" she squealed. "But is it true?"

"Is what true?"

"That you're not dancing anymore?" We moved together toward the edge of the floor, the better to talk and be heard.

I nodded. "Strictly sidelines. My afternoons are nothing but physical therapy. Which is as tough as dancing, except with none of the grace, and no gorgeous recital at the end."

"I figured you'd quit sooner or later, once you didn't get that part in *Chicago*. I mean, it was just a school show, not a community thing, but still."

I'd lost out on a part in a show? Oh. I'd conveniently blocked that little failure. I decided not to pursue it, for now. "How's school?"

"I never sleep! You need to come visit me; I'm in student housing—the Meredith Willson res uptown." Lissa was squeezing my fingertips. "Did you get my email? I know, I know, I should have written way more; I'm the queen of procrastinating. And this year, holy cow. It's nothing but rehearsals. Did I tell you Lafayette almost didn't let me graduate because I flunked math? Can you imagine anything more wrong than doing another year at Laf? I was in such a pickle—I had to take summer school—and then I ran away to Russia! For all the rest of the summer!" Her laugh was more bark, as if she were still shocked by her nerve.

"Russia? That's awesome! What'd you do there?" I was shouting over the music; I could feel my lungs working for the extra pumps of air.

"I studied with the Bolshoi, as part of their ballet exchange program. It was incredible. Anyway. Jeepers, *Ember*. I missed you." Her eyes bored deep into mine.

"I missed you, too." And it was true. I hadn't felt the tug of not seeing her till this minute, all these months later. And here she was, long-leggity Lissa with those same black eyes glittering like mica, her cheeks blotted tea-rose pink in her vanilla skin, her inky threads of hair wisping from her braids. No Lissa, no dancing, no Areacode—none of these prized, wild moments had been in my life since February, and I hadn't even remembered to yearn for them.

"And the mad scientists made you perfect again!" Now Lissa grabbed both of my hands and swung them out. "Jeez Louise, but I totally hate how your bangs hide your face!"

"Yeah, yeah." I had to smile. Lissa's bluntness could be as surprising as those quirky grandma expressions like "in a pickle" that she sometimes used. "I give up. What are you dressed as? Coppélia?"

"I'm dressed as myself—a crazy ballerina." Now Lissa dropped my hands to hold my shoulders. "This place is almost as packed as New Year's Eve! Remember last New Year's Eve?"

I smiled so I didn't have to lie.

"Hey, and I'd *still* buy that jacket off you, whenever you're selling."

What jacket? She couldn't mean the pink-bubble-gum coat—a boho girl like Lissa wouldn't be caught dead in that mess. But now something else was happening. Little bits of New Year's

Eve were beginning to flutter down on me like pieces of ticker tape. Sweet, tangled memory. Blowers and streamers. Gold, glittery top hats and oversized Happy New Year sunglasses. A crush of bodies—I'd been so warm that night. Claustrophobic—I could feel it again, the need for fresh air.

"Come dance." She tugged my arm. "It'll be like old times."

"I can't." I could feel myself ready to bolt. Not yet, not me—no.

"Of course you can."

"No, I can't. And, um . . . I brought a friend, see . . ." I looked around till I found gauze-wrapped Rachel, bendy-noodly in a far corner, talking intensely to equally noodly Jake, who was immediately recognizable despite his Spider-Man mask. They were standing close, right by the fire-escape window.

That view. That was the same fire escape where Kai and I had sat outside.

"Oh, come on. Five minutes?" Lissa pleaded.

"Maybe later," I apologized. "I have to hit the restroom. So good to see you, Lissa. But I gotta . . . go. . . ." And I leapt away from her bewildered reaction before she could find the words to protest.

13

You In or Out?

The bathroom was over-lit and unisex and crowded. When I finally got my turn and emerged from the stall, I had to smile. I should have known Lissa would follow me in. She was standing inconveniently in front of the towel dispenser, not paying attention to the others—who even went so far as to apologize when they needed to duck around her to pull down a paper towel. Lissa's outsized confidence was integral to her persona.

"You don't think you can do it anymore, am I right?"

"What are you talking about?" But I couldn't meet her eye. I unpeeled my forehead bandage to splash cold water on my face, wetting my bangs so that now they lay flat and dark, like some ceremonial costume hat.

"But you need to. You love this. I can't bear to see you not do the thing you love."

"You're wrong. I'm just feeling tired is all."

She stepped toward me suddenly, cupped my chin in her hands, and pulled me in to face her head-on—a Lissa gesture if there ever was one. "I'm right. But why am I right?" When she let me go, I stepped back and crossed my arms in front of my chest.

My dry eyes blinked. She stared back. She was not giving up on this. "My body used to be one thing and now it's another," I admitted. "I don't know if this body even knows how to be out in public, dancing. And if I can't, I might not be able to handle the disappointment."

"My brother-in-law Charlie in AA would say fake it till you make it."

"See, that's the thing," I told her. "I'm not even sure I can fake it. I have these images of falling and getting up and falling down again, like the scarecrow in *The Wizard of Oz*."

"And if you do, so what? But you won't know anything till you try. . . ."

I wasn't winning this one, and Lissa took my hand and pushed us out of the restroom and back into the heat and noise.

Desire had been overcoming my reluctance anyway, and the energy of the other bodies warmed me up. With Lissa's close, up-beat presence shadowing me, I knew that, after a couple of min-utes, I was okay. To the point where I stopped caring if others were watching me, or if I was dancing naturally, or if the accident had stolen my rhythm. And I wasn't Scarecrow. My muscle memory was deep for this. Then Rachel and Jake joined us, and then a few of Lissa's friends . . . and then I was lost in it.

Seeing Maisie pried me out again. I caught a glance from a distance. She'd pushed up her mask, and she was over by the drinks table, in a loose friend throng. I moved closer to see. One of the girls, long and dark-skinned, with that fluid, economical body that could wear anything—including the Cleopatra tunic and gladiator shoes she was in right now—seemed like a person who maybe I knew? When she noticed me, she waved, and I waved back, but it wasn't an invitation on either side.

I turned in, toward the center, where bodies pulsed together like a core of dark matter. Those weren't my friends. That was a whole crew of strange kids, who seemed only circumspectly interested in my presence here. Still, Maisie was my Anthony Travolo link, and I'd come all the way out here to find her. Should I approach her, and talk to her? Pry her for more information about Anthony?

It seemed almost too awful, a dread obligation—*go spend tonight learning everything you can about that guy you killed.*

By now, I'd stopped dancing. My feet felt leaden and unable. I stood, chewing my bottom lip. But I wouldn't go over. Rachel was right; this wasn't the time or place.

"Hey!" Lissa twined her fingers through mine. "Loosen up!"

As if she knew. As if she was purposely trying to make me stop thinking about it. I stole another glance at Maisie. If I wanted to find out more from her, I could. I'd Facebook her tomorrow. Yes, that would be better.

Then the music changed. A downbeat. The floor seemed to absorb air-mass noise sweat into one clammy thud and pull of motion.

My eyelids drooped, but now I was too tired—my limbs kept losing tempo, my mind was suspended with strange thoughts of Maisie and Anthony, all of them—when I looked up, I saw that Smarty was actually getting into it, too, though her dance style hadn't changed; she'd always moved as awkwardly as a baby foal. Her zombie bandages were, like mine, sticking to her T-shirt and leggings, and her bleached-white bangs were starfish-spiked off her head.

She was here because I was here.

Her quick, self-conscious smile nearly melted me. Smarty, at a dance club. She'd never have come if I hadn't wanted to go. My bestie. Holden couldn't have been right, that we'd been fighting. Even if so, it wouldn't have been a big deal. No way.

When the music transitioned again, I signaled to the others for my much-needed break. We stumbled to a table in the back. Jake procured our paper cups of electric green punch. Then the DJ layered a Weregirl loop over the next track.

"Ooh, Weregirl . . ." I was so happy to hear them, like a stamp of approval on the club, and our presence in it.

Out on the floor, Lissa was twirling like a punk sylph. Maybe it was Lissa who'd loved this band?

"Think we're gonna sit out a few." Rachel was tucked under Jake's arm. "Do not—I repeat—do not wear yourself out, Emb, okay? Your mom would have my head on one of these poles."

"I won't."

I could feel Rachel's gaze stay on me warningly. She could see how exhausted I was. She and Jake dragged a couple of folding chairs to a dark, far corner of the room that a few other couples had already staked out.

But I returned, relocated Lissa, tuned in Weregirl, found my-self. I'd never heard their music pound so loud, so mesmerizingly surround-sound. Here I was, pre-accident. And my old self was emerging delicate as new skin. But this one song was all I had in me. I couldn't keep pushing myself much longer.

"Embie, I need water." Lissa bumped up close to talk in my ear. "You too?"

The song wasn't over. I shook my head, but when she left, I felt unmoored.

Rachel and Jake were in the corner, out of sight. After an-other confused minute or so, I stepped backward until I'd moved off the floor altogether, sidling up to the back wall, fighting the impulse of my buckling knees before I lost the battle and slumped down to sit on the cold poured-cement floor. My blood was an electric blanket and my heartbeat drummed my skin. My muscles would feel pulverized tomorrow. I watched the other dancers; Maisie and her friends had pulled off the various masks and capes of their costumes, and now looked unknowable and anonymous, all in skinny tees and dark jeans.

And then out of the corner of my eye, I caught a glow of light like a firefly. I craned my neck to see.

He was lighting matches. Striking them against a matchbook and flicking them into the air, a spark of dangerous magic in the darkness. He'd been there awhile, behind the coat mountain.

Striking matches and watching me. I was sure of it.

Kai.

Oh my God.

My body was locked in the suspense of what he might do next. When he made his move, there was no shyness, no hiding, no explanation. I stood up, my spine bumping hard against the rough surface of the wall, as he approached—I didn't care, I just didn't care in this moment that Kai hadn't called, that he'd been an asshole, that he'd hurt my feelings. All I wanted was this now, *now*. As he closed the last bit of space between us to create a solid shape of just us two, he reached out and gripped me at my sides.

"You shouldn't play with matches," I whispered, wrapping my arms around his neck as if he'd held me just like this a hundred times before. His kiss made me know that I hadn't imagined the interconnectivity of that first kiss.

"You're right." When he pulled back, he was smiling. He flipped me the matchbook. "Here. Don't get burned."

I caught it one-handed, easily. "Thanks."

"I liked watching you dance," he said. "It made me think something."

"What?" I couldn't remember the last time I had been more curious for an answer.

"Made me think that whatever you end up wanting to do with your life, you're just going to attack it until you're the best you can be. You've got so much to give. You've got so much . . ." He let the last word go; he meant a lot of different words. All of them good.

"Thanks." I did the "whatever you say" shrug, though inwardly I was shining.

"Come with me?"

"I . . ." It seemed he'd tricked me out of the reactions I'd thought I'd have when I saw him next. The anger, the disappointment that he hadn't called—none of it was clenched inside me anymore. My bones had softened to paraffin. Was this the correct reaction? Or was I "miscalibrating" again?

I wasn't going anywhere with him. He'd hung me out to dry. I should hate him, right? We'd had no contact, nothing, after the fire escape. And besides, I didn't chase guys. Especially guys who didn't chase me back.

But it was as if I were in a trance, following him.

His hand, so warm, now reached to hold me behind my neck, before it dropped to the small of my back. I breathed him in. He was wearing the same shabby olive jacket and jeans. Not even the hint of a costume, plus, of course, he was an underage male—and he still got into this club.

"Ember," he whispered in my ear. "Your name's like this sign that's been blinking in my head. Ember, Ember." He smiled. "Don't leave without me, okay? Don't let me go." His grasp was sure, no arguments. He led me out into the main room and to the dance floor like we'd made some secret, previous arrangement to do just exactly this.

We were dancing slowly, our bodies pressed, but I'd been exerting myself for so long that I had to push my muscles to make them work. He held me tight. My eyes closed as the room spun, spun, and kept on spinning.

And then Kai was leading me to the exit doors. And I wasn't saying anything. No protest, no "I've got to find the others." Who'd I come here with again? I couldn't remember. It was happening and I was allowing him to do it, I was allowing myself to be pulled, crooked into the shield of Kai's arm as he maneuvered us through the crowd. First to the coat pile, then the exit.

Just roll with it. For three weeks I'd been obsessed with him. And now here he was, shoulder-shoving us through a side exit door into a stairwell that was lit but empty, and down flight after flight of steps. Sequined light pinwheeled in my eyes; I toggled up my coat.

Kai turned and kissed me again. I was rapt, basking in him. He was so real, so right. As my hands twisted up the fabric of his jacket, I couldn't stop from saying it. "Don't let me go, either."

"Never." His voice was hoarse. Then his mouth was on mine. Was I awake?

When I'd had my wisdom teeth pulled in ninth grade, they'd put me in a twilight sleep—I'd been present and yet distractedly not; the sound of the drill had been as drowsy as a bumblebee. I kissed him and I had no idea what else was happening around me. I couldn't hear the music, or the crowd on the dance floor. It was Kai and me and nothing else.

On the ground floor, we stopped to kiss again. I belted my arms around his narrow waist. His body was wiry, sinew and mus-cle. "Let's take off for my place," he murmured. "Hatch is there. I need to get back on the early side. I promised him spaghetti and old movies. He hates to be alone, especially on a wild night like this. We'll get a cab—if we can."

"Sure." I reached for my cell phone. "Let me tell the others."

I got Rachel's voice mail immediately. "Waffles, waffles," I said, and laughed uncertainly—was that our private joke? Actually, I had no idea why I said it; I felt sort of stupid, tipsy with adrenaline. "Hey, listen. Don't worry about me. I'm leaving now, but I'm with a friend."

Kai squeezed my hand. We pushed out the heavy door and into a bitter wind. I could feel myself wincing, shrinking—even my teeth hurt with cold. Traffic was brisk, but there weren't many cabs, and the ones we saw were all off duty or occupied. Kai stepped into the road and raised an arm to flag one down.

"It's freezing!" I called.

I should go back. I was doubtful now. I didn't want to lose Kai, but maybe this wasn't the best idea after all.

Another minute passed. My cell buzzed—Rachel, of course—but I didn't want to look at it, to be dragged back to the party. I wanted to go go go. And yet I felt unequal to the night, as if I were close to passing out. I just didn't want to let go of him again. My senses were looping like a hamster on a wheel.

A cab turned the corner, its roof light signaling that it was free. Kai whooped.

"Now, there's a lucky break. Never thought we'd get one of these so quick tonight." He opened the driver's-side back door. "In, in!"

I ran over to meet him just as my cell phone buzzed again. And again and then again. Texts from Rachel, of course. Now my ringer started. She was panicked that I was leaving Areacode without her.

The cabbie cracked his window. "Are you in or are you out?" he shouted at me. "Make up your mind!"

Kai was in the cab. My hand was stuck on the door handle. It had happened so fast. I shouldn't just leave the others like this. Should I? The building's fire-exit door slammed open. I jumped, turning.

"Goddammit, Ember!" Rachel was sprinting toward me, her zombie bandages streaming, with Jake in a loose gallop behind her. "What the hell?"

"I'm fine," I called.

"You can't do this to people!" She was at me in the next bound. "You can't do this to *me*!"

"I'm with Kai, we're just . . ." I looked back to watch the cab squealing off, the driver cursing. Kai hadn't gotten out. He'd left without me. No no no. My eyes teared and felt immediately icy.

"Have you totally lost your mind?" Rachel's veins were standing out in her neck. "Just to up and leave us?"

I nodded, shy and shamed, and rubbed my hands together, trying to extract warmth. The cab's red taillights were in full retreat. Now pinpoints, now gone. As quickly as Kai had appeared, he'd left me. "I'm . . . I'm . . ."

"You're nuts. Let's get you back inside."

I let her put her arm around me and turn me, though I cast another look over my shoulder. Would he double back, maybe? It seemed like a feeble hope. He'd really needed to go home.

We returned to the building, me stumbling between the other two like a culprit. But I was grateful for the heated stairwell as we entered.

Above the fire-escape doors, the words jumped at me. NO REENTRY ON THIS FLOOR. It was like a warning of something not yet clear.

"I feel sick," I said. Aware my voice was dry and toneless, as if I didn't care what had happened, as if the crisis were nothing to me as my mind sank blank and black and quiet. I was shutting down—burying my mixed-up emotions rather than dealing with them. Dr. P even had a five-dollar phrase for it, "habitual inurement," which I'd forgotten till now. Basically it meant that my brain couldn't pick what it felt like, so it desensitized itself and picked nothing.

"You might be bombed," Jake mentioned. "There's a rumor they spiked one punch bowl but not the other. Like a cocktail version of Russian roulette."

"And you most definitely got the wrong Kool-Aid," said Rachel. "Why else would you be shouting about waffles? Are you hungry? That message you left me was insane! You were seriously leaving the party with a stranger? What'd you call him again? Cal? Where's he from?"

"Kai," I said.

"I don't know any Kai," muttered Jake.

"He's not a stranger," I answered flatly. "And no, I'm not hungry." But Kai was gone, and my muscles were so cramped that it was hard to move. Pain was a burden in my body. I dropped to the bottom step, leaning so that my cheek pressed against the wall. Rachel took a seat beside me.

Jake offered a plastic bottle of water, nearly full. "Drink," he commanded.

Which I did, in long, messy gulps.

"Who was he, then?" Rachel asked.

"Just this guy I met," I managed, wiping my mouth.

"Do you realize how screwed up that sounds to me?" Rachel shook her head. "That you would have just taken off with some random dude who you hadn't even bothered to introduce me to, who you'd only just met tonight?"

"Actually, I *have* met him before. Let's talk about this later, 'kay?" I pushed back the damp tendrils of my hair.

"You're acting really strange."

"I'm feeling really strange."

"Hey, Ember." Jake knelt before me. His face doubled in my vision. "Your pupils look pretty dilated. I drove here, by the way. I'm parked about four blocks down. If you two wait, I'll bring the car around."

"That'd be awesome." Rachel's hand covered mine. "Oh, Embie," she said with a sigh once Jake had gone. "You just can't do that to me. If you'd left and all I'd had to go by was that crazy voice mail, I'd have had no way of knowing where you were heading or who with—or anything!"

"I'm sorry." I tried to access the right tone so that Rachel would know that I was. Mostly I felt so incredibly tired. "I don't know what got into me." Kai. Kai had gotten to me. Again. I did such incredibly stupid things when I saw him. All common sense—*pffft!*—out the window.

"If that was grain alcohol you were drinking," said Rachel, "then I'm just going to blame the rest of your bad judgment on accidental drunkenness. When's the last time you even had a drink? It must be close to a year ago, right?"

"Mmm-hmm." I rested my head on her shoulder. I wanted to cry now, to break down in a flood of tears like a baby. My emotions were in whizzing orbit. I'd obviously gotten the spiked drink. There was no other reason I was feeling shaken. And Smarty was also right that I hadn't had any alcohol since before the accident—my tolerance was probably zero.

"We're going to get you all tucked in bed with tea and toast—sound good?"

"Sounds good."

"Good. I just texted Jake to hurry." Rachel rested her fingertips on my knee. A dragonfly's weight. As if I were made of something less able, less capable than a regular person. Tonight, that was probably true.

14

An Easy Spin

The doorbell rang while I was on Facebook late that next morning, rubbing Bengay into my aching muscles and browsing Maisie Gantz's profile. One album had a picture of Anthony Travolo in it. I'd zoomed it to pixels, but I still couldn't tell what he looked like. He was wearing a baseball cap pulled low, and was standing in a long-view group shot of maybe a dozen kids with paintbrushes who were all posed in front of a wall, celebrating a city mural that looked familiar.

He'd been tagged, too, but when I clicked his name, a message popped up that told me his profile did not exist. My skin went cold at the words.

Anthony Travolo didn't exist in this world. But once upon a time, he absolutely, gloriously had. He'd been an artist; he'd helped create murals and a single, tiny, perfect painting that was good enough to hang in a sumptuous, multimillion-dollar Tribeca loft. I already knew such interesting things about him. What else had he been?

It wouldn't take more than one painful conversation with Mom to get his parents' email. I wanted to know about him, sort of. I wanted to step closer. I just wasn't sure of the cost.

So much about last night felt vague and distant. After I'd gotten home, I'd checked in with Mom and Dad, who were pretending not to be awake until I was home safe, and then I'd crawled into bed, letting Rachel give me a stern tuck-in, before she and Jake took off.

In bed I'd tossed and turned for hours, unsure if I was suffering the effects of alcohol or exhaustion. First Claude and then Maisie, then Bushwick, Lissa, then, finally, when I'd been almost too tired to process him, I cleared my head to fill it with Kai. That part of the night was confusing. A thousand moments crystal clear, a thousand others as dark as storage closets.

Why was the interconnection such a snarl? Why, in the bleak patter of this morning's rain, did last night at Areacode feel so immediate—and yet not part of any reliable whole?

Kai had said he had to get back to Hatch, who I'd revised in my imagination from thuggish wingman to somebody younger, more sensitive—maybe a brother or a cousin. So it made sense that he wouldn't have jumped out of the cab when I didn't jump in. But he could have called or messaged me anytime. Last night, or this morning—anytime. Though with every passing hour, my hope on that deflated.

As I glanced at my phone to see if someone was texting their arrival, the doorbell rang again, insistent. Mom and Dad were out doing errands, and I wasn't expecting anyone.

I raced downstairs, then unlocked the door and threw it open. "Oh!"

"Hey." The rain was a steady drizzle. I shaded my eyes. Holden stood on the mat, wearing the Driza-Bone that he'd bought years ago on a family vacation to Australia. I'd always loved that raincoat; it made him look edgy, like the bank robber hero in a spaghetti western.

"What are you doing here?"

He shrugged, a little self-conscious. "Can't a guy come check on his ex?"

"I guess. If he's feeling unloved." I crossed my arms and leaned against the doorframe. "But I thought college guys didn't need to make time for their high school exes."

His smile deepened. "Here's the thing, High School Ex. I was home doing my Sunday-laundry drop-off, and that's when I heard a voice in my head saying to go treat you to lunch. So my advice is you better hurry up and say yes before I realize I'm way too cool to hang out with you."

"You're serious, aren't you? I'd need to dig up my rain boots."

"No rush." He gestured to the cab idling at the curb.

"You are serious. Okay, hang on. Let me change real quick and leave a note for my parents. If they come home to find me gone, they'll freak."

113

I'd missed one cab last night—this time, I was getting in. Holden and cabs went way back, on account of the fact that he didn't like to drive. After I'd passed my driver's license test, I was always the designated driver, picking him up in the Volvo whenever we wanted to get out of the city. Of course, Holden was also always totally fine to bike, walk, or subway. But if he had half a choice, he defaulted to cabs, which wasn't very Brooklyn. I wouldn't say it was Holden's fault. His mom didn't even know how to drive; Holden and his older brother, Drew, had been given credit cards to pay for rides since they were in elementary school.

"Those Wildes have their heads in the clouds," my mom always remarked.

"Or up their arses," my dad liked to respond. Dad, who'd grown up on "old" egg-creams-and-Dodgers Brooklyn, thought the Wildes were a perfect example of everything that was wrong with "new" boutiques-and-cafés Brooklyn.

But Dad had a point. The cabs, the credit cards, and the endless supply of twenty-dollar bills had always set Holden apart from the rest of us. Even snotty Claude lived in a regular apartment with two parents, one sister, one and a half bathrooms, and a Murphy bed for guests. But the Wildes, who presided over the neighborhood from their five-story town house on Columbia Heights, had never known what it meant to want what you couldn't have. As far as I'd ever witnessed, being a Wilde meant that life passed in an easy spin of private lessons and extra-long vacations at their genteel-shabby lake house upstate.

I'd always dealt with the Wildes just fine, without ever warming to them. They could be arrogant, but they'd been nice to me— except right after my breakup with Holden, when Mrs. Wilde had pulled some strange moves. Like once she'd crossed the street right in the middle of Montague so she wouldn't have to talk to Dad and me. Another time she and Mr. Wilde both painfully, deliberately ignored me in line at Key Food. Since money couldn't fix our relationship, it was as if they'd made a pact to quietly reject me.

The Wildes would have been displeased to see me in this cab with Holden, after I'd hurt him so badly. Even considering all that had happened to me afterward. None of them—especially not Drew—was generous with forgiveness. Not by a long shot.

"So what gives?" I asked as we whooshed down the rainy streets.

"Rain makes me think about you."

"Ha. That sounds like bad Taylor Swift."

"We-ell, dang," he drawled. "You got me." Then Holden began to sing "Love Story" with a croaky country accent. Joking through the earnestness.

Don't let me go. Kai's words—I heard them again, rough and honest and deeply vulnerable in the moment. Last night with Kai was a bruise on my lips.

Last night with Kai, I'd never have thought that I'd be sharing my next day with Holden.

Who looked great as always, casually slouched with a knee knocked lightly against mine. Over the bridge, we watched the East River glide past, slate water touching the sheen of a pearl-soft sky. I couldn't help wondering (okay, maybe a little gloatingly) why Holden had decided to spend the day with me and not Cassandra. I knew they'd gone to Oktoberfest together. Plus a dinner-and-a-movie thing. Holden played a close hand with the details, but even from his bare-bones report I got a sense that he liked this girl. And while I wasn't sure how I felt about it, I'd resolved to play the role of former girlfriend with as much grace as I could.

We exited onto the FDR uptown, and then on Holden's instruction we pulled off the highway at Sixty-Third Street.

"Midtown, interesting. What's your master plan?" I asked.

"Serendipity."

"Aha." I settled back. Sweet. Serendipity was a well-known café slash ice cream parlor around the corner from Bloomingdale's. It was also where Holden and I'd had our first date.

The place was usually packed, and today was no exception. A ponytailed waiter led us to a table behind a fat potted fern.

"It's so cute here." I looked around as we sat. "You should have seen the dive that Rachel and I were at last night."

"Yeah. She told me."

"Ah." I could feel the smile drop off my face as I opened the menu to hide behind it. The Holden-Rachel cousin bond could wax and wane, but it was always there. Whether I liked it or not. "She told you everything?"

"That you might have had a disgusting green cocktail, and it impaired your judgment to the point where an hour later, you were jumping into cabs with strangers? Yes."

Over my menu, I wrinkled my nose. "It happened, it was awful, I guess I was following an impulse. What can I say?"

"There's not much to say, except I think you should just order the everything nachos and a frozen hot chocolate to share."

"Done."

He'd chosen the items deliberately. It was as if by unspoken mutual agreement we were taking a nostalgia leap two years backward. Back to the thrill of our first date, my sophmore and his junior fall at Lafayette, when we'd only known each other for a couple of weeks.

We'd sat right there, a stone's throw from this table. It had been so fantastically awkward. Staring at each other, sometimes laughing at each other for no reason, and then, over the shared frozen hot chocolate and everything nachos, seeking and finding the million things we had in common, including a mutual appreciation of anything dashed with cinnamon (from French toast to applesauce to gum), our dueling collections of retro board games, and our major sneezing allergies to pollen—which my mom was obsessed with and Holden's mother totally disregarded.

"I love Serendipity," I exclaimed in a rush of unfolding relaxation. Or else it was the Advil I'd taken just before I'd left, finally working its muscle-softening magic. "I mean, it's the coolest, dorkiest scene. You can be in first grade or grandparents, and you're never out of place." Other tables were filled with young couples, families, and seniors, all plowing through their sundaes and grilled cheeses and banana splits, plus the frozen hot chocolates that were the house specialty.

"So where does that put Dave and Busters?" Holden asked.

I laughed outright. "Unforgettable."

"Okay, for the last time. I had no idea that it was the Champion League soccer final that night."

"Mmm, I don't know, Hold. I thought it was kind of fun trying to talk to you over the sound of two hundred drunken grown men swearing and drinking Guinness."

"I'm amazed that I had a chance with you, after that night."

117

"I'm not." We exchanged a glance. What was happening here? It was light, but meaningful. And I didn't mind it. "So how was *your* Halloween?"

Holden passed me his phone. "You want the short story? Check out the last three videos."

I took it and watched them, mostly of a gang of guys roaming wild up and down a crowded dormitory hall, all wearing crazy hats (cowboy, Viking) and masks (monster, vampire) and mugging for the camera. At one point, Holden flipped the camera on himself to show that he was dressed like Jack Sparrow, which had been his go-to costume ever since I'd known him. It involved a gold clip-on hoop, eyeliner, and a skull scarf wrapped around his head.

"Why does college fun look so much better than high school fun?" I asked as I passed the phone back.

"Hey, high school fun has its charm. Just ask my ex."

Holden's beard scruff seemed to make his eyes three shades bluer. I knew that he also knew that these moments between us were peculiar, charged with memories, affection . . . maybe more? Whatever it was, I was relieved when the waiter reappeared to take our order.

And the rest of lunch was easy, as we launched back in time. Which felt amazing. I loved stretching into the weight of time re-membered. The day we went on six rides on the waterfront carou-sel, or when we crashed a party on the roof deck of Soho House. It was a nice change to reminisce easily, with no inconvenient blacked-out trauma section.

As we strolled out of the restaurant, Holden bought me a gi-ant lollipop from the selection of toys and candy at the cashier.

"I remember that wallet." It had been a gift, one of my first to

Holden, for his seventeenth birthday. Ralph Lauren calfskin, not on sale; plus it had cost another thirty dollars to monogram. I'd used up all my babysitting, allowance, and catering-with-Smarty money. It had seemed crazily extravagant, but with parents like Holden's, who gave him everything, it was almost like I'd needed to spend the extra.

"Yeah." He flipped it over. "If it ain't broke . . ."

"Your stash of twenties gets skinnier by the hour," I noted as I unwrapped my lollipop.

"Easy trade," he said. His smile was wry. I never liked Holden to feel that I was interested in him for his money, but the issue was always there, an unpleasant little twitch. He liked to treat; he liked solving problems with a credit card. Again, not his fault. It was like hailing cabs—it was part of his background.

As we stepped outside, I wondered what that would feel like, to have so many solutions ready via my wallet. This was where my mind had often drifted when I'd gone out with Holden. Smarty and I were always talking about ways to make extra cash. With Holden, it was as if those bills just appeared by magic. And yet it also took away another kind of magic—of scheming, of hoping, of saving.

The rain had stopped. Water dripped from trees and awnings as we strolled down Lexington.

"Thanks for this afternoon, Wilde. It doesn't even feel real. More like some gorgeous Sunday daydream."

"Anytime." Holden twined his fingers through mine. "Only thing is, I'm not sure I'm exactly ready to deal with my Sunday-night reality yet. Look, the sun's just about to break through—wanna walk to the park?"

"Okay."

It was a few blocks to Central Park, where the trees were in burning-leaf autumn glory. On a park bench, an old man was smoking a pipe. The woody tobacco smoke mixed in heady with the mushroomy, wet-soil scent of the park after a rain.

"Which way? North south west east?"

"Strawberry Fields," I said without thinking.

"The girl knows what she wants."

Yes, I did, apparently. Hand in hand, we took a rolling footpath that led north and westward across the park.

Why didn't Holden-and-me work out? The thought had been percolating in my head from the moment he'd picked me up. This day was a gold coin; it was shiny and perfect and I knew I would treasure it. I wanted to ask the question right then, with the sounds of raindrops plopping off the trees, the tobacco smoke in the air, and the whole afternoon hushed and serene.

What happened to us?

Holden was giving me another Raphael the RA tale. "This dude, I don't know what his hygiene issues are, but he's got a huge bucket—honestly, it's more like a bin—and it's just crammed with all his shower supplies. Shampoo, hair conditioner, bodywash, body oil, zit cleanser, back scrubber, washcloth, loofah, you name it." We were both laughing as Holden used his hands to try to describe it. "So one day, this other guy who lives down the hall, Jackson, so he and I decided that every night, we're gonna take exactly one item out of it, just to see if Raphael's gonna notice or put up a fight, if he cares or gets—"

It came at me like a handful of sharp stones thrown into my path, tripping me up—*swsssp swsssp swsssp.*

Let me take you down, 'cause we're going to . . . Strawberry Fields. . . .

He was singing it in my ear. I could hear his voice as if he were as close as Holden—*and nothing to get hung about*—because he was always singing, because he loved music, he loved Strawberry Fields and the "Imagine" mosaic and the wistful desire in John Lennon's lyrics and message.

In fact, that's why I was here. That's why I'd picked this place.

The voice was gone. I could feel that I'd locked myself up in tension—was this the whisper of another memory of Anthony Travolo? A song in my ear the way he whispered about his painting? Had he and I come here, to the park, together?

And if we had, so what? What good did it do me to think about it now? I could feel myself in a mental crouch, self-protecting and wary. So what? He was gone, and so was most of my memory of him, and today I was here with Holden, and that would have to be enough.

Holden was still talking, his voice pitched in a comic imitation of Raphael, though I'd utterly lost the thread of conversation. I blinked down at my rain boots. Grape-juice purple. I'd never buy these rain boots today.

"You still with me?" Holden reached an arm around my shoulders.

"Of course. So, hey, I heard about my breakup boots," I said. "And Tom called me a club rat."

"A tad harsh. Club-rat lite," said Holden. "But where are the mysterious boots? Donated back to the Salvation Army?"

"I haven't seen them. I'm sure Mom knows. She probably hid them."

"What got you thinking about your boots anyhow? Are your feet cold? Are you tired?"

"Not at all. Couldn't be better. But this coat must weigh three hundred pounds—there's all this loose change that's fallen into the lining. Can we sit for a second? I've got to dig out some of it."

"Yeah, sure." Holden found a bench and we sat. My free hand reached deep into my coat pocket. There must have been over three dollars in quarters, dimes, and nickels jangling around.

"Your coat is like your own personal wishing well," Holden observed.

"No joke."

Something else was lodged in the corner of the hem. I pulled it out.

A red and banana-yellow matchbook. In feet-shaped letters, the words EL CIELO were dancing a salsa above a Cobble Hill address.

"Oh. From last night." As I flipped open the matchbook, I saw that a number of the matches were missing.

Because Kai had used them, striking all of those matches before tossing the matchbook to me.

This morning, almost everything about last night had seemed unreal. And when Kai hadn't called me—*again*—I could feel the memory begin to tamp itself down to a disappointing near unreality. Just like our afternoon on the fire escape. But last night had happened. Kai had been lighting matches from this very book, tossing them into the air like tiny fire batons. My brain reshuffled and redealt the memory. He'd taken my hand and spoken my name. "Don't get burned."

He'd been shy, but also mischievous, as he'd flipped the

matchbook to me—and then we'd moved out of that room, our bodies nudging and jousting to be close and closer.

Had Kai come to the club with another girl, maybe? In the haze of my head, in the shadows of the cab, I'd had and lost Kai. He'd slipped off and out of my reach as if testing me.

"Ember!" Holden was shaking me. "Focus!" When I looked up, his eyes were flooded with concern.

I must have dishragged. My Serendipity lollipop had dropped to the ground, and I was holding the matchbook clutched to my heart. Heat in my cheeks and at the top of my head and the back of my neck.

"What's going on?"

"Nothing."

"Something. You were like a million miles away."

"I'm just light-headed." My fingers quietly slipped the matchbook into my jeans pocket. It was a comfort, to feel it lumped there. "It happens. It's nothing. I'm still tired from last night, I think."

"It's not nothing. You've got your doctor looped into this, right?"

"Yeah, of course." I broke the intensity of his gaze, then took a breath and rechanneled. "Speaking of last night, I saw Lissa Mandrup. We hung out a little. Kind of lucky—it wasn't a plan; I just ran into her. She had some warm and fuzzy New Year's Eve memories that I couldn't access, but I'm getting used to that feeling."

"Yeah, but the good thing about Lissa is she's a girl who's always fully committed to the moment she's in. Funny how after our breakup, you went for noise and I went for quiet. I spent most of that time in the library or holed up in my room." Holden's hand in mine was always so sure. I could feel myself returning to equilibrium. Safe. Holden made me feel so safe. "Guess we both went more extreme than we actually are."

"That's true. Anyway, it wasn't the perfect atmosphere for a conversation. I got really winded on the dance floor. God, Holden, sometimes it feels like someone else borrowed my body for a couple of months, trashed it, and gave it back with all these dings and scars and missing mental pieces." I was embarrassed to hear the shake in my voice.

But Holden knew me well enough not to keep making me talk. After a few moments, he stood. Pulled me up with him. We began to walk down the other side of Strawberry Fields. "My advice, for what it's worth?" he said after a few more silent moments. "Let go of all that. These lost weeks are only a ripple across your life line. How could they be equal to the amount of effort you put into worrying about them?"

"Right. I know." I nodded; I was resigned to the fact that nobody could truly understand. The kindness and the pep talks from Holden, Rachel, my parents—they were all so incredibly well-intentioned, and came from such a place of yearning for me to be better. But in my heart, I knew my friends and family were trying to solve a darkness that there was no way for them to mark, let alone dig into. "And I'm in good shape, considering," I told Holden instead. "I know I'm lucky. I'm obsessed with what I've lost. But the whole reason I want to be in this world, living my life, is because I know the value of what I got to keep."

"That's the Ember I know." He stopped, rubbed the pad of his thumb across my chin. "But there's no answer in that accident. There's nothing there, actually. You'll only make yourself unhappy if you keep looking back. So why don't you start to build up new memorable moments? Like today. Right? Today was amazing." Then he brushed my bangs away to touch the scar. And then, to my surprise, he kissed it.

I flinched. "Don't."

"It's a badge of courage. It's who you are now."

"Not yet I'm not." I ducked my head and turned away.

Horribly, somehow I could feel right in that odd, painful moment the wrench that Kai hadn't called, and that he wasn't going to. It was very likely he had a girlfriend. Or maybe he just plain wasn't interested enough in me. Beyond the spontaneous, electric combustion that seemed to happen during these chance meet-ups, there was no place for me in that guy's life.

At the next corner, I reached into my jeans pocket to toss the matchbook into one of the park's giant steel trash baskets. How silly to be so sentimental. Kai hadn't given this to me as some kind of romantic keepsake. I didn't need any reminder of a night that held no logic or meaning.

Holden was right. Let go. Some things were better off forgotten. Be the moment. Live in beauty. Seize today. Except that wasn't exactly how it worked. Life wasn't as easy as messages on coffee mugs sold in hospital gift shops, and I should know—I had a shelf of them.

At the last minute, with the basket in clear sight, the matchbook stayed in my hand.

125

15

It's Your Pandora Moment

"Hey, Mom, where are my accident clothes?"

"What? What are you talking about?"

"You know what. From February, from the bridge. The hospital people have to give you those things."

"Oh, Ember."

Mom looked so crestfallen that I returned my attention to the pot. Not exactly a happier view. The polenta looked like sludge, dense enough to bind bricks. Mom and Dad were both waiting at the kitchen table, set for three. But now, with this new topic, it was as if I'd lit a flare. We'd been discussing

Dad's golf handicap, right before. Which had been a breezier topic.

But I pressed on; I had to. "I want my biker boots back. People keep telling me about them. How I wore them every day. But I can't find them. They're not in my closet, or in the coat closet, or the winter clothes closet. I must have been wearing something on my feet that night, right? So I'm guessing it was those boots."

"Ember, please. Lower your voice." Mom took a sip of her wine. I pressed my lips together, then ladled out my sautéed button mushrooms and served the dish to the table. At least the mushrooms would sneakily disguise my polenta issues. "And you'll just have to give me some time to think about where I put those things."

"The boots have got to be here. I know you, Mom." I went to the drawer for the serving spoons. "You're two parts neatnik and one part hoarder."

Dad smiled. "The girl's got your number, Nat."

"I didn't want to start rummaging around in the basement and messing stuff up," I continued, "but I bet they're in one of the bins, somewhere between the Christmas tree lights bin and the summer patio cushions bin, and probably with an 'Ember—car accident' label."

Dad let out a whoop of laughter, but Mom looked perplexed. "It's hard to say exactly where I put—"

"Come on, Natalie. You absolutely know you stored them down in the basement." Dad swept a hand through the air as if swatting a fly. "If you want those things back, Embie, they're yours. I think it's actually a plastic bag on that back shelf near the ski poles. And I'll bring it up after dinner."

"Thanks, Dad." Though I sensed Dad's forced casualness, and Mom's silent discontent. But how could I not be curious? What boots had the power to bug Tom? What kind of jacket would Lissa Mandrup covet?

After Holden had dropped me off this afternoon, I'd gone through all of the upstairs closets with a fine-tooth comb. No boots, and definitely no style of jacket that Lissa ever would have wanted to buy off me.

I cut the polenta into slabs as thick as pound cake, as Mom refilled her glass. "Thank you, Ember." Though she refrained from saying "This looks delicious"—assumedly because it didn't—as she shifted forward to serve herself a precise, mathematical square. "Did you and Holden have a nice day?"

"We did." I sat up, spine arched and ready to field the Holden questions.

"He's become a real man," said Dad. "He wears college well. Matter of fact, I'd like to see Holden coming around here again."

"Will he be?" asked Mom.

"Sure. I mean, why not? We're still good friends," I answered.

"Good friends doesn't count for much if he starts dating someone else," said Mom. "And he's a lovely young man. Holden Wilde would be the One That Got Away, I'm afraid."

"And I bet he does pretty well with the ladies," Dad added.

I nodded in absent agreement. So parenty. "He's become a real man" and "the one that got away" and "does well with the ladies"—those were just the kind of dorky Mom-and-Dad-style lines that I might repeat to Holden later, so we could crack up. Holden and I shared a long-standing private joke that my parents' approval had always worked just a tad bit against him. And it wasn't completely untrue, either—though I never would have admitted it.

But even if I wasn't going to confess it to my parents, it was impossible to ignore that something had rekindled with Holden. When he'd dropped me off earlier, lingering on the steps as the sun set, the sky cold and bright and pale as champagne, he'd invited me to Drew's engagement party at his house this coming Thursday.

"Ooh, I don't know." I'd grimaced. "That could be all kinds of nonfun. I'm not tops on your mom's list."

"Please. It's gonna be all of Drew's Young Republican friends, and I'd really like you to be there, to even the odds," he said.

"Well, when you sell it like that." I laughed, then asked, "Is Cassandra busy?"

Holden paused before answering. He was seeing her, I could tell. Her name meant something private to him. "Look, I can't spring my family on Cassandra just yet. Or vice versa."

"So I'm the old hat, the ole pal?"

He stared at me evenly. "More like first choice."

"How about . . . I'll think about it?"

In response, he'd kissed me. A sweet kiss, on the lips. Not a dangerous, electric Kai kiss. But it gave me butterflies just the same.

And I couldn't deny that the prospect of my taking Cassandra's place as Holden's date, made me feel a touch smug. I'd been an unofficial member of the Wilde household for my entire sophomore year, plus that summer into my junior fall, and I wasn't sure if I was ready to jump off the diving board into the anonymous pool of girls who didn't matter anymore. Especially now that

Holden and I had been enjoying this new closeness. Serendipity, and the walk in the park afterward, hadn't been unromantic, and it had held all the memory of when we had been a couple. He and I were older now. We'd lived through things. Survived them.

Midway through dinner, the doorbell rang.

"I'll get it." Mom stood, and was back in a moment with Rachel.

"Yay! Perfect timing! Good job, me!" She whooped as she sprang into the kitchen and took a plate. "I must have a sixth sense. Because I just *knew* I wouldn't have to eat leftover pork fried rice tonight." Like me, Rachel was an only child, but Rachel's parents were both corporate trial lawyers, with all the crazy hours and long nights and last-minute meetings and work-slog weekends. Which meant that Rachel was on a first-name basis with every takeout restaurant in her twenty-block delivery radius.

Watching Rachel, seeing her ease and comfort here as she dished up her plate, I wondered what last year had been for her. Without me. Without my home to rely on. It couldn't have been especially great.

After dinner, we were excused while Mom and Dad handled cleanup. "It's only fair to give the chef a break," said Mom.

"Cool. You don't have to offer twice. Hey, and Dad? Will you bring me—"

"I will. As soon as we're finished here."

"Thanks."

"Bring you what?" asked Rachel as we grabbed ice cream sandwiches from the freezer and then hauled upstairs to my room.

"Just some of my old clothes," I said. "I need to do a closet cleanout."

"Cool. I'll help."

Rachel started to look through my clothes closet, which was stuffed with fluttery blouses and ruffled dresses. The other day, I'd sorted out everything into piles of "wear" and "never." On my chair was the wear pile: black jeans, broken-in boyfriend jeans, black leggings, brown leggings, plus two thin gray sweaters and one navy sweater from the bottom of my drawer. Voilà: my new neutral-palette uniform. I'd also chosen two white and one black long-sleeved T-shirts that were really just the tops to thermal underwear packs Mom had bought for me to use as pajamas.

"Birdie got me hooked on these," I said, remembering. "She was always layering undershirts and leg warmers, and when the dance studio got too hot, she'd unpeel herself like an onion."

"If you're ripping off her style, you should swing by her office and say hi," said Rachel. "You know Jake's little sister, Mimi, is taking dance this year? And she has a mad girl-crush on Birdie."

"Everyone does." It pained me. When it came to dance, there'd always been two things I'd wanted: Lissa's talent and Birdie's passion.

Rachel was still shifting hangers, examining dresses. "Remember how your mom used to come back from Loehmann's with armloads of clothes for you?" she asked. "She must be bummed you've gone and drained all the color out of your working wardrobe—again. See, even if you drop over a bridge and lose your memory, you still end up making the same fashion choices." She stepped back, hands on her hips, as she gave a final appraisal of the flirty girlishness that took up most of my closet. "Except I think this stuff is what needs to be on the chair, right? And the pieces you actually want to wear get the priority of the closet."

"I'm not sure I'm ready to do that to Mom yet. And full disclosure, my dad's about to bring up what I was wearing the night of the accident."

"Ooh. Creepy." Rachel dropped her last bite of ice cream sandwich into her mouth. "But I get it. Memory helpfulness and all. Hey, Holden texted me that you two hung out today."

"Mmm." I smiled.

"That sounds like a private *mmm*, so guess what? I won't be nosy. But guess what else? I went to the movies with Jake this afternoon."

"Ah. And?" I wriggled my eyebrows. "What'd you see?"

"Does it matter?" She smirked.

"So is this official?"

She shook her head in a vague non-gesture. "Too early. I will say that all tickets and concession-stand items were paid for by him."

"Nice to hear that chivalry isn't dead."

"I'm mostly happy that I'm hanging out with a guy who's not shorter than me. You don't realize, Emb, all the advantages of your shrimpdom. When I was going out with Patrick Case, he lent me his jacket and the arms were a little short. For a girl, that is distinctly not a cool feeling."

"Wait—when were you going out with Patrick Case?"

"You were at Addington. It was super casual, and it's way over. Hey, and Jake's asked me out for Friday, too," Rachel added shyly, "so I was wondering if I could borrow those Indian gold and jade hoops of yours?"

"Of course. Hang on."

Rachel and Patrick Case. I barely knew him, except that

his untied construction boots always made him look a little bit homeless. It wasn't important, but information about anything I missed while at Addington probably would always catch me off guard.

In my jewelry box, I'd placed the matchbook next to Kai's little sketch of me. As I plucked the earrings from their notched holder, I wondered if maybe it would be better to toss out the Kai items. He hadn't been in touch all day or night—clearly I wasn't someone he'd fixated on the way I'd fixated on him. Out of sight, out of mind and all that. So maybe I wasn't being fair to myself to hold on to these objects of defeat, keepsakes that were like my temp teeth—an impression hardened from a moment that had no permanent use in my life.

And thinking of Areacode was a little bit like thinking about Rachel and Patrick Case—a not-quite-reality. The night flowed back to me in a roar of noise, fake heads on spikes, toxic punch, fog and shadows, and me trance-dancing—with Kai and without him—light-headed and spaced-out.

I shut the jewelry box hard, to snap out the memory. "Here." I handed Rachel the earrings.

"You're the best."

There was a soft knock on the door.

"Sweetie? Delivery." Dad was holding a blue recycling bag, tied in a slip hitch—Dad's knot of choice when he wanted things to stay sealed. "Here you go, with love from me and Mom."

As he passed off the bag, his hug was hard, his cheek a quick press to the top of my head. He didn't want to do this. My heart clutched. "Night, Dad."

After the door shut, Rachel and I climbed up on my bed,

facing each other, the bag plopped between us. "You know what? I'm not sure I want to open it."

"Just do it," said Rachel. "It's your Pandora moment. And you need to know what's in there."

"Okay, you're right. Here goes." I worked out the knot, then I pulled up the items one by one. A thin, deep purple cardigan and a white T-shirt, patchily bloodstained rusted brown, and neatly sliced—probably by an EMT's sterile scissors. The softened jeans were also seam-sliced, the right leg cut to ribbons. Just looking at the jeans, I could feel a bone-deep tingling in my legs, and could see those monstrous purple bruises stamped on my skin. God, I'd thought they'd never heal.

Unlike my body, there was no salvaging these clothes.

"I see the boots," whispered Rachel.

I fished them both up with effort, as if out of a pond. Wide and blocky, the silver grommets were encrusted in dried river sludge. The boots themselves looked huge, too big to fill. But they were intact, and broken in, presumably to the shape of my feet. Rachel reached into the bottom of the bag and pulled out my black leather bomber jacket—*whenever you're selling*—ripped and water-stained, like an old carcass.

We were silent. My fingertips followed the wavy traces of water and rusted blood, plainly visible against the sheepskin lining.

"Go ahead," said Rachel. "Test them." She nudged a boot closer to me. I set them both on the floor and slipped one foot, then the other, deep inside. They were heavier than anything I'd worn all year—including my hospital Crocs, my tennis sneakers, my loafers, and my rain boots.

As I walked around the room, my steps as careful as a biker

Cinderella, Rachel folded the ripped clothing and tucked the items away into my bottom dresser drawer.

She would know that I'd need to hold on to them. They were my grim keepsakes.

Neither of us spoke as I slid into the jacket. Rubbed the sleeve back and forth against my cheek.

"You look cool," Rachel commented. "Okay, so maybe I wasn't loving it last year. But I'm revising that opinion. I think you grew into this look. Could be because you seem tougher, with the scars and all," she joked.

"I think I bought the boots on Canal Street." My words came as a surprise to me. I'd had to make a choice between these boots and a pair of vintage Doc Martens. I'd paid in cash. It had been freezing that day, the dead of winter. I'd marched straight out of the army-navy shop in them. Ready for anything and rushing toward everything.

The unexpected surge of remembrance was like a hug from a lost friend.

From my corkboard, the band members of Weregirl were observing me as if they'd been waiting for this moment ever since I got home.

"One step closer to the real me," I said.

"Embie, no." When I looked up, Rachel's eyes were as steady as stars. "You're so wrong about that. All parts of you, right this minute, are the real you, okay? With every new thing that you remember, don't let that be something you forget."

16

My Drowned Face

They had all gathered to watch the artist. A silvery afternoon in Carroll Park, chilled in silence. He had set up a picnic table. His concentration was utter, an invisible wall between himself and the crowd that had grown around him. Tubes of paints were spread out on the table. I remembered their names from my freshman art class—cadmium red, Chinese white, phthalo green.

I'd approached from a distance, lost in the audience while wanting to stay close. But he knew I was here. That was what mattered. I watched him squeeze paints, smearing color with a spatula-shaped instrument.

"The darklight on the silk screen will pick up the negative." His voice. Exactly that voice. It prickled the hair at the nape of my neck.

"Let me look." Had I spoken out loud?

And then I was aware of someone else. Someone watching us from the periphery.

The artist's voice reverberated in my head. But that couldn't happen—it was a distortion in my own brain. "Look. Look at you. You're my best work."

And now I saw T-shirts hanging like ghosts, caught in the bare branches. Some folded, others arranged to reveal images of me.

My own face, underwater. My opened eyes were sightless, my lips were a sealed slash of blood, my hair stood out from my face, unfurled like seaweed, snakes, Medusa.

When I opened my mouth to speak, all that I could taste was icy, dirty water—it filled my lungs, heavy as earth, pushing down on me, swallowing me—

I woke in a single hard motion, lunging forward; my eyes popped open like a doll's. A nightmare. That's all it was. It felt like more. My body was sweaty, the darkness impenetrable. For a few moments I couldn't move. I stared at the ceiling, listening to the sound of my heart in my ears. I couldn't have spoken a word if I tried, or moved a muscle. My limbs were collapsed like bent tent struts beneath the covers, my mind smoked like a just-tamped fire, my thoughts were still somersaulting, unguided, in a netherworld between air and water, dreams and wakefulness, life and death.

Let it stay forgotten.

The thought burst clean through me. Full awareness. I inhaled through the sharp kick of adrenaline. It had never occurred to me that I might not want to rip open every single closed stitch of my lost memories. That I shouldn't rattle and shake what ought to be left untouched, a pirate's locked and rusted trunk, long set-tled at the brackish bottom of my subconscious.

I rubbed my face and looked around. The Day-Glo dial of my alarm clock read half past one. My fingertips found my phone right next to it.

U up? alone? ok to call?
in 5

When Holden phoned a few minutes later, I was more than awake—I was wired. I could tell by the background echo that he was out in the dorm hall, where he often liked to hang out.

"What's up?"

"It seems stupid now. I had a nightmare. I shouldn't have texted. I was scared. I'm sorry. And now I feel like such a baby." Though I was comforted to hear his voice.

"Here I was thinking booty call." Holden sounded tired but amused. "So are you feeling normal now?" I could tell by the downshift in noise that he'd gone into his room. "You wanna tell me all about it?"

"It's boring, to tell someone your dream."

"Try me."

So I retold it quickly, as if it were nothing. "I was dead but I wasn't—and my drowned face was being sold as art on a T-shirt."

"Whoa." I could almost see Holden's wry smile. "Awright, to get philosophical for a second, maybe this isn't so random when you analyze it. I think we all need to think people will miss us if we die. Even people we hardly know. Who doesn't want to be memorialized on a T-shirt? There's a little bit of tragic-death rock star in everyone. And you got closer to the mortal edge than most of us. Right?"

I forced a small laugh. "Sure, I guess."

"So maybe you were just indulging a morbid fascination. Almost like you were attending your own funeral. If that makes sense?"

"Sure." I leaned back against the headboard. Allowing myself to deflate. "Yes, I mean. Yes, it does."

"Cool. I think this has been a productive session. I accept Visa or PayPal."

"Ah, shut up." But I was grateful for Holden stepping so easily into doing what he did best—smoothing out my world. By now, my eyes had adjusted and I could see the lumpy furniture outlines of my safe-room nest. "Here's something. I got back my leather jacket and my black boots tonight."

"The old new look." Holden cleared his throat. "You know, for a while, Ember, with the way you'd changed and all, I thought you broke up with me because you'd met someone else."

"No . . ." That last night with Holden. The flickering apple-scented candle, the warmth of Holden's body, my dragging knowledge that I didn't want him enough. And then I made myself ask, although this was a hard one: "I know we've been through this, but I wasn't extra depressed or anything back then, was I, Holden? Maybe about you? Or giving up dance? There wasn't some part of me that would have wanted to . . . hurt myself, that night?"

"Don't even, Emb," he said. "You got dramatically interrupted, but you never lost yourself that way. I was watching you. From a distance, sure. But I never took my eyes off you."

"Right."

"Seriously. I wouldn't say it if it wasn't true."

"I know."

Holden didn't have hard, fast answers. Just assurances. Right now, that would have to be enough.

It was like old times, when we'd loitered on the phone late-night and never seemed to run out of things to say. Holden talked midterms, and his mother's imperious insistence that he get a second fitting for the blazer she'd bought him for Drew's engagement party. I told him about the Jake and Smarty date, my flubbed dinner, the Theory of Knowledge quiz tomorrow I was sure to fail.

Eventually I could feel that numb, familiar desire for sleep roll through me.

"Thanks for staying on the line with me, Holden."

"Anything for you. I'm gonna get going on this conflict res essay, but I'll put the phone down and keep you on speaker. Just if you want some white noise?"

"Yeah, I'd like that." We used to do white noise, too. Stay on the line without actually conversing. It wasn't as aggressive as video chat, and it wasn't as insistent as IM'ing. It was a peaceful sound that held us together when we weren't quite ready to let go.

"If I leave my desk, it's just to take a piss or get coffee in the lounge. How's that sound?"

"Sounds like thanks." I stretched out, flipped my pillow, and burrowed into the covers with the phone next to my ear. I listened to the click of Holden's fingers swift on the keyboard, the dependable clearing of his throat, the whispery turn of a notebook page. If I dreamed at all again tonight, I hoped it would be of Holden's profile in this moment, serene and focused, patiently waiting for me to close my eyes and breathe the breath of sleep.

17

A Different Kind of Different

The next morning, when I clomped downstairs to the kitchen in my boots and jacket, my parents held their tongues. Which I was glad about. I felt a little bit self-conscious wearing all of it, anyway, like in those early months at Addington when I'd had to use a wheelchair. Gliding down the corridors or wheeling through the garden, I'd wanted to shout to anybody, all the patients, staff, visitors—anybody who spied me—that I was only in this contraption for a little while. That I was temporary damage.

Even with the long denim skirt (that I didn't love but didn't actively dislike, either) Mom had given me last Christmas, my boots and jacket made me feel a different kind of different. Not broken. The opposite. I felt braver. I felt like a girl who'd push back.

In homeroom, though, Claude lost no time. He was lounging with Lucia on the windowsill, his chest puffed to flaunt his Georgetown sweatshirt, though most everyone else in the entire senior class would have been cringingly superstitious about wearing their top-choice college in the months before hearing news.

"Check it out," he said, his smirk firmly in place. "There's a new sheriff in town. What do you call that look, Emb? Rockabilly goth?"

"Strong show of wit, Claude. By the way, Georgetown called—your sweatshirt got in, but you're wait-listed."

"Har-har." Claude rolled his eyes, truly unbothered. He seemed to have no nerve endings; he never cared if he got snapped at or chewed out.

As Rachel came rolling into homeroom, he shifted focus to her. "Hey, remember those jokes you made, Rachel? About Ember's makeover, last year? Looks like it's time for an encore."

"What jokes?" I asked.

"Claude, do you ever shut up? They were just dumb jokes." Rachel was eyeing me to see if I cared. "Exceptionally dumb. Plus I've gotten to appreciate the new-old-new Ember." But I could tell Rachel was embarrassed; she was visibly squirmy.

"Emb's better as a ballerina," Tom called over from the back of the room, where he was in the middle of a cram session but obviously had been dual processing with an eavesdrop.

"Except that I'm not even taking dance this semester."

"You're also better with Holden," said Claude. "Is it true you two are going for it again? That's got to count for double as physical therapy."

I laughed, sort of. I didn't want to get defensive. I had no comment, officially, on Holden. But Rachel was at him in an instant. "You know what, Claude? Why don't you take a time-out from this conversation? You've already hit the ninety percent marker for talking about things that aren't your business."

"Claude, *caro mio*, I agree. And I also like your jacket, Ember," piped up Lucia. "It's how all the students look, you know. Back in Firenze." Her liquidy dark eyes were full of approval, and I felt a surge of gratitude toward her.

"Hey, Lucia, I keep meaning to ask you—who was that girl at your Halloween party, in the yellow mask? Maisie, I think her name was."

Lucia shrugged. "I don't know any girl named Maisie. Maybe she was an artist. They come and they go; it's hard to keep track. My uncle likes the company of young artists and aspiring artists. He threw open his doors to them when he was here, and he would have these exhibits, these salons showing their work. And some of the students still come to the parties and stomp around and think they own the place."

"Kind of like you in those bossy boots, Emb."

"Enough already, Claude," I snapped. "They're just boots and a jacket. Not my personal manifesto."

But I was lying. They were important. In the hush of this morning's walk to school, I'd enjoyed how they anchored me inside my body, making me feel protected and mysterious and, for once, an older version of myself instead of the girl I was always trying to catch a backward glance at.

143

And yet in what should have been the comfort of homeroom, surrounded by kids who'd known me since grade school, I was feeling like an imposter. Was it really so impossible to change anyone's mind (including my own) about who I was? Then again, was I being too hard on my friends? I didn't want them to lie to me—I valued their opinions. But I wanted them to embrace that I'd changed—not to keep harking back to someone who didn't exist anymore.

And I wasn't prepared for Tom's confession when he fell in step with me on the way to first period.

"Hey, Ember. I was hoping I could catch up with you about something."

"Is this about getting a Saturday court time from Holden? Because I asked him already—he said no problem." Tom was a tennis player, but it was Holden's family that belonged to the local tennis and squash club. Tom and my dad always used my connection to Holden to reserve courts under the Wildes' account. It was technically against club rules, but Holden never minded; actually, he seemed glad whenever he could pull a fast one on the snobs who ran the club.

"Ah, that's great. Thanks. But this is about something else."

We'd been heading up the stairs, but as we swung through the door to the upper library hall, I sensed that what Tom had to say was more important than scheduling court times. We moved to the side, dropping pace for privacy and to let the other kids pass. But still Tom seemed to hesitate.

"What is it?" I prompted. "What's wrong?"

"Ember, I haven't been sure how to approach you about this. I don't even have a real handle on if you want to hear it. Then

I decided it was worse to keep it in. I can't keep it from you anymore. You need to know."

"Know what?"

"Here's the deal. I met that kid. Anthony."

"Oh." Beneath my ribs, my heart began to beat in that same, horribly pained way whenever I heard Anthony's name.

"Nobody else out of our friends did, so I never mentioned it to anyone. And I met him just by chance. He came to pick you up from school one afternoon. It was late—I'd been getting tutoring, and I think you'd been at a dance practice."

"Anthony Travolo came to pick me up?" I'd stopped walking altogether. My shoulder met the wall for support.

"Yeah, I think so. He was just outside the back entrance. He was waiting for you, and you and I came out together, and you introduced him as Anthony. We spent a few minutes talking ice hockey. But then . . ." Tom was facing me, his arms crossed at his chest, his head bowed a bit, like a professor lost in thought.

"What? What?"

He looked up. "Well, here's where it gets a little funky. A cop car turned in from Court Street. Not in an urgent way, not like it was on anyone's tail. But your guy, Anthony—he kind of flipped."

My guy. "You think the cops were there for him?"

"No, but I think he thought so. He got tense. And then he bolted. And you took off after him—you followed him down the street and disappeared. I just kind of stood there and watched the whole thing. But then the next day, you never said anything about it. So I didn't, either. I didn't want to blow it up into some gossip item. Get Claude all pumped up. So I left it alone." Tom gazed at me perplexedly. "Do you remember anything about that?"

"No," I admitted. What a strange story. I tried to picture it, and I couldn't, though my body was prickly as if I were once again about to give chase, again tailing the long fleeting shadow of Anthony Travolo. "I know he wasn't a stranger," I said. "But what was he, to me? What was our situation? Could you tell?"

Tom shifted his backpack. "I suck at these things, but, okay—my instinct was that you seemed with him. Like, *with him* with him. It wasn't any one specific thing you were saying or doing, but he hadn't surprised you by meeting you. You were happy to see him. Look, I don't know if I should have thrown any of this at you, Ember. But I feel bad that I can remember Anthony and you can't."

"No, I'm glad you told me." I touched Tom's arm reassuringly. He didn't like being out on an emotional ledge like this.

We started walking again, continuing until we'd stopped outside my classroom.

"You should do another Folly," he blurted. "Okay, last time was a bust. The thing to remember, Emb, is it was never about the food. We'd have come over and housed canned ravioli if that's what you served. We're your friends. We want to show up for you. And you've got to lean on your best stuff. Those nights were what made you *you*."

I could feel my eyes sting. "Right," I said helplessly. "Thanks." Was that true? For me, those nights hadn't been about me being me. They'd been about getting the dishes perfect. I hadn't looked through any other lens, or even much considered what Follies had meant to the others.

After Tom took off, I detoured to the bathroom, locked myself in a stall, and pressed my head against the cool metal door. Would last year always be a dark jungle that I was hurtling through, with only a single flashlight to guide me? I should be used to it by now. But I wasn't.

During lunchtime, I knew by the way Rachel kept trying to draw me into the conversation that I wasn't fully participating. The others seemed to feel it, too. At one point, Tom left the lunch table and bought me a peanut-butter brownie from the bake sale that was being held outside the gym. Later, when I hit my study carrel to work during afternoon free period, I found that Perrin had taped me a note—*It's me, Perry, just passing by & sending you xoxoxoxo love ya, Emb.*

I'd known Perrin since we did Camp Imagine in the summer after fifth grade. Tom's family went to my church. Rachel and I had been friends since the days of naps and finger paints. My crew was tight-knit and well known to me, familiar as every shelf and corner of the house I'd grown up in. And yet now I was expected to believe that Anthony Travolo had been in my life to the point where he was picking me up from school? That we'd been out together, but I hadn't considered introducing him to Rachel? Or to my parents? Had I been ashamed of this guy? Frightened of him? Was he really in trouble with the police? What had he meant to me? I'd checked and rechecked every email, every Facebook message. He was nowhere. One thing I knew about our connection for sure: I'd been keeping Anthony a secret.

Why?

There were little drafts of an email I kept saving, that I'd been writing to Anthony's parents. I'd been working on it for weeks. Starting it, restarting it. I swiped out paragraphs of guilt and sadness and replaced them with new ones. But I'd never gotten it in any shape to send. I was scared of it—scared that whatever sentiment I expressed to the Travolos wouldn't be correct or appropriate. That in trying to do something right, I'd unintentionally do something hurtful and damaging and wrong.

Dr. P and my parents didn't want me to push it. They wanted me to preserve my feelings, my sensitivity. When I'd written Dr. P about it, he'd written back to "stop perseverating on this letter. One thing at a time. Let it go for now." *Perseverating* was a term he'd used when I was at Addington, and it basically just meant to stop chasing the same worry around and around, with no meaningful way out. At some point, though, I knew I'd have to trade the chase for a decision.

In other words, I'd have to be brave and hit send.

The school day dragged, and I was glad for the end of it. All I had now was physical therapy. As I swept through the city in the underground, the anonymous subway ride felt both romantic and authentic. Alone, surrounded by strangers, and on my way to anywhere, I contained any and all of the Embers I might have been.

"New boots," Jenn commented when she saw me.

"Old boots. Reclaimed." I pulled them off and sat them on the bench, like a pair of dusty thug friends. They'd been all the way to the bottom of that river with me. Now they would stand guard over my physical therapy session. It was probably a stupid thought, but I liked to imagine that the boots were somehow encouraging me, subliminally, to push through this session—and to be grateful that I was here, alive, and able to do the work at all.

I'd been diligent with therapy since that first time I missed it, but over the next hour, as I pulled and stretched and bent into as many tilts, tucks, and planks as my body could withstand, I could feel that I was coming at this from a stronger place than usual. It beefed up my confidence, envisioning new muscles thickening my tendons and ligaments, promising me future power.

"Nice, Ember. You haven't even asked for a break! Do you realize that?" Jenn could give me at least a dozen variations of positive encouragement—and I was grateful for every single one.

"Okay, but I'm taking a break now." I dropped to the mat and let my cheek claim its sneaker-smelling surface. "It sucks how much it hurts, but I'm really trying to force myself past the pain. It's different than when I was at Addington—when I felt too close to broken. Now I feel like I can . . . endure."

"This time next year, I bet a lot of what you're calling pain will be more like a twinge. Like pain memory. And I'm not just saying that to psych you up." Jenn knelt on the mat next to me. Her face was serious sunshine. "You're so young, Ember, and you're naturally in such good shape that your body's snapping back like a rubber band. The prognosis is for a near one hundred percent recovery. In a couple of years, I'll bet you that—with the exception of your scars—that horrible night, and everything that came after it, will be completely erased from your body."

My smile was a cover, I hoped. I knew Jenn had meant everything she said in her most upbeat way possible, but as I left the Y, I could hear only that one word: *erased.*

Reflexively, I touched the scar on my forehead. It was like a secret monster, a hideous zipper beneath my bangs. No amount of scar gel and cocoa butter would erase the ugly rickrack of that mark. That night would take aim at me every time I looked into the mirror.

It was dusk when I walked up from the subway. Another cold

snap, but this one meant business. Winter was on its way. The clocks had turned back this week and the sky was wolfish gray.

I stopped at Carroll Park, revisiting the scene of my nightmare. Rachel and I had played here a lot when we were younger, two kids on scooters with Band-Aids on our knees. My nightmare wasn't waiting for me here, of course. There were no T-shirts on the trees. I lingered. The park was pearl-shadowed, luminescent. I watched different clusters of rowdy kids combine and separate, jousting for time on the swings or yanking for turns playing with grungy public toys strewn in the sandbox. There was a bench under a hunchbacked dogwood. I sat and found a curled piece of bark, rubbing it between my hands, letting it crumble.

It wasn't until I leaned back and looked around that I saw it from across the playground. It was the mural that had been on Maisie's Facebook page, the one that Anthony had posed next to. I must have known, maybe semi-subconsciously, that it was here.

The paint looked dingy and rain-weathered, and yet the beauty of the artwork—a canopy of green trees interlaced in blue sky—was still strong. But what caught my eye and stopped my heart was the lower corner. There it was, that sideways gunmetal A. Not as refined as the mural, yet it seemed to be a kind of signature. How strange that it would be here. I knew that it was all connected, somehow. I just didn't have all the puzzle pieces yet.

I stayed for a few more minutes, until the darkness forced the mural into murky shadow, too dark to see. Leaving the park, I cut through to Union Street, walking loud, relishing the knock of my heels, each foot neatly packed and protected. I kicked a new path through the hundreds of tear-shaped, butter-yellow dogwood leaves all mashed up along the sidewalk.

It wasn't on purpose. It wasn't by accident. It was something in between that made me do it. I'd memorized the address, and so I knew right where I was directing my boots as they crossed Court over to Smith.

El Cielo was smack in the middle of the block, with a picture-window façade. I peeked in on a bustling view of dinner hour. It seemed to be one of those all-ages restaurants, a few families gathered together while up front was a happening cocktail scene, with many barstools claimed by couples on amped-up date nights.

Most of the space was arranged with square and round tables, many set with sangria pitchers and baskets of blue-corn tortilla chips alongside painted bowls of red and green salsa. Strings of colored Christmas lights and framed black-and-white photographs—a few depicting haunting scenes from Mexico's Day of the Dead festival—made the wall space vibrant as an art gallery. But overall, the restaurant had the atmosphere of a beloved hangout that had withstood time and trends.

My heart was pounding repeatedly with a single question, a fizzy manic new thought that unnerved me but at least had replaced the meditative tone of my day.

Was Kai here? Was Kai here?

Of course that was a major leap. Even for me. Just because Kai had given me a matchbook from this restaurant didn't mean he had any reason to be here now, this minute. Or at all.

But what if he was? What if?

I hovered at the hostess stand, checking out a waitress as she unloaded plates of smoking hot fajitas for a huge family. She was older than I was, maybe college-age, with a soft pink face and hard pale eyes and yellow hair skinned into a bun. She was being helped by a busboy who couldn't have been more than thirteen. The boy looked familiar, too, sinewy and dark-haired, and when he noticed me staring at him, he stopped and turned away abruptly to haul an overfilled plastic tub of dirty dishes back to the kitchen.

I was being watched. I looked back at the girl, who now seemed to think she needed to deal with me. With her lips pressed and a quick "hang on" finger signal, she took the tub from the boy and lugged it away through a swing door to what had to be the kitchen in the rear. When she returned, wiping her hands, she seemed resolved.

"You can eat in back," she said. "It's okay."

"Thanks."

I hadn't planned on eating. But after my ninety minutes with Jenn, plus the walk over, I probably should. I was famished. And then I remembered that I had a twenty-dollar plus ten-dollar bill on me, though the money wasn't technically mine—Suzette Bodkin had owed yearbook for an ad. I'd tucked the bills into my jeans pocket, meaning to put them in the envelope in the business office. But I could use this money, and then I'd just bring in a replacement thirty dollars tomorrow from home. A sit-down dinner for myself at El Cielo seemed indulgent, but also exactly the right way to spend the next hour. Somehow I needed to be here.

My parents were out tonight with our neighbors. I wouldn't be missed.

"Follow me," said the girl. I had to move quickly to keep up as she led me through the narrow passage and to the rear of the restaurant, which opened into a festive kitchen of copper hanging pots and a brick pizza oven and one of those dinged brass bars that looks like it has seen its fair share of rowdy nights.

Then she left me to stand alone. Where was I supposed to sit? At this hideaway back bar? It felt presumptuous to just hop up onto a stool. I waited, watching.

At the stove, a tiny, grandmotherly woman was in full command of her kitchen realm. It included two younger male prep cooks, but she was clearly the leader, a dynamo who looked like she'd been shrunk while her clothing had stayed the same size— her silver hoop earrings nearly touched her shoulders, and her kitchen apron bagged at her ankles. She was all useful motion, moving in waltz-like grace as she bumped and reached from the sink to the oven to the chopping station. I couldn't decide if I'd ever seen her before, or if it was more that she looked like a grandmother from the movies, she was so vibrant.

The kitchen spices mingled with deeper notes of browning butter, roasting garlic, sautéed yellow onion, and sizzling grilled meat. I hadn't been to a restaurant since Serendipity, which had reminded me how much I loved to see all different people coming together for a delicious meal. It was what I'd always wanted my Follies to be about.

At first I had a distinct and unnerving sense that everyone working at El Cielo was aware of my presence. The feeling didn't leave, even when nobody singled me out. But in the haze of smoke and clattering overheated kitchen, there was real energy, enough so that I couldn't have been the true center of attention even if I'd wanted to. The old woman was lost in her pots and pans, the cooks were deep inside their shorthand dialogue, and everything was muffled by the roar of an electric range-top fan.

At the touch at my elbow, I turned.

The busboy stood in front of me. He was holding a rolled set of silverware. Wordlessly, he set me a place at the barstool. I hopped up.

"Tía Isabella," he said, addressing the woman. *"Ella está aquí. Para la cena."*

The woman raised her eyebrows as she officially took me in. The busboy darted to lift a pitcher and glass from the nearby busing stand. He filled the glass and brought it to me.

"Gracias." I felt geeky using my classroom Spanish.

"De nada," murmured the boy, before he slipped away again.

I went back to watching the cook. She was a real master, long trained in this kitchen. She was also so short that she'd invented a quirky choreography of kicking a stepladder along next to her as she went about her business, the better to leap up for cupboards or canisters, while muttering what sounded like *"entonces, entonces"*—words that I was pretty sure meant something like "and then, and then," but in this case seemed to be Isabella's own private magical incantation.

But there was a catch in her eye that I couldn't decipher exactly, when she finally paused to let me know that she was considering me. Of course, a seventeen-year-old girl sitting all by herself on a barstool of a crowded restaurant was probably not her usual customer. Without a word, she found a menu under the bar and passed it to me before returning to her work, but every so often she'd stop and tilt her head, stealing a glance. As if I might be something that she'd put into storage, who now had turned up in an unlikely setting.

And when she finally smiled at me, it was quick as a flower

tossed into an audience, and it disappeared just as fast. "What do you like?"

"Oh—it all looks great. I'll eat anything." True. My stomach felt scooped and empty and ready for whatever came my way.

It was the right answer. "Let me fix you something."

As I watched, I could feel myself mentally shadowing the woman's own movements, as she quickly heated a reserve of skillet oil for mushrooms and peppers, then added a couple of lethal pinches of chili pepper and a dried bay leaf to the sauce already simmering on the stove.

In no time, she'd served me up a platter of enchiladas, narrow as cigars, lightly drizzled in salsa verde and dolloped with sour cream, along with a side of black-bean salad and another of crispy fried zucchini.

Sinking in my fork, I had to resist the impulse to abandon utensils altogether and eat with my hands, and then to mop up the sauce with the extra plate of soft, warm tortillas. Stealthily, I let my boots drop to the floor, and I tucked my feet so that I could eat cross-legged, the way I loved to do when I was alone.

After a few minutes of relinquishing myself to what was easily my most amazing food experience in months, I could feel myself absorbing the enchiladas in a different way, as I imagined preparing them. I could feel my hand cover the spine of the knife blade, a technique I'd learned on a cooking show that had effectively demonstrated the cleanest way to chop and seed a jalapeño pepper. And there was, I remembered, a trick to the timing of the recipe, to juggling the sauce with the filling and the last-minute grating of the cheese—rough not fine—and yet this was a trick I'd forgotten. . . .

The dish was already spicy. My nose was fiery red and tears were slipping down my face. I'd doused it in hot sauce when it needed hardly any.

The busboy had reapproached me noiselessly and set down an extra napkin for me, which I used as a handkerchief. I watched him as he picked up a rack of dishes from a dolly, heaved them over his bony shoulder, and prepared to take them downstairs. At the same instant, another figure swung empty-handed around the corner. My heart stuck in my ribs. Kai.

18

Third Door Down

I froze. Kai didn't see me at first. He had paused at the touch screen to place an order. But for me, everything stopped—the hour itself seemed to come screeching to a halt, along with my pulse, my thoughts, and every single half-prepared scrap of speech I'd ever recited to Kai in my head.

Stop . . . stop . . . stopped. Numb. I was scared to blink, to lose him.

Kai worked here? My brain reeled to make this seem obvious and natural. Of course he worked here—the matchbook had been his clue to me. He'd wanted me to find him. He'd been expecting me to find him. In his element. Because he looked good working here, too, dressed in his waiter's tailored black pants and short black apron plus a golf shirt with the restaurant's red and yellow logo emblazoned on the front pocket.

As soon as he finished punching in the order, I was sure that Kai was going to turn in my direction. But I was jolted to watch him coast past me toward the front of the restaurant.

He'd sensed me, though. Of course he had. Nobody who gets stared at as hard as I was staring at Kai doesn't somehow figure that out.

So now what? *Do I just wait for him to come to me?*

I glanced down at the sauce and sour cream pooled on my empty plate. It was probably the lingering after-impression of all that spicy food, but I was heated up and close to tears; they threatened to wash out at any moment. Or maybe it was the old here-we-go-again panic slash exhilaration of being caught in another sort-of chance meeting with Kai. The matchbook had led me to him so easily. Too easily.

Okay, but now I was here. I'd found him. And he was less enigmatic now, right? Here was a huge new chunk of information. Kai worked here at El Cielo. *As a waiter.* Was anything less mysterious than that?

My heart thrumming, I kept my head downcast. I took tiny mechanical bites of the last tortilla, all too aware that Kai was wandering around in possible eye- or earshot. And when I twisted and craned, I caught him in angles as he tended to the tables, skirting between them, a purposeful back-and-forth from the wait stands and busing stations and then around again—to stack a high chair or bring a pitcher of beer. My vision of him was broken, occasionally, by the busy presence of the blond girl, who seemed to deal with Kai's tables as well as her own. Maybe he was just a backup waiter?

After a few minutes, I could relax almost to the point of enjoying him. It was a new power, to watch while I remained unobserved. Kai looked more boyish in this setting, and more sweetly earnest while at work. His white shirt set off the dark tones of his skin—a color I could semi-achieve if I baked myself in the sun all summer—and his hair was different, comb-marked like a little kid's on school picture day.

I stared, entranced, slightly dazed from too much dinner; plus my muscles were warm and now slightly achy from the physical therapy session. If there was ever a time to be equipped for another meeting with Kai, this was it. In one short month, I'd come a long way from my barely-rehabbed-odds-and-ends self. I didn't need Dr. P to tell me I was taking better care not to be some shivering girl on a fire escape, or that I'd even learned a lesson from my Halloween trancing in darklight to a downtown club mix.

El Cielo might be Kai's turf, but tonight I was strong enough to meet him on it.

I waited another couple of minutes, my heart racing faster than a Daytona mile as I thought up cute-but-not-cutesy icebreaker lines. The tension was killing me and I could feel doubt start to creep in. What if I had this all wrong, and he never came over?

Because I had to talk with him again.

It really needed to happen. It was everything.

After another minute, I slid off my perch and back into my boots, and then went in pretend search of the bathroom, darting a quick look around the corner where the busboy had vanished. The threads of my nerves were pulling and tweaking at me like I was a puppet. The restaurant was now packed.

When Kai materialized around the bar in a few sure steps to stand right there in front of me, I was pretty sure he knew I'd been here all along. His smile was halfway in hiding, but there was concern in his face, too. He was guarded but not unhappy to see me. Not at all.

"Hey, you."

"Hey yourself."

"You found me."

"No thanks to you."

He raised an eyebrow as if this might not be true. "I want to talk."

"Me too."

"Not up here, though. Cold storage, basement. Third door on the left. I'll meet you down there." He tapped his bare wrist. "I'm on the clock. Though I've got some solid backup who won't rat me out." He motioned to the busboy, who'd reappeared and was refilling water glasses.

I nodded. "Okay."

"You go first and I'll join you. Give me two, three minutes." Kai winked, hoisted a bar tray, and slipped past me as if we hadn't connected at all.

I hovered another moment by the archway that marked the stairwell. My eyes sliding right left right to make sure no vaguely menacing eyes were doing any spying on me—though why would anyone care what I did?—and then I bolted down the terra-cotta tiled steps to El Cielo's underground.

It was an instant atmosphere change from the warmth of the ground-floor crowd. Down here felt cooler, serene and unoccupied. It smelled musty, and I could hear a white noise—a water heater drum, maybe? Sound had shifted to a dull ocean roar. At the bottom of the steps I found myself in a hallway marked with opposing doors—one labeled DAMAS, the other CABALLEROS— plus two more doors on the left. I peeked in the next door, which was thinly cracked on a windowless office.

This third door was heavy, squared off like a vault. Breath held, I turned the knob and pushed. The icy air was almost menacing and the temperature seemed like a warning that this was a forbidden zone, that I wasn't welcome here. I bit my bottom lip and turtled deeper into my jacket.

There was a fluorescent glare here, too. From floor to ceiling, everything in the room was marble or chrome, with wall-to-wall steel cupboards and a refrigerator that had an industrial lever handle, while the fridge itself looked big enough to hold Noah's whole ark. Nobody else was down here, but I moved around like a burglar, anyway. The temperature drop made my brain and body sluggish, as the cold slipped and settled over me like a silk scarf.

The silence was lonely, too. I chewed at my cuticles. What if Kai didn't come? What if he was upstairs getting raged at because the waitress had been watching us? Or one of the line cooks? What if I got caught? What if Kai got fired?

No, no, no. He'd be down soon. And then everything would be okay. Kai wouldn't have told me to slip away and meet him here if he didn't think we could pull it off.

The overhead track lights were so white they made me see purple.

On impulse, I snapped them off.

Better.

Humming electricity was an absence that filled the darkness—sterile and antiseptic, delivering me into memories of the unyielding shape of that narrow cot at Addington. So far from my own soft bed and its sweetly shabby friendship quilt. Every room at Addington had a bedside call bell. I'd never used mine.

Press it, they encouraged. Press it and a nurse will appear at your side within moments to meet your demands. Help to the bathroom. A glass of water. A hot-water bottle. Anything.

I'd looked at that bell every night, wishing that it had the power to summon the people I really wanted. My parents, my friends. Those empty, lonely nights where all I'd done was stare up at the ceiling, waiting to heal, had seemed to drag on forever.

Cold was seeping into my bones. I moved slowly, feeling my way, ducking around the refrigerator and out of view in case the wrong person showed up. I sat cross-legged on the ground with my back against the wall. Then I closed my eyes, letting the freeze sink me. Adjusting to it. A minute passed. I heard the door open.

I exhaled. He'd come. I leaned around. "Hey! I'm over here," I whispered.

Silent as a panther, Kai found me. I could smell him, that intoxicating hint of him, as he slid down next to me in the dark.

"It's freezing," I whispered. "I'm not sure I can be here for that much longer."

"I know, I know. I can't stay, either. We're getting slammed. But I'm—wow, I can't believe you came by."

"Are you surprised?"

"Hell yeah, I'm surprised. A girl like you, wanting to hang out with a starving student slash waiter like me. What would your parents think?"

"What do you mean a girl like me?"

"A girl like you," he repeated. "I guess I could say a pretty girl, or maybe I'd say a girl from a fancy landmark district, who goes to Lafayette and buys lunch in a bento box, and can even use the chopsticks. But what I really mean is a girl who knows her own mind." He smiled. "Yeah, that's mostly what I meant."

"Oh." It was a cool thing to say, though I wasn't sure that's how I'd have defined myself. But it wasn't not true, in relation to Kai. For one, I knew I wanted to see him again. And I'd gone out of my way to find him. "Well, you couldn't possibly be starving," I said, deflecting his intensity even as I stored away his compliment. "The food's too good here."

"That's my aunt who heads up the kitchen."

"She's a genius cook. I'm surprised you don't weigh an extra hundred pounds."

"Put the blame on my good metabolism." Kai was fiddling with something. His flask, I realized. He unscrewed the top and took a long sip. I could smell the dark-roasted coffee, and I didn't have to taste it to know that it was strong.

"I don't think I've ever met a guy who drinks coffee from a flask."

"It was my dad's," said Kai. "The only thing I've got that's his."

"What happened to him?"

"Nothing, except that he ditched. Classic lost soul, and he's part of the reason why there'll only ever be coffee in my flask.

My mom died—cancer—when I was seven and Hatch was three. Isabella's really my great-aunt, my grandmother's sister. She's been raising us since I was in third grade." He gave me the information in a voice as flat as a glass of milk, but when he offered the flask, I had a feeling that he didn't let just anyone drink from it. I took the smallest bird sip.

"Coffee makes me nervous," I confessed.

"Yeah? Are you nervous around me?"

"Only because I think this is our last visit," I answered. "Honestly, I just can't tell if you really want to see me or if you're avoiding me."

"Both," Kai answered. So matter-of-fact it was almost jarring.

"Okay," I said. *"Both."*

"If you think I'm never thinking about you, you're wrong. Your name's been like an extra beat in my heart since I saw you. But the thing is, it's complicated. I've got a lot going on. Too much. My aunt isn't big on me getting serious with a girl, and my aunt's got a major vote in my life. I'm dealing with school, the restaurant, my kid brother. There's no room for me to screw up or screw around."

"Sure. I get it. Absolutely." I didn't at all. Was I part of "screw up" or "screw around"? "Actually, no, I don't get it," I added in a next breath of openness. "I can't stop thinking about you."

"Me either," he said quietly. "I'm not going to deny it. We connected. I feel like we want the same things, in a way. Like, I've got this theory about people—that there are people who stay and people who go. And you're like me. You want out." I could feel Kai watching me. "Because you're not in life to obey it, to stay stuck in a system and a rule book and a set of expectations that were predetermined practically before you were born. You're looking for more, right? So am I."

It was so true that it was jarring. I thought of my parents, sweetly prodding me to be their perfect ballerina. Picking out all the ruffles and flowers of my clothes closet. Nudging me, even, toward Holden—the perfect boyfriend. "Yeah, I'm going," I admitted. "I'm not sure where yet, but I'm facing in a new direction, and I'll get there. Eventually."

When I glanced at him, Kai's eyes seemed to glitter like mica in the shadows. When he slipped the flask back into his waiter's apron pocket, we were close enough that our shoulders touched, and it seemed perfectly natural for my hand to drift to his forearm.

"So, now that we got that outta the way." He laughed. "The real issue is that we're a coupla goofballs who can't stop thinking about each other."

From that, it took nothing to touch my lips to Kai's neck, allowing myself to taste his skin, the recipe of him. He turned to face me full-on, tipped up my chin and kissed my mouth. I kissed him back. More than a kiss. I felt drowsy and reckless, but what could I do? He transfixed me; he'd been stalking every corner of my mind since the moment I met him.

"I missed you," I confessed. "And when I saw you the other night at Areacode, I just knew—"

"Ever since the first night," he interrupted, his words cartwheeling over mine, "I've been writing about you."

"Seriously?"

"And sketching you, imagining you. Inventing you, sometimes even making you up as I went along. There's so much I don't know about you that I need to learn."

It was a strange moment for Holden to flash across my mind. And not Holden, the guy who was overly endorsed by my mother and father, but Holden, who knew everything about me. All of the friends and memories that Holden and I had in common, bumping in and out of each other's paths since grade school, when I knew him first as Rachel's cousin. Holden was a "stayer"—he'd never have the desire to leave New York. Even his college life was a stone's throw from home. But there was also something wonderful about Holden's being so known to me, familiar as a fingerprint. Whereas I knew Kai was tricky, like a fish swimming upstream, flashing in and out of my life.

"Don't lose me again, Kai. Please?"

In answer, he kissed me. Maybe it was because it was so dark, but I was immediately lost in him, in his touch and the scent of him, all mixed up with the onion-bread garlic smell of the restaurant. Kai immersed me completely. Anesthetized me. Nothing else mattered more than this moment.

"Hey, I've got an idea. Let's do something," I whispered. "Something planned. Something just us two."

"Sure." He nodded. "Yeah, I'd like that."

"I'm up for anything."

"Anything? Cost and time being no object?" Kai had shifted to a casual tone—did that mean he wasn't serious about this? "Maybe we could go out to Burning Man, in the Black Rock Desert. It's supposed to be a once-in-a-lifetime experience. Or we jump on a plane to England, hit the Glastonbury music festival. I've always wanted to check that out. And Barcelona, and Florence. But I guess first I'll need to get a passport."

"Okay, okay, very funny; I know you're joking," I said. "But I'm serious."

"And there's always ice fishing in the tundra," he continued, as if I hadn't spoken. "Which is about the same temperature as in here. Damn. Makes me sleepy." He turned from me to cover a yawn, and I could see his silhouette, the delicate notch of his neck and the joint where his jaw met his ear. He'd presented these destinations as jokes, but I had a feeling that his mind had lingered over each and every one of them. He was frustrated with it—the lack of money and time. He wanted so much.

"Let's go everywhere," I said. "I'm on for all of it. Nothing you've said sounds completely out of reach to me."

"I really do need to start hanging out with you."

"Exactly." I was perfect for him. He'd never find a better fit. I could dream any dream with him.

But my mind was also shutting down a bit, too. The dark freeze of this industrial-chrome storage room had cast a sleep spell.

"But for now, I wouldn't mind starting small." My voice was hardly a whisper into silence. "I'm more of a burger-and-a-movie girl. A walk-in-the-park girl. We don't have to go anywhere."

When Kai spoke, his tone was clipped. "Look, Ember. It sounds awesome now, but girls don't stick to me. I've hardly got anything to offer. No time, no money, nothing."

"So you've said. So what? I'll do anything, even if it's nothing. I just want to see you. I don't care what we do—it makes no difference to me." I couldn't remember any other time when I'd been so serious, or so truthful. I also knew that I was on a tightrope, and that the breath of Kai's rejection might blow me right over.

"Coney Island," Kai said suddenly.

That was a bit out of left field. "Coney Island?" I repeated.

"Yeah. Why not? I always wanted to see Luna Park in winter."

"Then sure. Great!" After all, it was a relatively simple destination. And I'd been to Coney Island once before, a long time ago, with my parents in the dead of August. The afternoon had ended in a massive summer thunderstorm. I'd listened to the ghostly sound of the wind whipping down the boardwalk, and I'd inhaled a corn dog from under a kiosk umbrella as we'd watched the storm sweep through, rain sluicing our legs and turning the cornmeal batter damp, which made it taste even better. It was one of those detachedly pleasurable memories of childhood, and it tumbled into my lap as true as if it had happened yesterday.

I could take the car. Flatbush, then cut across to Ocean Parkway. The possibility of this day was something to fight for. That scent of it, like Kai, was exactly what I craved.

The icy air of the cold-storage room was its own insistent counterforce. We had to get out of here soon. I yawned as I tucked my numb fingertips into my armpits. "Is this real, then? Coney Island? With me?"

"Ember, I don't even know how to be more serious."

Hearing my name gave me confidence. "Okay, cool. I can drive us there," I offered. I wasn't even sure if it was true—I hadn't driven a car since that night. And yet I had to do it at some point. Despite all my anxieties, I had to put myself behind the wheel and strap myself in and make myself go. Here was my perfect initiation. I'd drive to Coney Island with Kai, and in the process I'd reclaim my driving skills, yet another part of a precious whole I'd lost that night.

But I could get that back, I knew I could. The risk was worth it.

"Want to say Saturday?" he suggested. "Then I'll call you once I'm sure I can get the time off. But I better head upstairs, or I've got no job to get back to." As he leaned forward to stand, his mouth grazed my ear. Kai was so effortlessly sure that everything he did would be everything I wanted him to do. And he was right.

"How should we handle this?"

"I'll go first. You wait a minute."

In the shadows he was hard to see. He wasn't kidding about this, was he? "So . . . if you can get off, then I'll pick you up?"

"Uh-huh, that works. I'm in the dorm residence at the St. George—you know where the St. George is, right?"

"I do."

"Cool. We'll pick a time." He gave me another kiss that left my lips either heat- or ice-burned.

And then I was alone in the Arctic.

After a minute or so, surprise. The overhead light flipped on. It wasn't Kai. I covered my eyes against the fluorescent flash. I listened as brisk footsteps approached the walk-in. It opened and something was slid out. Then came the smack of the sealed door shutting. A pause—I held my breath. The stranger left, and I hadn't been caught. Whew. I looked down at my arms in wonderment. My skin was icy as a Popsicle, with a lacy formation of goose bumps making a purplish space-alien pattern on my flesh. I'd been down here a long time.

When I raced back up the stairs, I knew that Isabella, though she kept up her same waltzing pace, was also circumspectly watching me. So was the busboy. Not in the nicest of ways. Definitely with intensity.

"Your check is paid," he told me formally as he served me a

dish of custard that I hadn't ordered. His voice wasn't particularly friendly.

"Oh." Kai comped my dinner? I hadn't expected that. The general acceptance of my presence here was no small thing. I nodded my thanks to Isabella and tapped my fingertips to my heart in appreciation of her kindness. Then I looked the boy in the eye. "Thank you."

But I'd seen all I could of Kai; he was probably too busy to come talk to me again, though after I finished my dessert and left, I stayed another minute outside the restaurant. There, I could see Kai only as a swiftly passing shadow.

I stood quietly for a while, anyway. Looking in.

Walking home, I let myself unwind and process it.

I couldn't have told anyone, least of all myself, much about Kai. I didn't know his favorite color or what kind of music he listened to or his religion, if he was a cat or dog person, if he liked sweet or spicy, if he was finicky or mellow. I didn't know if he played sports or if he preferred M&M's or Twizzlers at the movies.

And yet the connection was so firm and so true. I also knew that no matter how many details I ultimately coaxed from Kai, his favorite breakfast cereal or if he played basketball or soccer or liked to swim or fish or whatever, none of these things would add up to the extraordinary whole of what I liked about him, and why he was mine.

Because he was. More than Holden, more than Rachel, more than anyone else I'd ever met, I knew that this guy, in his essence, belonged to me.

It was as simple, it was as insane, as that.

Dear Mr. and Mrs. Travolo,

There are no words to express the pain of your loss, and I am writing to you with a heavy heart.

To the parents of Anthony Travolo:

I have been trying to write to you for many weeks now, but every time I sit down and attempt to communicate everything that is in my heart, I realize just how limited language can be.

For Anthony's family,

I'm not even sure if you want to hear from me, but the longer I go without writing to you, the more disappointed I am in myself. And so I have vowed that as soon as I finish typing this letter, I am sending it.

I highlighted the next block of text and deleted it. None of this was coming easily. It wasn't coming through for me at all. Maybe I was just deluding myself that I had the skill to create a letter that could capture the core truth of everything that I wanted the Travolos to know. But I was no closer to hitting send. It might be better to check into whether I could get hold of a phone number instead.

Condolences by phone. It seemed worse.

What I really needed to do was to visit them.

19

Exactly Their Person

It had been one year plus one month since I'd been over to the Wildes' house. But when Thursday arrived, I was dragging my feet. Drew Wilde's engagement party was going to be stiff and uncomfortable. That was a given. The problem was, I'd ended up promising Holden again on the phone, and now here it was Thursday, and my word was my bond. I couldn't go back on it. Especially not to Holden, who lived by those honor codes.

But I'd prepared as best I could. I'd even bought an outfit for it, at a funky little consignment shop on Smith Street that was around the corner from where I did physical therapy. It was a plain black dress with cobwebby sleeves. Even on sale, it was a bit more than I'd wanted to spend, but nothing else in my closet made sense to me, style-wise.

A cobweb dress, check. Black tights, check. Plus the boots. Was me.

Mom couldn't stop all the black, but then again I couldn't have stopped Mom from hitting Floral Heights and returning triumphantly with two giant tiger orchids, which she told me I needed to present as a "hostess gift" for Holden's mother and for Drew's fiancée, Raina.

"This is too awkward," I'd protested. "I swear to you, Mrs. Wilde doesn't even want these. She's super picky about flowers." Privately, it also seemed as if showing up with big expensive orchids was kind of like an apology—and for what? For breaking up with her son last year?

Luckily, Rachel swung by to pick me up so that we could walk over together. And she wasn't into presenting an orchid any more than I was.

"Really, Nat?" she asked, deliberately using the nickname my mom disliked.

"And just so you know, I'm telling Mrs. Wilde *you* bought them," I called to Mom as we walked out the door. "So you'll have to take full blame for currying favor."

"Don't be so dramatic. This is just good manners," Mom insisted.

"Okay, executive decision: your orchid is for Drew, and mine is for Aunt Eleanor," said Rachel. "I'd rather puke on my shoes than give Drew anything. I mean, I had to grow up with that kid; he's also my cousin, unfortunately. He was such a bully to me and Holden back in the day."

"When I was going out with Holden, I lived in fear that Drew would be at the house," I remembered aloud. "All he did was tease us about hooking up. He'd shout from wherever he was, 'Hey, are you kids making out up there? Smoochy-smooch! Kissy-kissy!' And it was like he knew how much I hated that term, *making out*." I grimaced.

"Yeah, it's hard to believe he's any better. I say we stay for an hour. Jake wants to meet up at Floyd after. He's playing bocce there with some friends."

"And God forbid you and Jake go three hours without seeing each other."

"He makes me laugh."

"He makes you more than laugh."

"I know. . . ." Smarty smiled to herself. She'd been in a permanent Hollywood-musical mood since Halloween—nothing but smiles and a spring in her step, and it had everything to do with Jake Weinstock. In the halls, they were inseparable. If she wasn't texting him, she was waiting for his text to come in. All conversations seemed to lead down the path to Jake's name, and most after-school or weekend plans included him.

Which was fine by me.

She was intolerable, before. Calling me, texting me every hour to talk about Holden and insisting he and I give it another chance. I was just about ready to kill her.

The thoughts came unbidden and surprised me.

"Sometimes I wish I'd met Jake last year; then maybe I wouldn't have been so, I don't know, *invested*—while you and Hold went through your breakup." Rachel spoke as if she'd been reading my mind. "When I think about it, I wonder if I just ended up making all your crap worse."

"No way. You can't take responsibility for that."

"I know. But anyway, I think it's cool that you're giving it another try."

Another try? Is that what Holden had told her? This seemed like the perfect time for me to tell Smarty about Kai. To confess everything—our meetings, our connection, El Cielo, the fact that he whipped around in my head on a permanent spin cycle. I wanted to blurt out that I was walking on air today because I had a message from Kai on my phone, a message to pick him up this Saturday outside his dorm, the St. George, which was a few blocks from the Manhattan Bridge—and about a twenty-minute walk from my house.

Since yesterday, I'd walked there twice in the hope I'd accidentally-on-purpose bump into him. So far, no luck. Of course, he was self-admittedly never there, since he was usually in class or working at El Cielo—which was one place where I didn't want to drop by uninvited, no matter how much I wanted to connect with him. Not with his *tía* Isabella's unflinching eyes on me. I'd be pushing my luck.

But the moment of confession looped into another, less intimate one as Rachel and I walked on, our orchids occasionally tangling up with each other. Maybe Kai was still just a me thing. Maybe I just wasn't ready to share.

"This reminds me of that other time, do you remember?" asked Rachel. "Back when Holden hosted his junior class party, and we walked over to the Wildes' together carrying that double-fudge cake your mom had picked up at Betty Bakery, and all the fondant roses on the sides got smushed? Remember?"

"Kind of."

"And I was in my rebel smoking phase, and I had to hide my Parliaments in somebody's flower box when Aunt Eleanor saw me puffing away from down the road. And oh my God, the actual party, how hilarious it was? All the guys just sweaty and miserable in their outgrown blazers, and Holden kept making fun of Aunt Eleanor because she was obsessed that the mini-burger buns might not be gluten-free since someone—I forget who it was in the class—couldn't eat them, and she was scared of a lawsuit?" Rachel's face was lit up into the past as she called it all back.

"Emily Vaughn," I said. "It was Emily because she's got celiac disease, and Holden's mom kept announcing it to everyone, and Emily kept saying, 'No, it's cool; I'm not even hungry,' just to shut her up."

"Ha-ha, that's right. And then we went into the city to bowl at Chelsea Piers after, remember? Which was awesome."

"Yeah." I could see it vaguely. It had been such a nothing night, even the bowling. But Rachel loved Chelsea Piers and double-fudge cake from Betty. Funny how the exact same event could get folded up and put away in some people's memories, while it got shaken out in others', to be worn again and again.

"Hey, listen," said Rachel as we stood side by side at the Wildes' front door. "If the family isn't feeling too warm and fuzzy around you, I'm right here, okay? Don't let 'em get you down." Rachel knocked her hip against mine in solidarity, the orchids tangling a last time just as one of the uniformed caterers opened the door.

Lilies, peonies, hyacinths—the front hall was banked in them. Immediately my eyes and nose started to itch. My pollen allergies were not going to be friends with this party. As Rachel and I set down our orchids, I sneezed discreetly into my sleeve. I looked around at the crowd, the open view of an equally formal dining room and what Holden's mother always insisted on calling the "parlor."

I'd never liked this fussy house, and it set me on edge to be here again. And at Drew's engagement party, no less. It was odd to think of Drew committing to something as selfless as falling in love, since he was always such a prick to everyone. Not a prick like Claude, who targeted his words like a sharpshooter and was always hoping for a reaction. Drew was tone-deaf; he moved through the world in rudeness and oblivion, hardly ever recognizing that his insults and oversights were painful to others.

Across the antiques and coiffed heads in the Wildes' parlor, I spied Holden talking to his grandparents, who'd come in from Summit, New Jersey, for the weekend. Holden's eyes were also red-rimmed with allergic reaction; plus the beard was gone, and I suspected that his clean shave was the result of losing the argument to his mother. It disappointed me slightly that Holden hadn't held his ground on that one.

"Whoa, boy!" I crouched to accept Jolly's waggling, nose-to-tail, full-on doggy-greeting at our unexpected reunion—and nearly fell over backward in the process.

"The ewww factor just doubled," whispered Rachel on my side as I stood. "Claude's here. At least he's with Lucia. She makes him less awful."

"How'd he get invited?" I asked as we all exchanged fake-friendly waves across the room.

"Not him; her. Probably Aunt Eleanor heard that Lucia's family's got rocks."

"You know, even when Holden and I were going out, I always felt like Mrs. Wilde looked down on me," I admitted. I'd never confessed that before—it had embarrassed me. But now it didn't seem to matter.

"How so?"

"She just kept me at a distance. Like, for example, she never, ever let me call her Eleanor."

"Oh, because *that's* such a privilege." Rachel rolled her eyes. "First-name basis with the Wicked Witch of the Heights." She nicked an endive leaf topped with something cream-cheesy from another passing caterer. "Hey, this reminds me," she said as she crunched. "You know that every morning for breakfast Jake Weinstock eats a cream cheese and—"

"Girls!" Like a tiny shark, Mrs. Wilde was plunging through the parlor, heading for us.

"Annnd . . . here we go," whispered Rachel.

I put on my best game face as Mrs. Wilde pulled up at us with an air-kiss that barely made it within six inches of our heads. Her thin strawberry-blond hair was stiff-sprayed into what Rachel called the "party pumpkin," and she was wearing a cashmere sweater set paired with a leopard skirt—Holden once had told me his mother thought an animal print cast a wide net of dress-code acceptability for whatever anyone else showed up in.

"Aunt Eleanor, congrats. I can't believe someone's actually going to marry Drew." Rachel said it in such a way that I knew it was hard for Mrs. Wilde to tell if she was kidding. Which of course she was not. I bit my bottom lip to stop my smile.

"The house looks great, Mrs. Wilde," I said.

"Ah. Thank you, Ember. And you are looking . . . wonderful."

Mrs. Wilde was unapologetically checking me out. "Wonderful"—she trilled the word again—"that you're here with us, Ember."

Here, as in here on earth, as a car accident survivor? Or here, as in ex-girlfriend with a possible second act? Or was Mrs. Wilde just being one hundred percent insincere as usual, and madly wishing that she hadn't allowed Holden to invite me to her oldest son's engagement party after all?

It was so hard to gauge fake people.

"Girls, please don't whisper and giggle with each other all evening, all right? Try to mingle. It'd be such a help to me." Mrs. Wilde flashed an oversized smile; her Botoxed forehead stayed indifferent. "Ember, my goodness! We must catch up once I finish the rounds." And with a parting pat on my shoulder, she glided back into the crowd.

"Promise me you will never let me turn into someone who 'finishes the rounds,'" whispered Rachel once Mrs. Wilde was out of earshot.

"Now, now. No whispering, no giggling." I frowned. "Mingle, minion!"

Which cracked us up all over again.

The Wildes had stocked their party with the usual suspects, mostly soft-faced, parent-aged couples in woolly blazers and tortoiseshell glasses. Holden's older brother, Drew, looked fancier in his pinstripes. When I saw him in the back of the dining room, chin up and ready to rumble, an unexpected unease washed through me. I'd never liked Drew, and I really didn't like him now, pumped with pride over his engagement, which he probably just viewed as another milestone in his smug, accomplished life.

As if sensing that eyes were on him, Drew glanced out. The heat in his stare, when he found me, made me want to run.

"Ouch. Did you see that? Drew just threw you some mean shade," Rachel whispered in my ear. "What's the deal with his deal?"

"You tell me," I said carefully, distracting myself by kidnapping a crab cake from another passing tray.

Rachel sighed. "Drew probably thinks you're going to dump Holden again."

I swallowed. "How can I dump Holden again if we're not going out?"

"You know what I mean. Anyway, Drew's a stuck-up conservative jerk, so maybe he's just practicing his standard jerk glare. Isn't it amazing how everyone finds exactly their person?" Rachel wagged her head in wonder. "I mean, Raina is the best fit for Drew. The girl is wearing a freaking Minnie Mouse polka-dot headband and has tiny bows on her shoes."

I studied Raina, slim and elegant at Drew's side. I knew what Rachel meant, but I didn't completely agree. "Maybe she's dressing that way because she thinks people expect her to dress that way. I think there's a much more fun, twinkly, non-corporate-lawyer version of Raina who is dying to get out and karaoke."

"She'll be sad to learn Drew Wilde is one hundred percent twinkle-free."

"Then he can borrow her twinkle on Saturdays." Was I imagining this, or had Drew just scowled at me again? Of course, he had one of those naturally inverted mouths that made it look like he was annoyed pretty much all the time.

Still, I could feel my face go blotchy with embarrassment.

Seemingly aware of my distress, Holden finally detached from his grandparents to join up with me. He threaded his arm loosely around my shoulders and bent for a quick cheek kiss. "You're awesome to come to this. What can I get you to drink?"

"Ginger ale?"

"Strong stuff." With a nod to Rachel, he added, "Let's go." I wondered if other people noticed Holden's arm. In some ways, it was a confidence boost and made me feel like I belonged here. On the other hand, I wasn't sure if I wanted to give Holden such bold arm-to-shoulder rights. On the other, other hand—I was probably giving this too many hands.

"Are your parents okay with me being here?" I asked in his ear.

"You're sweet to care about what my parents think," he answered. "I don't."

"Clean-shaven liar. Of course you do."

Holden rubbed his chin. "Touché. But Mom's too wrapped up in the party and Dad's too wrapped around the bourbon."

"Holdie, fix me a Diet Coke with lime?" asked Rachel.

"You got it."

Suddenly it struck me that this was how it would be if Holden and I got engaged. This would be our party, with Rachel bopping next to us, and Mrs. Wilde using the very same catering company and ordering up the same polleny flower arrangements. Holden's sparrow-boned Wilde grandparents would be here from Summit, too, along with those quirky next-door neighbors, the Rossiters, who often dressed in matching safari-esque suits—and tonight was no exception. And then Mr. Wilde would drink too much, and Drew would scowl with his scar-thin mouth, and the entire event would be spread in sticky layers of politeness, and would go on way too long.

"Light on ice, heavy on the ale, right?" Holden handed me a ginger ale with just two cubes and clinked his imported beer bottle with my glass. He looked super cute tonight. Even with the clean shave. Effortlessly adult—I practically could see him at age thirty. I imagined us dating on and off through college. It wasn't so out-there; we were natural friends, always had been. We'd never exactly said "I love you" to each other, but still. I'd never felt unloving or unaffectionate with Holden. And there were times I could get stupidly weak-kneed, staring at the chiseled angles of his face. If Holden and I ever did get back together—a big if, but not stratospherically impossible—would we ever have enough reason to break up again?

I felt the puff of Kai's breath in the cold-storage room, the damp animal-shine of his eyes in the darkness, the way the side of his body had pressed mine, the rumble of his voice lulling me—

"Ember!" Mrs. Wilde's thin fingers had latched my wrist. "Let me introduce you to Raina."

"Perk up, dish-Raggedy Ann." Rachel gave me a nudge, and Holden reluctantly relinquished me, as Mrs. Wilde led me to where Raina stood in front of the fireplace.

"Raina, I wanted you to meet Ember. Who has been a special friend to Holden." This was classic Mrs. Wilde—to take something awkward and make it way more awkward. *Special friend?* Seriously? "I think I told you about her horrible year?"

"Yes. Of course." Raina's eyes widened. "What a thing to live through."

Up close, I didn't mind what Smarty had been mocking.

Raina's polka-dot headband and super-feminine shoes seemed to suit her. Plus her eyes were gentle as a child's. "My brother, Ian, was in a bus accident," she confided, "and no matter what anyone said, I swear he was never the same after. Oh—but I didn't mean it that way." As Raina touched her shell-pink manicured fingers to her lips, I noticed her engagement ring, sparkling with new ownership. "I only meant that you . . . I mean, you look perfect to me." She laughed apologetically. "Not a scratch on you."

"Oh, but I've got a couple of scratches," I admitted. "Mostly on the inside."

Raina nodded. "Sometimes those are the hardest to heal. With my brother—"

"Hey, Rain, I want you to meet some of my cousins." Drew was at us like a wolverine in pinstripes.

"Good to see you, too, Drew." I cleared my throat. "Congratulations."

"Thanks, Ember." He hardly looked at me. "Nice of you to come." And then he patrolled Raina away by the elbow as if I were some kind of playground predator. I was relieved to join Smarty, who was now hanging out with Lucia, and, thankfully, no Claude.

"*Ciao, Ember,*" Lucia greeted me in her lilting Italian—did she sound delightfully musical, I wondered, even when she got angry? "I've been meaning to tell you something. Remember when you asked me about that girl, Maisie, from my Halloween party? And I didn't know her? Last week, I was speaking with my uncle on the phone, and I asked about her. He said Maisie has a partial art scholarship at the New School. A scholarship that he helps to fund."

"Oh, that's cool." I kept my tone casual. Lucia's uncle probably knew Anthony, too. I wondered if he had come up in the conversation.

Lucia shook her glossy hair dismissively. "He says she is not very serious about her art, not like some of the others." When she got imperious, Lucia sounded kind of like Claude. She had slipped into his skin in some ways since they'd started dating, the way so many couples did. "Uncle Carlos also helped to discover Alice de Souza," Lucia continued. "Do you know of her?"

My heart leapfrogged. "Alice de Souza? Of course!" I'd just seen the piece in the arts section of last weekend's newspaper, an article about this brilliant new young artist. The photograph had been one of those arty shots, and it had rung a distant bell, as I'd studied that image of a girl standing, speculative in her long spattered T-shirt, one foot planted on either side of a slab of linen canvas on the floor.

I'd figured it was just one of those oddly indefinable déjà vu things, but Alice de Souza must have been Maisie's friend Alice. The picture snapped like a rubber band in my head—Alice in the Cleopatra costume and gladiator sandals at the party was also the same Alice from that day last year, too—*we'd been trooping through Tribeca and then we'd stopped by the apartment on North Moore Street, and Alice was egging us on, "Let's go up, just for a minute," and then we were spilling through those giant rooms, looking for Anthony's painting. . . .*

On Rachel's "Earth to Ember!" with accompanying finger flick, I was back.

What was wrong with me? Second time tonight.

I was still standing between Lucia and Rachel, but they

weren't looking at me. Everyone was listening to Holden's dad give a toast. His arm swung his glass of champagne as he spoke, and his voice was reedy in his strain to amplify himself through the rooms. I fixed my attention. Mr. Wilde wasn't as glammed-out as his wife; in fact, he looked more like a bath-toy version of Holden. Round, buoyant, and even a bit damp.

". . . and to be as happy as Eleanor and I have been these past thirty-four years. Marriage is the most important decision you can make. It takes work, it takes commitment, and it takes one incredibly important sentence: 'Honey, you're right.' "

"He sure packs in the hammy clichés," whispered Rachel.

"Drew, my son, I hope you know that your family thinks you knocked the cover off the ball with this girl."

"Yikes, with a bonus sports metaphor," I whispered back.

"So please join me in raising your glass as we wish Drew and Raina health and happiness." Mr. Wilde swiped the air before he drank deeply to the scattered applause and *hear, hears*.

"Thirty-four years, gawd," said Rachel, with another sly check on her phone. "Doesn't that sound like a gruesome amount of time to be married?"

"It sounds like a gruesome amount of time to be anything," I answered.

"Check it, Jake just texted that he's at Floyd with the guys and he's ordered a couple of pizzas. So we can head over—want to say in forty-five minutes?"

"Sure. My allergies can't take too much more of these flowers, anyway."

The conclusion of the toast had rearranged the room into different conversation nests, and I watched as Holden broke from

185

one of them to give Raina a brotherly embrace before he beelined for me, sidling up and looping his arm around my shoulders in a tight squeeze. He might have had another beer, I could sense from the way he kissed the top of my head—casual, almost goofy.

"Come to my room," he said, his voice thick and hopeful in my ear. "Away from all these poison weeds, right?"

"Ha, no kidding." I sensed my friends pretending not to notice Holden's and my closeness. Their tiny nudges, their spidery-watchful energy. This was how it had been. This was how it was supposed to be, in everyone's minds. Friday Follies and parties and everyone together forever, all the way up to Mr. Wilde's sweaty champagne toast, for the rest of our lives.

But would the Wildes really and truly think their son had "knocked the cover off the ball" if he wanted to spend his life with a girl who had broken his heart? A girl who'd dropped everything she'd been, and then one night driven herself over a bridge, killing someone else in the process?

Or would they be (more likely) endlessly brooding and suspicious, always ready to expect some act of self-sabotage or reckless-ness, the very worst of me?

Ice, fever, ice. I felt light-headed as my resentment seethed. It wasn't for the Wildes to decide. Holden was mine and I was his, if we wanted each other. And if a future together was our landscape, it was a personal map for us to unfold, for us to plot the journey.

"Yes," I whispered. "Let's go."

20

One Guy, One Decision

Holden's room was just as I remembered, but at the same time it felt antiseptic. There were a few things I hadn't seen—the graduation picture, and Holden's cobalt-blue Lafayette mortarboard hung rakish over an old Super Soccer Stars trophy. Except it was a phantom presence of Holden here now. I could sense it in the stark surface of his desk and in the absence of his personal presence, that stuffy yet comforting, lived-in bedroom odor of gym socks and sweat and aftershave and a hint of fast-food French fries.

Noise pumped upward through the floorboards. If the Wildes

knew one thing about a party, it was how to keep it going. But I never liked the sound of adults getting silly on red wine. Which would be most of the Wildes' friends. It was yet another way that Holden's parents and my parents were different. And while mine might be less "fun," at least they never became giggle-boozy like Mrs. Wilde, or made dirty jokes with a hot face like Mr. Wilde. I was always surprised that Holden wasn't more irritated or upset, but I guess he was used to them.

Holden clicked the door shut. We each yanked up a few Kleenex—the flower arrangements were killing us—to get control of our weeping noses, laughing grimly about our shared allergy issues, before lying stomach-down and side by side on the bed, where we pored over the Lafayette senior yearbook. Holden got up once to get his iTunes going, and to lower the light. My body was a squeeze of nervous anticipation as Holden returned to the bed and then pushed away the yearbook to pull me close.

I could taste warmth and beer as Holden kissed me hard—there was something defiant about it. I wanted this, didn't I? I shifted position. I was having trouble relaxing; I couldn't seem to find the right place to put my arms and legs. Holden slipped my dress over my head, then undid the clasp of my bra and scooped a hand inside.

"Oh!" We hadn't hooked up for real in such a long time. Of course I'd agreed to it. Just in letting Holden's index finger link mine as we'd stolen away up the stairs, there'd been acknowledgment. We'd been flirting all night, wanting to end up in just exactly this space, alone together.

But now did I want it? I didn't want to overthink it. I wanted to be loose and warm and untrapped. I kissed him back as I cracked open my eyes to stare at Holden's shadowed face. He was undeniably cute. That tousled hair, the slight cleft in his chin—it all worked.

Holden was tugging down my tights—I helped wriggle and peel them off, dropping them over the side of the bed. Sexually, I'd gone pretty far with Holden, nearly all the way to actual sex, and the funny thing about that was no matter how much time had passed, the unspoken rule now seemed to be that all the things we'd done before were ours to do again, speedily, and only because we'd done them all before.

He kicked out of his gray flannels, and I helped him unbutton his shirt, and here we were down to nothing but underwear, facing each other in newly unwrapped shyness. Our mouths met, skin on skin. I could feel his fingertips trailing my spine, finding the bolt—though I'd shown him before, I hadn't let him pause there. In the heated, heavy darkness, his fingers learned and accepted it, and then he carefully rolled over on top of me. His body on mine was a familiar excitement.

Was I betraying Kai tonight, with Holden? The thought triggered another future, only this one was not the Wildes' parlor. Kai's life was less ordered, less safe; his world was explosive with the dry, glittery desert heat of Burning Man, it roared with the baseball crowd in Yankee Stadium, it trekked the green farmlands of the Glastonbury music festival, it teetered at the apex of the Coney Island Ferris wheel. In a split second, I saw all of it distilled as clearly as if a fortune-teller had let me gaze into her crystal ball.

"Holden," I whispered, unlatching my arms from around his back.

He didn't answer. Gently, I pushed his hand off its hopeful

back-and-forth skimming along the elastic band of my underwear. "Holden, I've got to go."

"What, to Floyd? No, you don't," he mumbled, catching and twining my hair around his finger the way he used to. "Nobody needs us to be there."

"It's more like . . . I don't think I can be here."

"Huh?" A little dazed, he pitched up on one elbow to regard me. His free hand stroked my cheek. "What's wrong?"

"I'm not . . . It's too soon, I think. Being here with you." Not quite true. What I was really thinking was how bizarre it was, after a year, that Holden and I were right back at this same knotty moment. Except this time there was no apple candle, no snoring Jolly at the foot of the bed, no frost on the pane. Only the catch in my lungs that made it hard to breathe through what I knew I might say.

"I felt like we were moving closer," he said.

"Maybe we are." I wasn't being totally honest, and if I wasn't being honest, I wasn't being fair. "But I think I just want more time," I qualified. That was honest. Wasn't it?

"Okay." He half laughed, then rolled off me so that we were side by side, innocent as toy mice in a matchbox.

We stayed like this for another minute or so, and then Holden jumped off the bed, moving toward the chair stacked with folded clothes and rummaging for his jeans, which he then yanked up in one rough swoop.

"Where are you going?"

"I think I'll hit Floyd."

"Oh." I stood, picked up my dress from where it had puddled on the floor. "Holden, I know you're upset."

"A little bit. That's normal, right? What do you want from me, Ember?"

"I'm not sure."

"The thing is, I can't be anything more than I am. And I'm one guy, one decision. So make it or don't. Let me know when you do."

He sounded weary, and I didn't blame him. This wasn't supposed to be the end of this night, with me tossing Holden off as if I were a child who'd grown bored with her amusement. I struggled with the zip of my dress. Holden had snapped on his lamp and was now leaning over his desk, facing away from me and clicking through emails on his laptop.

"Hold?" I whispered.

He didn't turn around. "You coming with me to Floyd?"

"I don't think so."

"Okay, cool." His back still facing me. I hated to think of the tears that might be in his eyes. Holden put up a stoic front, but I knew better. "I'll call you later."

"Sounds good."

He was hurt, and I couldn't undo it. So I left him; I had to. In the front hall, a number of guests were starting to leave—it was easy to slip out the door unnoticed. Head tucked, I found my coat, then clipped down the front steps and around the corner. Withdrew my cell phone from my bag and keyed in the numbers.

I was walking too fast and I couldn't stop; it was as if I'd spent the past couple of hours caged.

It went straight to voice mail. I spoke in a whisper. "I know this is probably crazy and violates our rules and you're not there and whatever, but I'm coming over. I'll be in the lobby of your building. So just text me whenever you get in from class or work." I paused. "Because I need to see you, Kai. I'll wait for you."

One guy, one decision. But hadn't that decision been clinched the moment I'd met Kai on the fire escape?

Quickly, I sent Rachel a text—pls pls cover for me if my folks call—before I turned off my phone and began to walk purposefully toward the St. George.

It was the right thing to do, to leave Holden. I couldn't hook up with him—not mindlessly, and especially not with full awareness—if I didn't feel it. Worrying and regretting and puzzling and *perseverating* over us was all just a waste of time. I didn't regret it, but I longed to make it better. And yet I couldn't.

I quickened my step, as if I could outpace my emotions, and checked my watch. It was only ten o'clock. If only I could see Kai again. Even if it was just for a few minutes. So what if he worked and took night classes, so what if he didn't have enough money or free time or whatever? Those were excuses; they weren't real reasons to stay apart.

And I was tired of being apart.

I broke into a run.

21

Waving, Worried

"There you are! It's almost midnight." Mom didn't sound upset. Good, Smarty must have provided an alibi. I exhaled in relief.

"Is it? I must have lost track of time. Sorry." I was shivering from the long walk home. "Mrs. Wilde says thanks for the orchids."

Mom peered at me. "Your cheeks are pink. I'll make cocoa. It got cold out, didn't it? It's going to be like this all through the weekend. You know, sweetie, I realize it's only six blocks or so, but I would have picked you up from the Wildes' if you'd called."

"Nah, I was fine. Cocoa sounds good." I rubbed my chapped

hands together, then pulled off my boots and stomped my feet. The temperature had plummeted. It had even been drafty and uncomfortable in the lobby of the St. George, where eventually I'd fallen asleep waiting for Kai, who never showed.

As soon as the kettle was boiling, Dad appeared, "yawning" in the doorway. Whatever. I knew them both too well. They'd both been awake, a couple of insomniacs, ruffling their feathers, waiting for me to come back to the nest.

"Your cheek is creased," Dad observed. "You've been sleeping?"

"Yep, I was. Over at Holden's."

It was a delicate moment of embarrassment to stew in, but I'd rather have them think that I crashed in Holden's bed than tell them the opposite—that for the past couple of hours I'd been curled up on a plastic couch in the St. George's dorm lobby, roused only when the security guard had shaken me and demanded to see my student ID—and then tossed me out like an orphan when he learned I had none.

Kai hadn't been in touch at all. I felt unbearably dumb.

"Tell me about your night." Mom spooned out the cocoa mix. "Starting with, what's Drew's fiancée like?"

"She's okay."

"Oh? Just okay?" Mom added the boiling water while Dad found a pack of campfire marshmallows in the cupboard and landed one in each mug. We slouched around the kitchen table as we had a thousand times before.

"She's the best Drew could hope for." My hot mug felt good in my cold hands, and I hunched down to let the steam bathe my face. "Listen, I'm glad you both waited up for me, because I need to talk to you about something." I sipped slowly, aware of their unsettled silence. "I think I need to start driving again."

My parents were wearing coordinating pajamas. Probably not on purpose, but it seemed too coincidental to be pure chance. Mom's were moss-green flowers on a butter-yellow background, and Dad's were butter-yellow with moss piping. They looked like people from one of those comfort-living catalogs that sell pj's along with wind chimes and chenille throw rugs. Mom and Dad had been married forever, and it was hard to imagine what they'd been before they morphed like cookies in the oven into this warm, sweet pair. Yet they were incomplete without me; I was their Everything. I sometimes felt like each hug came with their assertion in my ear:

"Ember, you are everything we dreamed you'd be!"

"Ember, we love you more than life itself!"

It had always been a weight on me. A loving weight, but heavy anyhow.

And it made conversations like this extra hard. I could feel both my parents' instant, snap-to-it attention at my mention of driving, and I'd have bet anything they'd been wrestling endlessly with this topic in private for a while now, of how I hadn't expressed any desire to drive since I'd come home.

"See, because I think the longer I go without driving," I continued, "the harder it will be for me when I do."

"Absolutely! If you think you're ready! Let's get you back in the saddle!" Dad's voice was loud, to cover his all-too-evident doubts.

I nodded along with him. "I'd like to take it out Saturday. If that's okay."

"Where are you going?" Mom was pushing a spoon around and around like a windup toy in her cocoa. Hydration was not helping her on this one. "And just to point out, you've never handled the Prius. Wouldn't you like me to go along with you? We could test-drive together, and work up to a big trip."

Maybe that wasn't such a bad plan. Mom had taught me to drive the first time around, and she'd be a steady presence in the passenger seat. "Sure, tomorrow would be good," I decided. "I should probably get in some practice before Saturday."

"Wonderful." Mom beamed. "Does that mean you and Holden are going somewhere Saturday?"

"Uh, yeah." It'd be easier to let them think that I was spending Saturday with Holden. Though my parents' worry practically had tentacles. Sweet as they both were, their protective instincts were like a monster they'd expertly conjured together. I could almost see those waving arms reaching for me through the air, plucking me up, curling around to hold me in a lock, and then my parents whispering in my ear that I was their very best thing, and that I must never, never leave home again, ever.

"You and Holden! I can't say I'm anything but glad about that!" Dad's voice was cheerful enough to scare the neighbors.

"He's a good guy."

"And he must have walked you home tonight, yes?" Mom looked over her shoulder, as if half hoping that even though I'd been home alone for twenty minutes, Holden might suddenly materialize in the doorway.

I colored, half nodded. After I'd been tossed from the St. George, I'd checked my texts, only to find a smattering of notes from Smarty. Nothing from Kai, and of course there'd been no new messages from Holden. No matter how hurt he was, Holden wasn't the type to push for extra rehashing of what had just happened between us. If I said I wanted time, then time was what he'd give me.

"So what special thing are you two doing this Saturday?"

"Not sure yet."

"But you know that you need the car," Mom said, arching a brow.

"Where are you going *in general?*" Dad squinted at me.

I was starting to squirm. I made myself stare at him directly. "We were planning to take Jolly out to the beach, if it's not too cold."

Dad liked that answer. They both did. They also figured I meant a day trip to Lawrence Beach, out in Rockaway, where we'd always gone as a family, and a route I had practiced on back when I'd first gotten my learner's permit. A very smooth, safe excursion up the Belt Parkway.

I'd let them think it. Spare them the anxiety.

Kai or no Kai, a driving test had to be conquered.

Up in my bedroom, I checked my phone one last time.

One more from Smarty. Nobody else. Not that I was expecting different.

22

She Knew, and She Pitied Me

"Howdy, stranger. You should have come out last night." Rachel had pulled up abruptly beside me as I walked down the hall. Despite Smarty's chirpy tone, there were thunderclouds in it, a warning of her temper.

"Sorry about that. Thanks for covering for me."

"Sure, no problem. But I also left you a few messages. Did you get those?"

"Uh-huh." Three, to be exact. The first—hey where are you, I want to go to Floyd now. The second—just checked my text, why are you making me cover for you, are you showing up here later?

The third—oookay, fielded your mom's call, so you're good. But you're not coming to Floyd at all tonight, huh? Holden's here and he looks depressed. What happened? Call me back! And then a couple of missed calls.

"But you didn't answer any of them." Rachel was waiting for an explanation that made sense.

"I was tired." I fell in with her deliberately slower step as we moved down the hall. At the end of the stretch, which felt like it was thirteen miles long, I knew that Rachel would hook right for AP Biology, and I'd turn left for the Friday yearbook meeting.

"Tired," she repeated.

"I'm sorry," I said again. Except that "sorry" wasn't cutting it. And she was right, anyhow. It had been strange and rude to just drop out on our plans.

"It's just I thought we'd agreed on Floyd."

"I know; you're right. We had."

"So I guess what I'm trying to say is that I think it was totally not cool that you didn't show up."

"Smarty, I'm sorry. I wasn't trying to kill your night. I needed to be alone. Don't you think it would have been worse for me to come out with you all if I wasn't up for it?"

"If you say so."

"Go ahead," I told her. "You want to rage at me. I'm listening."

"Fine. Okay." Rachel stopped walking and planted herself squarely but gawkily, as if she'd been given a stage direction she wasn't sure how to implement. "Here's the deal. When you first came back from Addington, I know you were unsteady, but I swear, I felt like I finally recognized you. You'd been so distant, so out of touch those weeks before your accident. Right in the beginning, we were back. We were real, true friends again."

"Of course we're real, true friends, Smarty—this is, like, a blip."

"It's not." Color stained all the way across Rachel's cheeks. "For you to take off from the party last night. For you to keep me in the dark while you make me cover for you. For you to not be in touch, to totally drop out of our plans together—how's that supposed to make me feel? And it's not just about last night. What about Halloween? What about your wonderful idea to jump in a cab with some stranger and leave me to deal with that?"

"You had Jake," I said faintly.

"Whatever, Ember. I'd just started hanging out with him that night. You didn't know if or how that was working out. But since we're speaking of Jake, sometimes when I tell you I'm doing stuff with Jake, you look relieved. As if you'd way rather be by yourself. I guess the point I'm trying to make is that I feel like you're disappearing from me again." She gulped, braving it. "Why?"

I had to tell her; there was no real reason not to. "Smarty, I've met someone," I answered. "The guy from Halloween."

"That same one, Kai, who was in the cab that took off?"

I nodded. "And I don't know exactly what's going on between us. But I do know he's been on my mind a lot, I guess. More than our plans, more than school. More than anything else. It's hard to explain."

Rachel crossed her arms and stepped back. To anyone else walking down the hall, she'd have seemed casual, in control. But I knew the agitation of my best friend's gaze on me. I'd seen it since she was little, when she used to worry that I'd use up all her yellow paint, since that was her favorite color. "So this person, Kai, is someone you don't ever want to introduce me to?"

"It's more like he's not someone I want to share right now. Not while I'm trying to work things out with him. I guess what I'm saying is I need my space."

Rachel flinched, as if my words were a stick that had poked her. "Fine, Embie, okay. I can handle that. He can be your secret Mr. Wonderful; I've got no problem with that. But don't shut me out completely, either. I mean, come on . . ." Her voice trembled, and I knew she was trying to keep it together. "Best friends since kindergarten should count for something. And I still want to be friends—if you just tell me how."

But Rachel had said this to me before, last year. We'd had this fight . . . I could feel the reverberations of it, a distant ripple through my brain. "Let's talk about all of this later, okay? Or I'll be late for yearbook," I said. "I'll come find you after, and we can hang out."

"Only if you want," she said quietly. "Don't do it as a favor to me, Ember."

I nodded. "Right." She knew me too well, knew that I ached to make it better. But in half confessing Kai, I'd put her on guard, and I was thankful that I didn't run into Rachel again—though it took some careful footwork, including leaving campus to hit the corner soup kiosk for lunch and skipping my last afternoon class.

Mom was waiting for me as I walked in the front door.

"So I thought you could take me on an errand!" She tossed me the car keys. "I need to get to the post office. I already took the car out of the garage, so we're set."

"Oh! Cool." I'd assumed that Mom was either going to

"forget" about my request to drive today or put up a resistance when I reminded her. "Let's go."

Unlike the station wagon, the Prius handled light and silent. Sort of like maneuvering a paraglider after steering a barge. With Mom buckled in, I eased it gingerly out onto the road, then began the journey by inching around the block, and finally onto Cadman Plaza.

The cold snap was here to stay, and there was a threat of rain in the wintry air; plus the Friday-afternoon rush hour was in full trafficky tension. Similar, I realized, to the conditions of *that* night. Which was not a good thing to dwell on.

"You can go a little faster," Mom murmured. Mom was a good driver, and I'd liked to think I'd inherited her skill. I wondered if I'd ever be considered a "good" driver again.

A guy behind me zipped past me illegally, honking long as he leaned out his window.

"Learn how to drive, you idiot!"

"Some people." Mom sighed. But as I pressed and released the gas-brake-gas, I knew that I was going too slow, second-guessing basic actions and overly attentive to the road rules. By the time we pulled up to the post office, I was sweaty with the effort.

"Stay here. I'll be right out," Mom promised.

I nodded, but after a minute or so I got out of the car myself, to buy a coffee at a corner food cart. I felt shaky, and flashbacks of this afternoon's conversation with Smarty weren't helping. Through my nerves, my longing for sleep was like a brick wall I could feel myself hurtling toward.

Back in the car, I leaned against the headrest and closed my eyes. The rapping on the window startled me. Hot liquid sloshed from my cup onto my wrist—"Oh!"—as I pressed the button to unroll the window.

It was Isabella from El Cielo. She looked even tinier in her street clothes—a beige plastic raincoat that flapped past her calves and a clear rain hat that poked up like a wizard's cone to accommodate her bun.

"Ember." Her eyes on me were a complicated fixation of sorrow and curiosity—the same as when she'd seen me at El Cielo.

I nodded.

"It was good that you came in, that night."

"It was?"

"Yes. You were right to come."

I stared, shy. My brain was a thick fog, offering me no certainty for what I was supposed to say next.

"And I want you to come back again," she continued. "Come assist me in the kitchen. I watched your hands—how you wanted to chop, to work. I saw it in the way you were watching me. You want to learn. I will teach." She touched her fingertips to her heart. "*Ayúdame*, and it will help us both."

I laughed, a bit anxiously, a dry, sandpapery sound. "Me, working at El Cielo?" That was crazy; it would be like stalking. "Thank you. Thank you so much. But I would be an inconvenience. A trouble to you, even. Underfoot and all that. And I'm really busy with school. So I'm not . . ." My barricaded defenses sounded false. Isabella could see right through me. I looked down at the reddening scorch mark of coffee across my wrist.

She knows about the accident.

Looking back into her black eyes, I was sure of it. She knew about Anthony Travolo. She knew what had happened, and she also knew that once I'd loved to cook, that cooking had been my joy and comfort. She knew, and she pitied me.

"It would be the right diversion," she said.

"You're very kind. It's amazing that you would offer me your kitchen. But I . . . I don't think I can."

Such a weak response. All that I wanted to say and instead I said nothing. Mom was exiting the post office. Her brow furrowed when she saw that I was speaking with someone. Isabella straightened, turning to follow my gaze.

"*Entonces*," she said quickly. "You have the address. We are open six days, six nights a week. Closed on Monday." She hurried off. Her head—nearly doll-sized and much too fragile—was bowed against the wind as she pushed in the direction of the subway.

My hands gripped the steering wheel; I was braced for Mom's questions.

"Who was that?" she asked as she opened the car door.

"Some lady, asking for directions."

"But you didn't know her? You seemed to know her."

"Nope."

Thankfully, she said no more. We drove home in silence. Whatever sliver of nerve had given me the confidence to think I could drive this car—even poorly—was gone. I'd lost. I bumped the curb twice and almost turned the wrong way down a one-way street. At least Mom didn't say anything, for which I was grateful.

"You think I'm not ready," I said once I'd gotten us into the garage.

"Practice will help," she answered. "But maybe you and Holden could figure out another, nondriving plan for tomorrow?

And then you and I can practice again together. We'll ease into this."

"Sure." No way. I was going, and I was going with Kai. If Kai was with me, I'd be my best me. For driving, for everything.

Inside, Dad had made enough tacos to serve a soccer team, but soon I grew weary of him asking me if I wanted to have Holden or Rachel over for dinner.

No, I didn't. I couldn't. I wouldn't.

Upstairs in my room, the night stretched empty.

I played and replayed my saved voice mail.

"Hey, Emb, it's me. We are on for Coney Island—I got Chris to cover my shift, so . . . totally looking forward to Saturday. Got me thinking, too, that I haven't been out there since I was like, what, eight years old? Okay, so I got class in twenty, better roll. Looking forward to it. Said that. (with a sheepish laugh) Awright."

My lips moved along with his words. I smiled every time I heard him laugh. Each time I played the message, it was like the very first time. Over and over and over again, and it never got old.

My body was sleepy, but my brain was avid for more activity. I resaved Kai's message, did some homework, then spent a bit of mindless time online. My usual searches, my usual obsessions. I went into my mail. I'd been searching my in-box archives for so long that I thought I'd covered everything. In my downloads, there'd been some other invitations to art exhibits, to a documentary showing at the Landmark Sunshine, and an invitation to a student group show at LaGuardia High School, where Anthony Travolo was listed showing his work along with a bunch of other kids, including Maisie.

But I'd placed this email in a folder marked "Travel."
It was the only email. It was from him.

Okay, you wanted a story about something from fifth grade.
You are kind of freakishly specific sometimes, Leferrier.

But I'm at your service.

So here it is: An All-True Fifth-Grade Story by Me,
A. Travolo.

First time I struck out with a girl was fifth grade.
Anna-Luisa Renaldi. I knew I'd caught her attention
earlier that day, with my mucho kickass oral report on
Ralph Nader (an A-minus, my only A that year). Me and
my swollen head were on the playground at lunchtime
recess when I saw: it was time to make my play.
Problem was, I had *nothing* to offer except a few lame
Jet Li moves. I'd practiced jujitsu over the summer. The
more Anna-Luisa watched me, the stupider and riskier
I got, until in my final action-hero sequence, I jumped
and swung out into a high-kick slash half-gainer.

Instant wipeout. Face, meet pavement. Pavement,
face.

No way to recover from that one. I blamed greasy
monkey bars. I blamed my no-friction tennis sneakers.
I blamed Anna-Luisa's shiny eyes. I blamed all of her
schoolyard girlfriends for chattering and pointing at me
like a pack of monkeys.

But she pretty much never looked at me again.

I'm too old for the monkey bars. But now I think
there's a pattern to the insanity. When I saw you that

night, I remembered every single thing about Anna-Luisa, and what I'd thought was love. Or at least my best fifth-grade version of it. I knew it all over again times a thousand.

I'm not wiping out this time, Ember. And when I see you next, I'm gonna show you my best Jet Li. Watch for it.

His email address was there in the address bar. On impulse, I sent a blank message to the account. It bounced back to me—null, of course.

My heart pounding, I printed his note, folded it, and buried it in my jewelry box along with everything else. His story knew how to make me laugh. It was sweet and charming. It was Anthony, talking to me so easily, so winningly—this guy and I had connected, and I couldn't or wouldn't look deeply enough in my heart or my mind to find him there. The boy I'd killed. Something was wrong with me—more wrong, even, than what Dr. P and all the Addington staff and my parents and Holden and Rachel and every last person in my orbit could begin to understand.

How could I have forgotten him? I was a freak.

23

Blink and Gone

I woke up in a fog. Finding Anthony's note last night had spiraled me into a dark and restless mood. I hadn't been able to complete my homework, or even a clear thought. Instead I'd roamed around the house, accepting Mom's cups of tea and half watching television, and I'd gone to bed unsettled. Awake again, I was wrapped in a thinner skin of the same depressed confusion.

It was still dark outside. Not even 6 a.m. But today was the day. My entire body was tingling as I looked out my window on the blue cold sky. As I showered and dressed, it began to distract and then take over me, winding me up like a cuckoo clock. It was like Christmas morning, when I was the only one awake, slipping and slinking around the house, silent as a cat.

There was my whole entire life to dwell on Anthony Travolo. But today . . . today was another kind of day. And since it was here, I wanted to reach for it with both hands.

I left my parents a note:

Went to the beach. On my cell if you need me.

They'd be frightened. They'd be furious. But technically, they hadn't forbidden this. As I pulled up in front of the St. George, I knew my hopes for the hours ahead were what was giving me driving confidence. My thoughts were splintery with anticipation.

Of course I was here much too early. It was a little bit silly. Almost the moment that I turned off the engine, the need to sleep taffy-pulled at me, and eventually I succumbed to it, though for how long I don't know, because my eyes opened to see that the sun had broken its clean gold into the sky. And there was Kai, walking out the door of the St. George, right on time.

Same green jacket, but this time he'd thrown it over a pewter-gray sweater, along with faded-to-charcoal jeans. His hair was sticking up sweetly and everywhere like a baby hedgehog, and his skin was scrubbed to a deep glow.

Kai had shown up. Why would I have doubted him? And now the reality of what this day could be sparkled. I yawned, stretched, struggled to sit up. A needle-shower of excitement, relief, and disbelief was spiking my skin as Kai opened the passenger door and climbed in.

"Hey, you."

"Hey yourself."

He fastened his seat belt, docked his iPod, pressed play.

No way. Although, hadn't we been talking music that first time, out on the fire escape? I must have mentioned Weregirl. It was too obscure otherwise. "Good choice," I mentioned after a minute or so.

"Yeah, I'm kinda fan-zoning Weregirl right now," he said.

"I downloaded them a few weeks ago, and now I know every song by heart."

"Me too."

"There are no coincidences," I joked. And while the day felt like fate, as if the stars had all lined up just for us, I hadn't bet on anything. I hadn't gotten my hopes up. When it came to Kai, I knew better. I just had to hold on to the tentative belief that so far nothing on the horizon pointed to this day going terribly wrong.

Coney Island was forty-five minutes out, according to my GPS. Almost the length of the Weregirl tracks twice through. Every song belonged to us. The music took Kai to the same place—I could tell by his fixed yet soft expression as he stared ahead, and by the way he sang along. His voice was low but clear, and totally unself-conscious. I loved the sound of Kai's voice over Weregirl. I wished I could record it—I made my brain try.

The boardwalk was almost deserted. We parked and fed the meter, and as we headed up the wide-planked herringbone walk, Kai caught me off guard, picking me up and spinning me around. My eyes closed, I was transported, my fingers tested his pulsing throat, the sides of his face, as he kissed me and set me down again.

"Ooh, look . . . cotton candy!" Suddenly shy of the moment,

I turned away and broke off from him toward the cotton candy cart ahead, trotting up the walk to buy a twist of spun sugar from the pudgy old man in the striped hat, who twinkled at me as if we were old friends. "A pretty girl, and all alone," he said. "That's no good."

"No, no. I'm with him." I pointed to Kai, but he'd drifted a ways down the boardwalk and was staring out at the sea. He looked so all by himself out there, so unattached to anyone, that I felt greedy claiming him just for myself. Especially when he didn't seem to belong to anyone.

The cotton candy man gave me a funny look along with my twist as if he, too, thought I was mistakenly attempting to claim Kai. I took my change and bolted, running hard to catch up since he'd walked even farther ahead, so that by the time I got to him I was out of breath, and the candy was beaded up in crystallizing sugar.

We split the treat, the sticky blue staining our lips. Kai bought tickets for the Wonder Wheel—and we cranked up up up in the swinging seat until we were suspended at the top. Kai's kiss was brine and salt and sweetness that melted on my mouth.

Then we wandered Surf Avenue, stopping for a corn dog at Nathan's for me and a hot dog with everything for Kai.

He let me try his first—"Gorilla-style! With peppers and onion, the best!"—and then he finished it in the next three bites. "Watch out, true believers. I'm going for another one. Best hot dog in New York."

"Only because it belongs to this day." Though the walking, the delirious excitement was catching up with me. My reserves were beginning to ebb.

Somehow Kai knew this. He took my hand and guided me, without speaking, to the dunes, where we stretched out side by side, staring up at the sky as we laid our lives bare. When Kai spoke, I got the sense in his hesitation and his stammer that he didn't confide in too many people.

And yet here I was, and I was listening hard.

His dad had been troubled, he told me. His few, dim memories were of a well-intentioned but angry guy who couldn't be anchored to a sick wife and two sons. He remembered his mom more vibrantly, with her coaxing voice and her spill of curly black hair, a comforting presence until she was abruptly gone. "But it's my aunt who's really taken care of us all," he said. "Mom died knowing Isabella would look out for Hatch and me. That's why I owe it to Hatch. Pay it forward and all that."

"You two seem close. Are you a lot alike?"

"Nah, Hatch is a practical dude. I'm the one chasing rainbows. Even if it means working sixty hours a week at El Cielo, scrounging for grants and loans for school. Which reminds me." He slipped his phone out of his knapsack. "Let me take your picture? It's for a project I'm working on."

I was instantly self-protective, shielding myself from his phone lens. "Really? Now? Me? I don't know, my hair's all frizzed out from the Ferris wheel and the salt—and I haven't looked in the mirror all day!" But Kai just laughed, didn't seem to notice or care, and he seemed so happy for me to be in his lens that soon I was laughing, too, as he clicked shot after shot.

"Enough!" I put up my hand, ducking away.

"One more, then the torture's over. I think you gave me some interesting moments, anyway." As I sat up, Kai did, too, mirroring my position, knees knocked and toe to toe. Holden always took a different angle, he liked to keep an arm over my shoulder, protectively herding me into enclosures as he warded off all and any danger. But Kai met me as my equal.

Ever since my ordeal of recovery had begun, I'd had to hear the refrain about everyone's confusion about that changeling self I was evolving into right before the accident. Holden, Rachel, my other friends, and my parents all spoke about it. How I'd been pushing them away. Leaving them behind. On this beach, with this guy, I knew that I must have been pushing in a new direction, toward another destination—and not just because I'd felt rebellious. I was acting on the impulse that Kai himself had spoken of, that evening when we'd huddled together in the cold-storage room. We both craved experience and variety and change. I, who'd been given so much, and Kai, who'd been given so little—we both needed something more, and we were going to figure out how to get it.

Kai had gotten me to remember that.

For a while we stayed out on the dunes, listening to the gulls, the tips of our ears and noses lightly frozen, the sea wind riffling over us until we were goose-pimpled and hungry again—and then at some point there was funnel cake and a burger that we inhaled with a shared bottle of water. I closed my eyes as Kai caught me and pulled me deep into the long grasses up the dunes. We knocked against each other, playful, then we quieted as we watched the sun burn off the end of the day.

The sea and sky looked like crumpled aluminum foil. I could feel my body's familiar desire—insistence—for sleep pulling and enfolding me. It was only natural; I was healing, and it was safe here besides. I settled my cheek into the crook of Kai's arm and stared out sleepily over the horizon. In my mind's eye, the Volvo was a plastic toy pirouetting weightless over the bridge.

A moment of time, blink and gone. And yet nothing could have stopped it; the forward momentum of that car was its inexorable destiny, bridge to water, life to death. I let the icy *what-if* sweep through me, submerge me. I didn't speak, didn't move. Kai's presence was indivisible from the air I breathed, and I couldn't bear to say the wrong words, or any words at all. Not if it meant that I would break the spell.

24

A Fancy Way of Saying

I was home in time for dinner, though I wasn't hungry. In the kitchen, I found a box of takeout pizza with two slices of plain cheese saved for me, plus a homemade three-bean salad. My parents were downstairs watching a movie.

When I joined them on the sectional, Dad scooted over and patted the space on the couch between them. "We just started, if you want to join," Mom whispered with a tiny, hopeful smile.

As if everything was fine. As if they were completely relaxed that I'd taken the car out all day, and that I'd only answered their nervous, attempting-to-be-measured texts (such as Mom's I hope you're being careful, Sweetie) with the occasional one word (yep, ok, soon)—depending on the question.

I knew my parents better than that. They were in no way mellow about my falling off the radar. In my absence, they'd had discussions, they'd made a plan. And after the romantic comedy was over and I'd said my good-nights and retreated to my room and opened my email, I found my answer.

A note from Dr. P.

A note that had my parents' agitated phone call to him all over it.

Hey, Ember—

Just checking in. Hadn't heard from you in a bit. Happy to hear that you are continuing to make strides with rehabilitation. (Your mom keeps me posted.) And I wanted to congratulate you on getting behind the wheel again—that's good forward initiative. I'm all for it!

At the same time, I wanted to take this opportunity to restate something we talked about in terms of maladaptive reaction. Which is just a fancy way of saying "not as easy as it seems." Not that any of this is "easy" for you, but I think I should put you in touch with a wonderful cognitive behaviorist, who also happens to be a great pal of mine—Dr. Linda Applebaum.

Her office is right on Front Street, so that's walking distance from you. She's easy to chat with, and I think you'd truly benefit from a therapeutic alliance with her.

A professional analyst would be a constructive alternative to the well-meaning bias (hey, I'd even go so far as to say INTERFERENCE) of family and friends. I've spoken with Linda myself just this evening, and she's got a great way of talking anyone down from a tree or out of a jam. She's waiting for your email or call, so whenever you're ready to do this on your own steam, she's there.

Are you looking forward to Thanksgiving?

Best,

Dr. P

Dr. P strikes again. I could almost see him going through the first draft of this email, adding in all of those friendly parts, the "hey" and "pal" and those homey Lissa expressions "out of a tree" and "in a jam," plus the end mention of Thanksgiving. The real question was: did my parents and Dr. P really think I needed a shrink, just because I'd borrowed the car?

I'd done therapy sessions three times a week at Addington. My psychiatrist there had been a really cool guy, Dr. Lawrence Lim. Everyone called him Laurie, which reminded me of *Little Women*. Who didn't trust a guy named Laurie? And my Laurie was no different. We'd gone through some of my Anthony Travolo issues, my shock and guilt—though at some point I must have shut it down when I'd stopped talking about Anthony completely.

But now I pictured Laurie's spotless office, his glass bowl of loose Starbursts, his comfy armchair that I always got to curl into with my handful of Starbursts and my daily troubles. I hadn't thought much about any of that until now.

My parents were right. I was never going to talk with them about Anthony, or the night of the wreck. I'd always be rearing up and away from them. They didn't know how to reach me, either, no matter how good their intentions.

"Sorry, just checking in. You need anything?" Dad might say, poking his head in my bedroom door. "Are you all right, Ember?" Or I'd wake to feel my mother's papery hand on my forehead. Reassuring herself that her daughter was alive and breathing—and hadn't slipped into another coma.

But I didn't need a "therapeutic alliance," either. I was doing all right. Didn't today prove it? No speeding ticket, no fender bender, no side-of-the-road meltdown. Why would I need any more outside help than I already had? Sure, Rachel and I had hit a bump, but we'd repair. We always did. And Holden and I would never be less than friends.

And everything I had with Kai—even if I always wanted more—seemed to sustain me just enough until the next time I saw him. If I were going to talk to anyone, maybe I would prefer it to be someone without that bias, someone who hadn't been with me through this ordeal, or had only known me after I'd lost Anthony—and I had a bleak feeling that my loss of Anthony was bigger than my conscious brain was prepared to reckon with.

The next morning, my parents were cautious with me.

"What are you doing today, sweets?" asked Mom.

"Homework, maybe see a movie with Rachel."

It wasn't the answer they wanted. But they'd obviously made a pact with Dr. P not to talk about yesterday's disappearance. I waited until they'd stepped out around the corner to their favorite diner for their usual Sunday brunch, and then I took out the car again, down to Livingston Street, just to think. I pulled into an outdoor parking area near one of the main federal courthouses.

I bought a coffee and donut from the food cart. With all the car doors locked, I ate my breakfast. It was maybe five minutes, maybe twenty, but unlike last night, this sleep came with real peace in the lingering closeness of yesterday with Kai. He hadn't called or written, but I was getting used to this rhythm. The way we spent time together didn't obey the natural laws of dating. Instead I'd have to tap into the dream, find the brine and beach sand, and the sweet softness of that particular memory.

When I woke up, it was clear to me that if I was really in the "jam" that Dr. P had mentioned, I actually did know someone who I could talk to. So obvious. It seemed silly that I hadn't called Lissa before.

25
Drive It

Juilliard students and School of American Ballet students all shared dorm space together in the Meredith Willson Residence Hall in Midtown. Literally hundreds of kids were auditioning, rehearsing, dreaming, despairing, being made into stars or accepting rejection all under the same roof. It was like a mini-kingdom of dance, fueled on talent and protein bars.

Monday afternoon, I took the subway to Columbus Circle and walked the block up Sixtieth. I signed my name at the lobby desk and pushed through one of the four industrial turnstiles to the equally impersonal elevator bank. My heart quick-jumped at the proximity of all these students—dancers, every one of them. I'd never been talented enough to take dance to the next level, but there'd been a time when I'd loved it just as much as Lissa. It was exciting to be around all that focus and energy, even if it was bittersweet, knowing what I knew now, that I'd always be relegated to the audience.

Lissa was in 1517, up to the fifteenth floor and then down an endless, dingy corridor of pill-bug-gray carpeting. The windowless hall smelled overpoweringly of lemon air freshener.

"Waffles, waffles!" Lissa answered the door with a whoop—but where had I heard that before? Then I remembered—I'd left that as a voice mail message for Rachel, on Halloween.

Why had Lissa said it?

"I'm so happy to see you!" I blurted. And I was. Lissa was wild as always, dressed in her signature unique style—a LITTLE MISS DIVA T-shirt, shredded jean shorts over rainbow sockless tights, taped feet, and a dozen blue stripes like jaybird feathers in her long black hair. Lissa's cupid lips were almost always ruby red, meant to be seen from the theater's nosebleeds. At any given moment, she could have been Giselle, or Coppélia, or Snow White.

"You're the best to come visit. Nobody does; I'm simply not exotic enough. University of Vermont, or Berkeley—now *that's* where everyone wants to go, to ski or the beach, or some stinky fraternity party. None of which is happening *chez moi.*"

I smiled, remembering something Holden had said—that Lissa looked like the future and talked like the past. "Believe me, this is plenty exotic," I assured her. "It's like *Fame*—the next dimension."

"I wish it were that glamorous. But look—speaking of a new

dimension," Lissa said, lifting her T-shirt to reveal a line of script running up her side.

I squinted to read it. " 'I don't want dancers who want to dance, I want dancers who need to dance. —George Balanchine.' " I laughed. "Nice ink. I've never heard that quote before."

"It's such a lovely thought, though, yes?" Lissa traced the loop-de-loops of the words with her finger, then raised an artful eyebrow at me. "Is it too earnest? Do you think I'll regret it?"

"Lissa, you're the most earnest person I know; plus you don't regret anything."

"True." She grinned. "Kick off your shoes. Ooh, and you're wearing my jacket. Name your price, remember."

"Not for sale. Sorry." I hung up the jacket on the wall peg, then pulled off the boots and left them at the door as well, sliding in on my socks. Lissa's studio was just what I would have guessed—a few wobbly sticks of secondhand furniture, a lot of center space to move in, plus a great sound system now tuned to something that I would have termed as vaguely experimental jazz.

"All mine, and no roommate is the sugar on top." Lissa gave an airy wave. "Except I'm never here. I told you I'm in the corps for *The Nutcracker* this season, right? And next year I'm an understudy in *La Sylphide*. They're even paying me real money, of all ginormous luxuries. Want tea? I was just about to have some; right now I'm in love with one called Sunday Saturnalia. But I bet they won't arrest us if we have it on Monday."

"Sure." I collapsed into a jalapeño-green beanbag chair, flinging out my arms and legs. A ballerina barre had been built against the opposite wall. Over it was a poster of Nureyev leaping through space. I breathed it all in.

"How's school? Is it such unimaginable weirdness to be back, just hum-de-hum, like nothing happened, after everything you went through?"

"There's good days and strange days," I answered honestly. Today, when I thought back on it, being a strange one. At school, Rachel and I had shared lunch, and things felt to me as if we were in more of a truce than any real burying of the hatchet. I still hadn't been in communication with Holden—or Kai, for that matter. I'd been feeling vaguely off center all day. But I'd been right to come see her, because Lissa, besides being a breath of familiarity, also seemed like the answer to something.

"Except for that dying cactus on the windowsill," I said, "I've got to admit, I'm pretty jealous of you. It must be so cool to know what you're doing with your life."

"First of all, he's not dying; he's hibernating. Second—jealous? You?" Lissa glided from the kitchenette across the room to hand me my tea. "Last time we talked about the future, you had dreams of heading off to cooking school in Paris to learn how to poach the perfect egg."

"Paris?" I sat up to take the mug. "Seriously? When did I say that?"

"Well, I mean it's not like I can *pinpoint* it. You were always talking about it. But I think that it was something you started in on sometime after you bombed that audition."

"What audition?"

"*Chicago*? You don't remember? You wanted Roxie, and you made chorus." Lissa dropped gracefully onto the futon. "It was back in December, and Birdie was working with Mr. Cutts and all the drama department people. I didn't see your audition, but you weren't happy about it. You were definitely pegged for a shot at the lead. I landed Velma—it was a lot of work, especially for my senior spring." She rolled her eyes but she didn't mean it; knowing Lissa, she had loved each grueling rehearsal. "Jeepers creepers, Ember, you could not be giving me more of a blank stare. You don't remember? Well, you were a really good sport about it, but I think you were also feeling kind of like, okay, time to move on. Resolved, I guess. You had other plans."

"Like culinary school . . ."

"For sure. Do you still cook? During winter break, you made me this scrumptious box of homemade truffles. It was like heaven. But I was surprised you didn't get Roxie, personally. Gadzooks, but that all feels like a long time ago." Lissa swung her long legs around, pulling into a seated stretch, her calves flexing *élevé, relevé, élevé.*

Chocolate truffles. Paris. An audition for *Chicago.* Nope, no recall of that. My tea tasted like hot, sweet campfire smoke. "I can't remember. What about 'waffles, waffles'—what's that about?"

Lissa laughed. "It happened one afternoon after practice. We'd been planning to be all healthy and go to Siggy's for those quinoa salads we always craved, but then we got there and checked out the menu and nothing looked particularly delicious—"

"Oh, wait—and we both said 'waffles, waffles,' at the same time!" I could feel the afternoon, a real-true click, the two of us hunched in the wooden booth at Siggy's. "We wanted waffles and pancakes and French toast and muffins. Mountains of carbs."

"Yes!" Lissa clapped her hands. "That was just the phrase you used. 'Mountains of carbs!'"

The afternoon unspooled in a gust of wind and woolly scarves.

Dashing out of the restaurant. Jumping on the subway to get to the IHOP over on Flatbush Avenue. "We were crazy; we must have each eaten for two," said Lissa. "But that afternoon was hilarious."

"And then we paid, big-time," I remembered. We hardly ate a thing the next day except for carrot sticks. Dancers can pick and choose from eating disorders, but a satisfying afternoon of pancakes is just not in the game plan.

"Not your favorite part—the next two days of denial." Lissa was right. I loved to cook, and I loved to eat—a simple pleasure, but any appetite, for a dancer, was a problem with a world of consequence.

Then I remembered something else. "So that was why we started saying 'waffles, waffles' to mean a spontaneous, off-the-radar new plan."

"Yep."

"Ha. I love it," I said. It felt great to have it again, too—it was a small, happy gift, like finding ten dollars in the pocket of my jeans.

Lissa stared at me over her mug. "Is this like a brain-damage-memory-loss thing you've got, from the accident? Sorry, not to imply you have brain damage. I mean, because you don't, do you?" She squinched her nose. Lissa relied on her innocent adorableness to save her from her innocent tactlessness.

"I think of it more as missing pieces. Not damaged pieces," I explained. "And I do get jolted back into memories. Like when I saw you at the club back on Halloween, I could feel these—*sparks*, I guess I'd call them—of what we did last New Year's Eve. We hung out together that night, right?"

"New Year's Eve, sure." Lissa sighed. "You came over to my

place before. We got dressed together. . . . Let's see. . . . Oh, and that's when I saw your leather jacket for the first time; you'd just bought it. And I made us mozzarella sticks, do you remember that? No? Or what about that stand-up mirror in my room at home that makes everyone look like they're in a fun house? It was definitely shooting down our confidence, that mirror."

"You're from Williamsburg."

"Uh-huh. I am." Lissa gave me a quick double take. Probably astounded that I could misplace such a huge fact. But nothing was clicking with mozzarella or the fun-house mirror, and I had only a dim recall of Lissa's home of old-fashioned furniture and flocked Victorian wallpaper and sconces that threw off blotted light.

"Okay, okay. Moving on to Areacode, which was where we went next," continued Lissa, all business. "You'd been joining me on the club scene for a little while, and this dude—or wait, no, it was his *brother*—had given you a flyer earlier that week, up in Manhattan. You were dying to go—but you didn't really know the dude. And you were kind of shilly-shallying about it, hoping he'd be there but trying not to get too excited."

"Did the guy have a name?" I braced myself. "Anthony, maybe?"

Lissa shook her head. "No. I'd remember that because that's my dad's name. Who's Anthony?"

"Just someone . . ." I breathed out. It was a relief in a way, every time I slipped a link to Anthony Travolo. It unnerved me to brush up against possible connections that I couldn't recall. It also seemed disrespectful to his memory.

"No, I don't think you knew this guy's name. But I think you knew his brother's name? Which is failing me. Now, I'd know *that* name if you said it."

"How about Kai?" I said it just to say it, the way Rachel end-lessly brought up Jake.

Lissa's face stayed blank. "Last name?"

Did Kai have his dad's last name? "Kai Ortiz?"

"No. Nothing like that."

I shrugged. "I'm all out of names."

"Okay. Well, anyway, we were super happy to get into Area-code. The sound was so hot, and I wanted to meet the DJ, or—whatever he called himself—*sonoric artist*. He was sublime."

Where did Lissa get these expressions? Not even my parents said *sublime*. "So did it work out? With you and Sublime?"

"For that night, it did. Although it seems that now I've blanked. What *was* his name? DJ London, Londoner . . ." Lissa shook her head and sipped her tea, leaving an electric red–lipstick smile on the rim. "And you found Romeo Late-Night, he was no slouch, following you around, acting pretty love-struck."

"On New Year's Eve," I said, "I guess everyone wants to be a little love-struck. But it feels like such an epic night for me to just . . . lose."

"Don't look so sad. Most people don't remember New Year's Eve." Lissa snapped her fingers. "But there was one other thing—at some point, you told me you were going out onto the fire escape, and you didn't want me to think you'd left. Because I remember thinking that it was crackers of you. I mean, since it was freezing. The coldest night of the year."

Blood rushed to my head. "Oh my God, Lissa, you can't be-lieve how strange that is! Because it must have triggered me to return to exactly that spot a few weeks ago. Wow, so I guess that wasn't a total coincidence."

"Speaking of triggering." Lissa was studying me. "Have you been back to any dance rehearsals at school? Dropped in to see Birdie or anything?"

"No." I could feel myself get tense. "I keep meaning to. It feels so complicated, seeing her."

"She's a person, not a jigsaw puzzle. Go see her. She'd love to see you. What about Bowditch Bridge? Have you been there?"

Bowditch Bridge. Even the name made me think of a blade, recarving my scars. "I'd definitely brave seeing Birdie before I went back to the bridge."

"It might not be a bad idea, Ember. Especially if you want to reboot." Lissa's voice was soft with care. "There's a term for it, right? 'Exposure therapy.' Like the fire escape. Or you sit in on your old dance class, or visit your old dance teacher. Or you drive to the bridge, the place where it all happened. Even if, psychologically, it's like running back into the burning building." She tapped her temple. "Because these blackouts that you're talking about—they're all in there. They might be hiding in a really dark spot, Ember, but they're not lost."

"Right, I know." My mind wouldn't stop the whirligig of imagining Bowditch Bridge again. I was acutely conscious of my heart's acceleration, the idea clenched like a fighter's stance in the core of my body. "I don't know. What if I freak out?"

"And so what if you do? Revisit the dance, step by step. That's what a dance teacher would say. You were going somewhere upstate, right?"

I nodded. "I was on my way to see my aunt. I guess it must have been a kind of thrown-together plan. I'd called her a few days before. And I'd been up there a few times in the fall, a couple of times before that in the summer. So I knew the route. But it was a really bad storm that night. And . . . I wasn't alone." I exhaled a shaky breath.

"Right, I know. You want my advice?" Lissa paused. "Drive it."

"What? Drive to the bridge?"

She nodded. "That's the real burning building. I'd go with you, if you want."

Drive it. "I'm not sure." I shivered.

Coney Island was one thing. The prospect of this drive was terrifying. And yet, if I were going to do it, I'd have to do it alone. No Kai, no Mom, no Smarty, no Holden or even Lissa. This would have to be my journey.

Reflexively, I checked my texts just to see if Kai had left me anything. No. But it wouldn't stop me from checking again, in the next half hour.

"Maybe you'd find the flow of what happened," said Lissa. "Or maybe you'll find the flow of all of these other moments that you're missing. But jeez, you look white as a ghost, Ember."

"It scares me," I admitted. "Terrifies me."

"Look, I don't think you should do any of this before you're ready. Go see Birdie first, maybe? Touch in with what you know before you head out into something you don't. Just to make sure you're strong enough, physically and mentally. You've got to be careful with yourself."

"You're right. I get it." I nodded. "Actually, you kinda sound like my mom," I told her. "In a good way, I mean."

"It's been my experience that moms usually mean it in a good way," Lissa answered.

26

Ember Was Here

I sent Birdie a note late that same night, once I got back from Lissa's—after hanging out a while longer in her apartment, we'd located the closest IHOP uptown, where we ordered silver dollars with whipped butter and strawberry syrup.

"You'll come watch me in the pageant? And then in the spring, I get to dance as a witch *and* a bridesmaid! Who could ask for more, right?" Lissa seemed homesick as she hugged me good-bye.

"You're incredible, Lissa. Of course I'll come clap for you."

She pulled away, her face unguarded pleasure. "Seriously? I'm not too far away?"

"What are you talking about? You're eight stops on the L."

Independence was a process, it seemed, and it struck me that Holden was just the same as Lissa in that way. Sometimes he'd seem incredibly independent, and then other times he'd reach out for me as if he were stuck out alone in a field and needed that quick reassurance of cover. "*Nutcracker's* opening night is December fifth," Lissa said softly, "and then it's March twelfth for *La Sylphide.*"

"Promise, promise to both. I'd love to come see you."

On the Lincoln Center subway platform, I'd absently checked again for messages from Kai—none. But I knew it was knee-jerk, that I'd only looked as a way of making myself feel better. The rhythm and tempo of Kai had been established. He happened when he happened, he answered to no rule, and I was coming to an understanding that no matter what I did, I couldn't control him.

As the train pulled into the station, I saw the letter spray-painted on the column on the opposite side of the platform. The casual sideways A, in gunmetal silver. My heart leapt—what did it mean? It was like a silent wave, or a smile, the signal of his presence. How many of them were here in the city?

The thought troubled me all the way home, where for once—probably due to my scrupulous texting—my parents were pretending that they'd been tucked up peacefully in bed. Dad reading, Mom knitting.

"How's Lissa?" asked Mom.

"Fun. . . . Committed," I said. "She's really in it."

"Well, I don't envy her. Dancing is such a hard life."

"Not if it's the only one you'd ever understand."

Dad, who slept closest to the door in old-fashioned protector style, now reached out his hand to cover mine. "Was it difficult for you? To see her? To be there, around all those kids?" If Mom was right that Dad's voice was the window to his soul, I could tell from the way he asked that a small, quiet part of his soul had been crushed I'd given up dance.

"Not as bad as I thought. Good night," I answered softly, leaning down to kiss him quickly on the forehead before I turned and left the room.

Birdie's reply to my question was immediate, pinging my in-box by the time I'd come back from brushing my teeth in the bathroom.

Hi, Ember—

Hooray! I was so happy to get your email message. I've really been hoping that you would come on over to the Fine Arts building and say hello. It's not the same— and for sure quieter—with you and Lissa both gone.

Also, Ember, I have something to show you that I think you will want to see. Drop by tomorrow after rehearsal—but not too late.

I would love to reconnect. Sooner the better. xx B.

I clicked and reclicked the message like a lighter all the next morning, during and in between classes.

Then I let my fingers send a quick ok see you then! at lunch.

Walking out of the cafeteria, Rachel and I made a plan to hang out this weekend, which was a step in the right direction— but things between us still didn't feel exactly perfect, so I nixed asking her to come with me for support, for my very first visit back to the dance studio. Dance wasn't Smarty's cup of tea, anyway. What we needed most was some real time together out of school. No Jake and no Holden; in fact, nobody else at all running interference. We'd make our way back to the right rhythm, because we always did.

I also called Jenn to reschedule my physical therapy. My afternoon was now clear, and with the school day over, I killed the next ninety minutes in the library. Schoolwork was not the same this year—I could feel teachers giving me leniency on papers and quizzes. I'd never been a spectacular scholar, or even a scholar at all, but now I struggled for my B-minuses and C-pluses. It was trickier, since the accident, to lower myself deep enough to reach those hard, fixed places of concentration.

Paris. My conversation with Lissa kept nudging at me. I'd wanted to take off even before last February. The land of shiny copper pots, of soufflés and flambés, and recipes that needed careful, close instruction. I'd have been in a country where I didn't know the language and didn't have any friends, and far from my parents. Was that what I'd been dreaming about, when I'd confided to Lissa?

At half past four, I gathered my books and left the main building, then headed down the block to the converted church that Lafayette used as its Fine Arts Center. The place of my old dreams.

It was the first time all year that I'd walked up the worn steps and through the arched front door. The entrance was the only place where you could smell the building's previous holy days. That dry-papery, ancient-wood, furniture-polish churchy smell. On the way through, I pressed my hand to the scar ridged beneath my bangs. It gave me courage—I was older, I was different, I was returning to the studio not in failure but with resolution that my past was my past.

I'd heard a rumor that some new hit TV show about ballet dancers had caused a major uptick in Lafayette freshmen taking dance as an elective, and the front hall of locker banks did seem extra crowded with girls in wraps and leg warmers, packing up and heading out. But from the deep cream walls and the lost-and-found basket at the front desk to the corkboards crammed with local auditions, everything looked the same as it always did. It was both exhilarating and strange to be here again.

Stranger still was that I was all but unrecognized by the freshmen and sophomores.

In H studio, I peeped in on a couple of mirrored dancers lingering at the bar. The floor was dusted in cornstarch, and Birdie's favorite Café Europa radio station was playing Charlotte Gainsbourg in a remix. Laughter drifted from the more casual "green room" next door. And even though there was no reason for it, the sound left me feeling unsure of myself, as if I'd been deliberately left out of the joke.

I walked down to J studio, where most of the one-on-one choreography happened. The protocol of J studio was silence, no music, and it was usually more intense, too, a controlled randomness of small groups and individuals working piecemeal through routines. Some of the dancers were beating out their eight-count combinations, while others performed in pairs. In back was a nest of freshmen stretching through their end-of-practice cooldowns.

With no Birdie in sight, I sat in a spare folding chair by the door.

"Ouch!" The seat was too hard; I winced as pain jolted up

my spine. It was like a reminder that the place where I really belonged was in my physical therapy class—not here.

"Ember! You okay?" Marianne Polzone, skimming past, paused to check me over.

"Hey, Marianne. Fine, I'm fine."

She nodded and resumed the complicated steps of a floor routine. Marianne was a senior, and she'd always been somewhat robotic in her style, but she'd really changed this past year. As I watched her, I had to respect how far she'd come from "Marianne Plod Zone," Lissa's smirking name for her.

After a minute or so, Marianne even dared a small, pleased glance at me, as if hoping that I'd noticed how much she'd improved. I smiled back. Yes.

Wade Adams, working on some difficult choreography on the other side of the room, was just as rubber-bandy and intuitively brilliant as always. His older brother, Chester, was a principal with the ABT, which is where Wade himself very likely would end up. Wade and Chester both looked like young, tall, red-headed Woody Allens. Not exactly leading-man types, but you forgave them their shortcomings in the looks department when they started to move.

I relaxed deeper into my seat, as Hannah Thwaite bounced into the studio. Hannah! I'd hardly seen her at school—she probably lived in the Arts building. Hannah was one of the best dancers at Lafayette, a natural despite her round, blow-up-doll figure that she liked to emphasize. Today she'd been highlighting her assets with a plunge-neck leotard, and as she sprang to the corner of the room to retrieve her shrug, she noticed me.

"Eeek! Ember! A little Birdie told me you might drop by today. But you're so late, you missed practice. You look amaaaaazing with your hair like that—I saw you the other day in the hall and totally meant to tell you." Did Hannah speak like that on purpose? Or did her fake sweetness sound okay in her own ears? "You've been such a stranger here! We were all starting to feel offended! But I guess you keep away because you miss it so much. It's incredibly brave of you to come by and show some support."

I gave Hannah's boobs a quick smile. "I always think of you as having plenty of support."

Hannah pulled her shrug across her chest and raised her eyebrows. I wasn't usually bitchy, and I was annoyed that I'd sunk to her level, but of course now Hannah had her claws out. "Well, if it's any consolation, it's been hugely competitive this year. So it would have been really hard to make the cut."

"Then I guess it was pretty smart of me to stage that debilitating car accident."

Hannah looked only slightly embarrassed. "Oh, Emb, I'm obviously not trying to be—I mean, I feel incredibly sorry for you. For what happened, I mean. We all feel bad." Her smile was awkward—she wasn't being fake now, but her sincerity didn't come easy, either. "You used to put in so much time here. Jeez, I feel like after one thousand or so hours, we should each get to tag the J studio wall, you know?" As she pretended to shake a can of paint and spray. "Like, 'Hannah was here!'" She snorted. "'Ember was here!'"

"Right . . ."

Just then Birdie swept through the door. Her eyes lit brightly on me. "Ember, oh good. I thought I saw you come in!" When she hugged me, the buttons on her long-underwear thermal shirt met the buttons of my long-underwear thermal shirt in a compatible click. "Wow." She smiled as she pulled away. "As I live and breathe. Okay, come on upstairs with me."

"See ya, Emb." As Hannah shot off, I stood to follow Birdie out of the studio and then up a flight of stairs to her cramped dormer office, the site of many late afternoons for some of us, after dance practice.

It still seemed that the room hadn't received the spring cleaning Birdie had been threatening to give it since I'd made my very first visit. It could never be termed a hangout office, but I'd spent a few afternoons here with Birdie and other kids, sardine-packed on Birdie's shabby brown velvet sofa, where we'd all gossip and watch *Dirty Dancing* or *Footloose* on her ancient TV while eating burnt microwave popcorn.

Ember was here. Hannah's thought, now planted, was never going to uproot.

"You had something to show me?"

"Behind here. Come closer." Birdie's computer screen was glowing. She dragged a straight-back chair—thinly cushioned, thank God—over for me. As I sat, she flopped in her own swivel chair next to mine and then gathered herself up in it, propping her chin on her knees. "Can you guess what this is?"

"Nope." I had no idea.

"It's your audition for *Chicago*."

My whole body prickled. "Oh."

"We taped everyone, so that the dance and drama departments could watch together, later. I think it might help you set the record straight. All year, I'm sure, you've had people feeling bad for you. Assuming that this accident had derailed your dreams. And I imagine it's been a difficult adjustment. But . . ."

237

Her hand hovered above the cursor arrow, as if waiting for permission. "This is from December."

"Yes. I'd like to see." Although I wasn't sure, exactly, if I was ready. But I nodded, swallowed, braced.

She pressed play, and there I was. Full screen.

Was it only a year ago? But I was so much younger! Unformed and soft in a way that I knew I wasn't anymore. In that thin pink terrycloth sweatshirt that I'd just donated last week to Grace Church. My legs looked too thin for my baby-blue leggings.

"Do you remember this?" Birdie murmured at my side.

"I'm . . . not sure."

My audition was standard, an *All That Jazz* dance sequence. I was prepared for anything, but mostly for failure.

Except I was good. I was great, really. Campy, sparkly, I was selling it, but I owned it, too. My voice was trained and suited the role, but my dancing was a cut above. Each move I made was clean and punctuated, and as I watched, I could feel my muscles remembering it—the swivel, the jump and land. I knew this routine. I'd been in such amazing shape. So limber and confident, and almost naive in my innocence. I thought I'd be in control of that body forever.

I watched that girl, the girl I had been. I watched her hit every line, every mark.

And then she/I stopped. A second later, the music stopped, too, in an abrupt and discordant break.

Off camera, Birdie asked me what was wrong. If I wanted to start again. There was an echoing moment. The cameraperson sensed that a drama was unfolding before her, and the lens-angle view jumped over to Martha Cutts, who was Lafayette's pinch-hit piano player and Mr. Cutts's wife. She was watching me, clearly puzzled, and then with eyebrows firmly raised, she began the piece again.

The camera jiggled back to me. Thirty-two beats, and when I stopped for the second time, Birdie leapt on camera. I watched her, compact yet sleek, as she picked up the routine, performing as if we were in it together, a duet.

"Come on, Ember, you know this cold!" Now the camera zoomed somewhat mischievously, I thought, into a close-up on Birdie's face. She looked strained. As if urging me to get into the spirit of it. *She really wanted me to get the part.*

I watched the muscular cut of Birdie's arm and the spin of her body as she took up the routine. The capable flex of her hard calf muscle as she landed a jump. She embodied Roxie fully and thrillingly.

Then the camera swiped another look at me. Next came a quick camera pan of me watching Birdie. And now I was speaking. The camera swiveled and closed in on me like a predator. It shocked me a little bit. There I was. My forehead was clear of its scar, my hair loose and Rapunzel-long, and my voice was soft and strangely girlish. ". . . because I don't, I just don't want Roxie. I don't want to be trying out for her if I can't commit to all of this work."

Birdie's profile was impassive as she answered. I picked up the general gist of it—something about trying out again, tomorrow, maybe. When I was more up to it.

"I want chorus." My voice came in a decibel stronger. Clear enough so that there was no confusion. "I just want chorus; that's all I can handle, Birdie."

Birdie must have made a joke or something. As I turned away, the camera sneaked in to capture my uncertain eyes.

"I'm sorry," I said, half to the camera, half to myself. "I'm done."

And then the screen cut to black.

I glanced at Birdie, who had obviously looked at this video clip many times.

"So, yeah. That's that." Her voice was kind. She wasn't harboring anything. No hard feelings. Not then, not now, not ever. She'd always been such an excellent role model, and my exit from dance never would have diminished that.

"Lissa said I bombed it."

Birdie shrugged. "Yeah, it was funny, that's what you told everyone. Maybe it was easier for you. You never attempted to reschedule the audition. I put you in chorus, and you were fine with it. You were worried about your parents, and their disappointment. But you knew what was best for you. You said you'd rather razzle-dazzle with a perfect four-cheese lasagna." She smiled. "And then you actually brought in a lasagna, and of course none of the dancers would touch it. Maybe that was your point. Anyway, I had a big wedge of it." She winked. "And it was delicious."

Just sitting here with Birdie, talking with her again, was an old familiar ease. "I'm sorry I've been avoiding you," I said. "But I didn't want to deal with the fact that being part of this world isn't a choice anymore. Maybe I walked away from dance once, but I could never reclaim it now, even if I wanted to." I rolled up my sleeve, exposing the scar. "My body just can't do what it used to. And I don't have that extra determination that would push me past my obstacles, to try and become what I'd been."

"You have to let your training serve you better than that. It was the one thing I gave you that might have qualified as advice. I told you not to let the fact that you weren't studying dance mean that you had to put away your passion for it."

I thought of Areacode, my nights out with Lissa. "I think I took your advice."

"I'm glad. You were wonderful to watch. But it's not what the audience sees that counts. It's what the performer feels."

Once upon a time, all I'd wanted to do was perform. Once my life—just like Lissa's and Hannah's and Birdie's—had been cleanly divided into timetables of dance schedules and rehearsals and steps to memorize, all for a chance on stage. I'd breathed daily inside that choreography. I'd followed the rules, made mistakes, and tried harder next time. I'd put my hours in, and then at some point center stage had not been what I'd wanted after all. Whereas in a kitchen, backstage was also the spotlight. Still, I was relieved to know that I'd made the right choice before the choice had been made for me.

"Thanks for this, Birdie," I said as I stood to go. "It means a lot to me that you showed me that clip. It was kind of painful, but also a relief to see it."

Birdie's gray-blue eyes met mine in empathy. "Thought that might be the case," she said. "And you'd better not be a stranger around here, okay? And maybe next time you come bearing gifts? I can't stop thinking about lasagna."

"You got it."

And we let our smiles hold the promise, before I reached for the door and she turned back to her computer screen so that I could steal away in peace.

27

Chop Chop Chop

Carroll Gardens was a considerable distance. I ran it. I wanted to see it again. I cut around back; the symbol was far away, that dry splash on the bottom of the wall. The silvery, fallen-down A—the same one I'd jotted on my hand, on the Halloween scrap paper, those first early days back from Addington, and the same one that was at the Lincoln Center subway stop.

Quick as an infielder, I shifted direction to sprint toward it.

A *tag*, Hannah had said. A way to show you'd been here. A territorial mark.

Obviously, I'd grown up seeing all kinds of tags, all over the city. I'd just never really paid attention to them. Not till now.

Why did I keep finding these tags? They haunted me, but how could Anthony continue to shadow new places I went to, when he was no longer here and couldn't possibly have known about the direction of my life now?

I stared at the mural, willing answers. Defiant but good-humored, the tag also seemed smart-ass—with a dash of light-hearted. I touched the grimy drywall and traced the symbol. The pad of my finger came away blackened. There were no more answers here.

I turned and left the park.

El Cielo had just opened, but it was too early for customers. Some 1950s rockabilly music—my dad's favorite, Chuck Berry? Yep, I was pretty sure—was blaring tinny from the speakers. At a corner table, the busboy was rolling silverware into individually bundled settings. He looked up and tipped his head toward the back kitchen.

Deeper in, I caught sight of Isabella, as if she'd never left. She and the prep cook guys were busy with kitchen work. The blond waitress was making pots of regular and decaf coffee for the busing stands. Kai was nowhere in sight. His shifts were erratic and depended on his classes. I hadn't seen him since Coney Island, but I knew if I came back here, it would only be a matter of time before we would intersect.

But even Kai didn't matter right now. Right now, I just needed it back. The secrets of this kitchen were mine if I was willing to work for them. I had to be part of the kitchen theater. To feel the heavy handle of the knife, to bisect onions into tom-tom drums, to decrown parsnips and send potatoes and shallots off to their translucent sizzle.

When Isabella murmured something to one of the cooks, he immediately stopped what he was doing and unhooked an apron from a peg near the stovetop, balled it tight, and lobbed it high through the air to me. I caught it and shook it out, slid it on, and secured it by its long ties.

They would allow me to be here, and being here was all I needed.

Isabella, kneading dough for tortillas, waved her flour-dusted fingers at the heavy bouquets of carrots and the bin of red, orange, and yellow bell peppers up from cold storage. I nodded, reached for the cutting board, and attacked a Spanish onion; good-bye top, good-bye base. Right from the first moments, I began to tear up.

"I'm fine, I'm fine," I muttered to nobody in particular, wiping my watering nose on my sleeve. Stinging in my eyes and bluesy electric guitar in my ears. This music was even older than my parents' era, but at least it did me the favor of conjuring up no memory, nothing at all except the cheerful, jangly background noise to a much-needed blast of right now.

In this kitchen, I was beginning again. I was turning into me. Not a dancer. But someone else. I'd catch up with myself; I'd retrace my steps any way I could, even if I wasn't able to see my own old footprints marking the path.

Working the knife across the board. One-eighth cuts, presto. Tears were dropping off my face and rolling down my neck. Here was my passion—I chose it once, and I'd choose it again.

Dice dice dice, mince mince mince, chop chop chop. The sound was rolling motion and maybe I was on my way.

28

World Hold On to Me

The moon was a scrubbed white dish—or possibly it only looked like that because five minutes ago, I'd unloaded, oh, at least forty scrubbed white dishes from the industrial dishwasher—by the time I left the restaurant. I didn't like walking by myself anywhere after ten, when Smith Street seemed to change hands from a café and restaurant crowd to a rowdier bar scene. I texted Mom and kept up a quick pace.

There hadn't been much for me to do after all the prep work. So I'd polished off another of Isabella's customized delicious dinners at the bar—fish tacos, along with tiny avocado bean cakes—and afterward she'd let me go without a word. The acknowledgment that I'd be returning was unspoken.

"Hey! Wait up!"

"Hey, you." My chest constricted. Kai. He hadn't been at the restaurant all night. I truly hadn't thought he'd be there, though I'd yearned for him, of course, and had been half watching for him around every corner. Seeing him now, I could feel myself ache with joy and relief.

"Got an idea," he said. "What do you say we hit the theater down the block? It's all film geeks who run that place. We won't have to pay, for one, and they're lax about letting you sit in the balcony."

"Sounds good." Maybe it was because I'd bailed on the physical therapy earlier, but I felt pulled as a puppet from being on my feet for hours. The prospect of sitting down for a movie sounded perfect.

Kai's presence was gravity. I was conscious of the heavy lift and fall of my boots, the weight of my sleepy eyelids as we ducked inside and slipped upstairs in the creaky old Cobble Hill Cinema, and then settled ourselves into the astoundingly comfortless iron seats. A movie was playing—something in German with subtitles, one of their typical esoteric offerings.

And there it was. Scratched onto the exit door, not to be missed, like a smirk.

Excitedly, I pointed to it. "It's you, right?" I asked. "The graffiti tagger? The sideways-A guy? It makes sense that it's you. Is it?"

"The tagger," he repeated.

"Come on! Don't play innocent! You keep putting them where you know I'll find them. There's a tag below the mural at

Cobble Hill Park, and one at the Lincoln Center subway stop. There's even one on the boardwalk on Coney Island."

"Ha, listen to you. Are you an undercover cop?"

"Except that you are looking very guilty. You did it, I just know it. I thought it was another letter, an *A*, but it's a *K*—a *K* for *Kai*, right?"

"Okay, guilty. *K* for *Kai*," he admitted, but he seemed pleased that I'd figured this out.

"How many are there, in all?"

"Two hundred? Two hundred fifty?"

"Seriously!?"

"Yeah, around there. I don't keep count."

"Kai." I sat back, knitting my fingers under my chin, contemplating the city as a city of silver *K*s. All the ones I'd found and all the ones I had yet to find. "That's a lot of tags. What's the deal? Is it some kind of project?"

"It's more just something I've always done, since I was a kid. It was my thing, a way of owning something that can't be owned. Call it a way of feeling special, maybe. Or call it, I don't know, my way of making the world hold on to me—till someone scrubs me off the wall and back into oblivion." He waved a hand through the air, as if it was all the same to him.

But it was personal for him, these tags. He wanted to talk about it, but at the same time he was self-conscious. He pulled out his flask and passed it to me. I took a tiny sip of coffee.

"I'm going to start looking for them," I decided. "I bet there's some at El Cielo—I'm starting with the men's room." I passed back the flask. "And I'll check some key warehouses in Bushwick, for sure. And around by the St. George and . . . I can't think where else."

247

"There's plenty more places. I guess you're just going to have to get to know me better, if you want to find them all." He leaned in to steal a kiss, ending the discussion.

We stayed until the movie was over, though neither of us had any idea what it was about. Kissing in a movie theater—it was so stupidly, deliciously middle school, but with Kai the act also became a high-octane thrill.

Afterward, he walked me home, all the way up to my front door. The casual nearness of him made me dizzy. I was conscious of holding my breath. "So what exotic locale is next for us, Mr. Bond?" I asked. "The Carnival in Rio?"

"How 'bout Central Park?" he suggested. "Cheap and easy?"

"Sure," I answered. "I go where you go." I fished out my keys. "From the minute we met, I knew that was true."

When I looked up, I saw in his face the promise of a response, but then he didn't give me one. We stood together, not speaking. Kai used his finger to delineate each of my features in simple strokes, sketching me in the air but not touching me. We were so close that his skin radiated warmth, his eyes shone by the light of the streetlamp. He wanted to tell me something, I could feel it. But at the last minute he decided to kiss me one last time instead.

Then he turned, down the steps, moving swiftly.

"Wait—when? When are we going to . . . ?" Too late. Kai was a ship out to sea, swallowed up in the night horizon.

But the smile remained on my lips, fading only when I opened the door to find both of my parents standing in the hall. This time, they weren't even pretending that they were occupied with anything else. They were as alert and aligned as two arrows in a quiver.

"Really, folks?" I forced an easy tone. "I checked in with you three times since after school. There's absolutely no reason for drama."

"Your last call, you said you'd be home before seven," said Mom. "Here it is, almost midnight. And when we tried you, you'd turned off your phone."

"Mom, I sent a text saying I was going to a movie. That's almost the same as a call. And there *is* also such a thing as overly checking in on someone. Every fifteen minutes, it felt like. I had to turn off the phone."

"Which movie? You never answered. Were you really at the movies, Ember? And what were you doing before?"

"Of course I was. And before? Before I was just . . . around." Obviously, I hadn't told them anything about El Cielo. I couldn't. The idea that I would now balance schoolwork, yearbook, and my physical therapy with an after-school job might tip them both over the cliff of parental outrage.

"We worry about you. We worry a lot." Dad's voice was a tiny bit accusing, and yet at the same time he was entreating me. As if he couldn't make up his mind which attitude to own. "You're so far away from us lately—and it feels like it's getting worse and worse. Locking yourself in your room, or driving off to the beach, or out till all hours."

"It's becoming just the way it was before," added Mom, and yet she, too, was conflicted—there was weariness along with the quiet reproach that by now I was used to. "Just exactly the same patterns. Last time, when this happened, we didn't step in, we didn't do anything. We felt helpless, of course, but we left you alone. We made that mistake. But this time, please, Ember, please don't lock us out. Let us help. We want to help. Dr. P says that you should call that woman, that colleague of his; he said he sent you—"

"If you really, truly want to help, you need to stop micromanaging me," I interrupted. "And if you'd really look at me, you could see I'm making progress—real progress. Not just talking out my emotions to sock puppets, or progress the way you think it should be happening. Like trust-falls with Dr. P's contacts."

"Ember, you're all we have," Mom protested. "How do you expect us to behave?"

"But it's like you're punishing me for being all you have. I'm sorry I almost died in February, and I'm a million times sorrier that someone else did! But you can't fix anything here by guiding me along what you think are the right ways I'm supposed to heal. All you're doing is smothering me, if you want to know."

"Smothering you?" Mom's face was crumpled in hurt. "Is that what you think I'm doing?"

"It's not that I'd think you'd want to, Mom," I told her. "But yes. Sometimes you do, anyway. You really do." And while I knew we hadn't talked it through to Mom's satisfaction, hadn't come to any kind of family resolve, I also knew there wasn't a solution. The rest of my life did not get fixed in one night, and it wasn't fair that my parents wanted me to pretend that I could make that happen for them.

Instead I pushed past them—plowing up the stairs, leaving behind yet another situation that would have to mend eventually, but I just couldn't deal with it right now.

29
Inner Circle

Holden hadn't been in touch since our bumbling, semi-mistake hookup at Drew's engagement, and I'd waited a few days to call him. I had to see him again, to make things better, even if I couldn't make them all the way perfect. I was finding myself in this situation a lot, it seemed.

Another offshoot of last night was that after I'd gone to bed, my parents had contacted Linda Applebaum themselves. When it seemed they couldn't get to her through me, they just went around another way. They couldn't resist.

So far, she'd left two messages on my cell phone plus one in my in-box. So much for "my own steam."

I needed Holden. I needed his reliability. But apparently he was needing me, too.

"Listen, I'm glad you called. I've got a favor to ask," he began. Less than two minutes into our call, and he'd jumped into it. "We're doing this family dinner at the River Café tonight for Nana's eightieth birthday. I know it's short notice, but can you come? Just as my bud? It'd sure as hell take the edge off."

"Oh." This was not what I'd wanted.

"Please? Eight sharp but we'll make it quick; Nana gets tired."

"Um . . . well, sure. Who am I to blow off your eighty-year-old grandmother?" Stilted events never seemed to stop being part of the deal with Holden. His family was so ceremonial. In the years I'd known him, there'd been a cousin's christening, a couple of high school graduations, the ballet, a Broadway revival, and once, even, a painfully boring family trip to the opera for Mr. and Mrs. Wilde's anniversary.

I'd also sneezed my way through Mrs. Wilde's fund-raising event at the Brooklyn Botanic Garden, and I'd walked through at least a half dozen fussy furnished town houses when she'd chaired the Brooklyn Historical Society's private homes tour. In these situations, Holden had always reached for me, as if the best option was for us to endure it together.

I'd seen old Mrs. Boughton—or "Nana," as all the Wildes called her—briefly at Drew's engagement party, and had kept out of her sight. She was the twenty-five-years-older original version of her daughter, bright and false and practically humming with judgment.

That evening at a quarter past eight, her hard eyes followed me as I walked across the restaurant in the same black dress I'd worn to Drew's engagement party.

Another thing I was reminded of, when it came to being part of Holden's life: I was often required to wear a party dress.

"Hello, everyone."

"Ember," said Mrs. Boughton, in her trademark withering tone. "You're late. We've ordered drinks without you."

"That's fine," I said, knowing that she didn't like that answer, because it sounded friendly but semi-implied that it was fine that I was late. I'd always enjoyed needling Mrs. Boughton, who wasn't as claws-out mean as her daughter—mainly because she was always so shocked anyone would dare be rude to her.

Next I presented her with my birthday present—an overpriced lavender candle, specially gift wrapped at the store. "Here you go. I'm afraid it's not very useful," I said. "But I remembered how much you liked lavender. So, happy birthday."

She inclined her head to acknowledge the gift, though Mrs. Boughton was the type of person who would almost rather be irritated to receive a rose or vanilla candle than accept that someone had attempted to be considerate. Meantime, all of the Wilde men had stood formally as the waiter pulled out my chair. I remembered how that always used to unnerve me. Still did.

I sat. They sat.

Mrs. Boughton pushed the gift to the side as if hoping someone would take it away. She raised a haughty finger at me. "Why did you cut off all of your hair?" she demanded. "And those bangs! Why, I can hardly see your face."

It seemed that nobody was going to step forward into

explaining anything about my surgery. This was when Holden's natural quietness kind of got on my nerves. Anyway, I wasn't about to give old Mrs. Boughton the whole spiel. "Yep, I changed my style. I like it, so I guess that's what counts." I tucked a few strands behind my ear—and then snapped my napkin into my lap.

It was going to be a long night.

Holden's dad rolled his eyes amicably at me. Deep into his cocktails. It was clear he'd decided to let this night, like so many others, just float past him in a dream.

"Good to see you again, Ember," said Raina, and then she and Drew resumed talking about whatever lovey-dovey thing they'd been discussing so privately that their foreheads nearly touched.

Under the table next to me, Holden gave my knee an appreciative squeeze. His eyes were already red from the fresh-cut roses on the table, which of course nobody had any intention of displacing. It was always kind of astounding how alone Holden was in his own family. As much as the Wildes could annoy me, and as cautious and unassuming a wingman as Holden was, he really did need me.

Within minutes, I was glad I'd shown up for the food, too, which started to interest me right from the lobster panna cotta. Followed by goat-cheese ravioli, and then pecan-crusted bass on a bed of sweet-potato puree. The panna cotta was a teeny bit jellyfishy, the ravioli was on the bland side but I finished it, and the fish had been sitting under the hot lamps a few minutes too long. But the sweet potato was fluffy as a cloud, and made with cinnamon—yum.

This was my first fancy dinner in forever, and I tasted everything excitedly, with interest and respect, like a chef. Like the chef I once told Lissa I'd planned to become. And I knew my newly-woken-up curiosity was really because of El Cielo. I'd put in another shift yesterday, and it had ended with my sampling more of Isabella's best dishes. It wasn't Parisian cooking, nothing as fancy as that, but it had its own complications, its unique difficulties to master. And in its own way, it was every bit as exotic.

"You have a real appetite," Isabella had told me. "And I see how you want to try new things, too. You remind me of my nephew."

It was her first reference to Kai. Her words had turned my blood to ice, and I hadn't mustered an answer, but afterward when I was putting on my jacket to go, she'd looked up and said simply, "Come back," and I knew she meant it. In spite of Kai, I could come back.

And of course I would. She knew I would.

The unfortunate penalty of tonight's dinner, wonderful as it was to taste, was that I had to listen to the Wildes. Had they always been this boastful? Between Mrs. Wilde's fairly creepy self-praise of her decorating decisions, Drew's reference to his promotion, and Mr. Wilde's telling anyone at random that nobody could beat his backhand, there was enough hot air at the table to power up a balloon.

But never any bragging from Holden. He asked the questions the others wanted him to ask, and he didn't look too bothered when Drew undermined everything, from how he looked ("Dude, how are you surviving that haircut?") to his college ("NYU sucks, it's a rip-off; plus it's overcrowded with wannabe hipsters").

A couple of times, I bumped Holden's knee under the table in solidarity, while above the table, I pretended to think Drew was not being a massive blowhard jerk but merely a young man of persuasive opinions.

Afterward, the town cars were waiting for us.

"Come over, hang out for a while?" Holden's arm on my shoulder was strong. "No pressure . . . just, y'know." He cleared his throat. "As friends."

"Sure, why not?" Doors were being opened and the others were climbing in—Mrs. Boughton had her own car-plus-driver to whisk her back to her apartment in the city. And I had nothing else to do. I'd called Kai's number a couple of times today and listened to the preprogrammed machine message. We hadn't made plans for a next time. Of course.

"That was too much, right?" Holden murmured in my ear, so low that Raina, on his other side, couldn't hear. "I lean on you too hard."

"I'm used to your family; they don't scare me," I whispered back. "And more importantly, you know I'm here for you." It felt great to say. Maybe because it had been such a long time since I'd been the one to offer strength—to be, finally, the someone who got leaned on.

Time tonight with Holden was restoring the balance, too, after what had happened last Thursday. What I hadn't counted on was a late-night dose of Drew. Who, at the last minute, decided he didn't want to head into Park Slope with Raina—since she had to wake up early for a 7 a.m. business breakfast.

"We'll watch the fight on pay-per-view," he said, pummeling Holden in the ribs.

"Not sure that's what Ember signed on for," said Holden in half protest.

Drew's answering silence made me feel as though I were the evening's interloper. And once Mr. and Mrs. Wilde had padded off to bed with their whiskey nightcaps, leaving me alone with Holden and Drew, I began to wish that I hadn't come along after all. There was something needling Drew, and it had to do with me. He was showing me all the same behavior that he'd put me through at the engagement party. He was pent-up annoyed by my presence—I could tell by the way he avoided looking at me, his eyes shifting off hard when I made a single comment, and by the way he charged past me in the den to grab the remote control, then fixed way too much attention on the boxing. It was all so unnerving, well past the point of unkindness.

When Holden went upstairs to get waters, I braced for it. Here was Drew's opportunity to pounce.

I was right. With his eyes beady and determined on the television screen, he cut right to it. "So does this mean we'll be seeing more of you, Ember? Family dinners are usually pretty inner-circle." By the flicker of the television light, it struck me that Drew did share some resemblance to Holden, only fattened up and with a melty chin. I'd never thought so before.

"Last I checked, it wasn't a crime to hang out with your ex," I answered lightly, resisting my urge to leave the room altogether. But part of me wanted to hear what Drew had to say.

A split-second glance at me, and then Drew focused back on the screen. "Nothing personal, my dear. I wouldn't mind at all, except for the inconvenient fact that my brother's still in love with you—and you're not in love with him." His voice was indisputably bitter. "You know that I saw you both?" he continued. "Last January. You and that punk street kid. I was coming into the city in a cab, and you two were walking the footpath over the bridge, in the opposite direction. We passed head-on. You saw me, too."

"What? Drew, what are you talking about?"

"Like you don't know. You can't fool me, Ember. You're the walking wounded, broken up with the street kid—or maybe he broke it off with you—and you're rebounding with my little brother. Giving it another shot because you know he'll do any-thing for you. How much plainer can I make it?"

"I'm not—" The Brooklyn Bridge, a shred of clouds, a bitter breeze, the weak winter sun on my face—it was kaleidoscopic. Yes, I had seen Drew that day—his face tight, shadowed through the taxicab window. I'd felt him staring at me, and I'd turned. And I'd been stricken with guilt as he'd held my eye, even though Holden and I had been over for months. It all came back to me in an electric pop.

"Holden might be your runner-up, but what really gets me is that you've always been his first choice." Drew reached for me so quick I didn't expect the grip of his fingers around my wrist. "So if you had any heart about this, you'd do the right thing and go home."

"Hey, come on. Enough." I shook off his damp hand. There was an acrid taste in the back of my throat. The sound of my boots, the view of the skyline—I was in it again, that beautiful day. . . .

But Drew wasn't done. His face was a sneer, and I'd never disliked him so much as in this moment. "Just one more thing." He paused for effect. "Do you ever think about her?"

"Who?"

"Cassandra. The girl who's losing her chance with Holden because you've decided to keep him on your back burner. He likes her. A brother knows these things. And I know you're sabotaging it for both of them."

"I'm not! I haven't done anything like that."

"You are—you know you are—by being too weak to cut ties."

It was beyond hurtful. But was it true? "I probably should thank you for being so blunt," I said, recovering my speech a little as I stood up to go, "but let's just agree that you don't need that particular compliment."

Leaving the room, I nearly collided with Holden in the doorway.

"Hey—what's wrong?" When I didn't answer, Holden put down the water bottles and followed me as I skimmed up the stairs. "Seriously? You're going? It's Drew, isn't it? What did he say? Some cheap-ass shot, right? But you can't go because of him, he's always—"

"No, no, this time he's right—and it's not his fault." I spoke over my shoulder; I couldn't stop moving, but at the front door Holden sidestepped in front of me, blocking my way. "Please stay. Please, Ember." He moved closer, taking up my hand. "This is bigger than Drew. I really want to give us another shot. Last week, maybe we pushed things too quick. And I'm not trying to rush or force anything with us, really. I want us to come back together naturally. I'm betting hard that we can."

Drew, Rachel, my parents, Holden himself—everyone thought we had a chance, because I hadn't been strong enough to make a decision. Drew was right. This wasn't fair to Holden. I had to take responsibility.

"Holden, you know that you're one of my very favorite people who has ever come into my life." It was getting harder to breathe, my words felt so clumsy and misshapen to this moment. "But honestly? I think that the best that you and I can be is friends. That's how we make the most sense. That's who we should be for each other."

"Wait—are you for real, Ember?" Though he released my hand. "I know how much of a strain you've been under, trying to get back on track . . . but I guess I thought I was one of the beneficial side effects."

"You are; of course you are."

"So what is it? What's wrong?"

"It's not that anything's wrong. But it just can't go back to the way it was."

"I'm not that stupid. I don't want it the way it was." But Holden knew what I was delivering. He leaned into the support of the doorframe, his voice softening. "It's only . . . after everything we've been through, I feel like we could be stronger."

Why was this so hard? Because I wasn't making the right choice? Was there any way to be one hundred percent sure? "After everything we've been through," I said, "I think we'll just become ourselves again." I took a breath. "I'm so sorry, Holden. And I'm really sorry that it took your brother, of all people, to realize how much I was hurting you."

The moment struck me as nearly unbearable. I was ready to run—my usual solution. But Holden knew that. He caught me, his arms folding me into a hug as true and loving as anything I'd ever known.

And so I let myself drop into it, and it seemed that our whole world together was held within it, along with the knowledge that just because things have to end doesn't mean that they didn't matter, because they will always matter, and whatever we'd been to each other would build the next phase of what we were supposed to become, apart.

It was all there, and it was nearly impossible to let go, but I did.

30

Sooner than Later

Late that night, sleepless in bed, I craved my clicker again. I hadn't thought about it in so long, but my morphine clicker had been a critical part of those early couple of weeks, when pain had been deep and sudden as a flashing knife, or throbbing like a constant scream trapped in my body.

"The patient usually best understands her own pain management," one of the faceless nurses had told me, wrapping my fingers around the metal instrument that was no bigger than a piece of chalk, the communicator between my vein and my IV drip. "Each time you press the button, this activator releases the morphine. Try not to do it unless you feel it's absolutely necessary. You don't want to get dependent on the drug." She patted my shoulder. "And I bet you'd rather get outta here sooner than later, am I right?"

Right. My throat had been too dry and sore to answer.

Click-click-click. The morphine was colorless but swam heavy in my bloodstream. I imagined I could hear a scold in every click. *Click-click-click* meant that I wasn't strong enough to handle the pain. *Click-click-click* masked the reality of what had happened to me, to us.

Of course I wanted to get out of there sooner than later. But I also needed relief from the agony of the moment I was living through.

The thing was, I'd been pretty disciplined at weaning off the morphine. Because I did want to heal. I did want to go home. After that first week of *click-click-click*, I'd allowed my thumb to rest on the round-button surface of the clicker. But I'd hold off pressing it.

Hold hold hold and then sometimes *click*. Rarely *click*. No *click*.

My brain had been a clicker of sorts, too. It had flooded me with sleep and daydreams, it had activated scenarios that forbid reality. Sure, I'd circled it. I hovered over the surface of it. I knew I needed to make contact with it. But if I was actually ready to handle my truth in full, if I really was strong enough to find myself, then I had to return to Bowditch Bridge.

By daybreak, I'd decided it.

I put the plan into motion using one of the recipes I'd learned at El Cielo. It was an apple crumble, a dessert item at the restaurant, but I prepared it with less brown sugar and half a cup of oatmeal. I thought I might be able to trick it out as a breakfast food.

"Morning, Mom."

"Oh. You're up early." She gave me a quick look—my presence had startled her—then she recovered with a smile as she poured a cup of coffee from the pot I'd just brewed. No flies on Mom. She knew I was up to something.

"Just thought I'd make you some breakfast." And when I opened the oven, I was instantly gratified by the bubbling apple, oats, butter, brown sugar, and hint of clove.

"Mmm, smells good." I could tell Mom was surprised. She was ready to call a truce, especially over baked apples.

"Here, I'll fix you a bowl. Oh, hey, also—if it's okay by you, I'm going to take the car into Midtown tonight to sit in on Lissa's *Nutcracker* rehearsal."

"The car," she repeated dubiously.

"And it's really easy to get parking up there," I continued as I ladled out a serving. "Morning, Dad. Right on time. Here, sit down, both of you. Enjoy."

Dad was sniffing the air like a bear that had woken from hibernation. I dished up a generous serving for him and set the bowl next to Mom's. It had been a while since I'd last put on my chef's hat—and after the other night, I had a hunch that both of my parents were searching for any way to find the middle ground with me.

"What if we give you taxi money?" Mom bargained. "I thought you and I had a deal, that we were going to practice driving together."

"Mom, I know how to drive. I have my license. And I'd much rather work on my driving while I'm feeling good about it." I turned on the spigot, focusing on my sponge and suds as I cleaned out the mixing bowl. Letting them work out their private eye and hand signals.

"You know where the keys are," said Dad after a pause. "Especially if there's seconds on this crumble for me."

Relief. "Thanks."

"Please, please be careful." Mom was not fighting the decision, but she wasn't enjoying it. "This is so yummy, Ember. It reminds me of something . . . something you might have made . . . before."

Might have made before the accident. It was hard to keep my smile to myself. "Thanks, Mom."

The school day felt eternal. The words *Bowditch Bridge* seemed to either fog up or slice through every moment. After classes and physical therapy, I took my homework to Tazza, a sandwich shop where I had a cup of coffee. Would coffee forever make me think of Kai? Probably.

Dance practice had always been finished by six. On the night of February 14th, I'd started the trip upstate sometime after seven.

And if I'd been picking up Anthony Travolo, then where from?

I refused the clicker. I closed my eyes.

From Pratt, of course. You'd take the subway, and then you'd walk over the bridge together. It was a way to catch his little bit of free time.

Not too much dissection all at once. I could feel my body shut down like a power plant. *Click-click-click.* My sweat cooled.

One more coffee, one more check on my watch, and maybe I was ready. All along, I'd been leading myself to this night, listing toward it as a final phase, that last known place.

Because it was waiting for me. It had been waiting all along.

Weregirl had been playing that night. I'd hinted about the concert we'd be seeing next month. I was never good at surprises, and this gift had thrilled me. The two ticket printouts were still in my desk drawer; I'd found them under a bunch of papers just last week.

Tonight, the car seemed overly large and powerful to be handled by a single person. I drove slowly, listening to the GPS even though I knew the way. Exiting off the George Washington to US 9, briefly onto the Palisades. There weren't many cars on the road as I pulled onto the roundabout leading to Mountain Road. Another ten minutes, and it was truly desolate up here. Being a city girl, a city driver perpetually sharing the streets and claiming my space, I was struck by how so many roads upstate were lonely and unlit.

Tonight, my vision was illuminated by three-quarters of a moon in a cold black sky. It would have to be enough. I hunched over the steering wheel. Turned up the volume on one of my favorite songs—"Half-Life," the title track.

That night, I'd hit the bridge at a quarter past seven—the emergency call had come in at 7:21. There'd been a snowstorm that afternoon, three inches in the city by four o'clock, followed by sleet. Ice on the bridge had made it a slippery hazard. I'd known that.

If I'd been older, more cautious, more experienced, would I have crossed the bridge safely? Would I have been able to hold on to us?

A businessman named Jim Lyford, in the car behind us, had been on the way back to his house in Fishkill after a dinner in the city. He'd been in the coast guard, a detail that probably made all the difference in the outcome of that night. He'd just turned onto the bridge when we went over, and his series of reactions to what he'd witnessed had been instant and flawless.

He'd moved with the precision of a specialized task-force member, calling it in as he pulled off to the side of the road, then bracing for the dark water, plunging through and diving deep. Wrenching open the car door once the pressure equalized, and then using his CPR training when he'd got me above water . . . Later, he told me that the best way to save a life was never to doubt that you could.

Jim and his wife, Diane, had visited me in the hospital a couple of times in those first weeks. I barely remembered them outside the haze of kind voices and hovering faces. When I could, I'd written him, and he'd written back, and there had been a couple of back-and-forths since—it was one of those highly bizarre relationships crafted from a completely unprecedented situation.

But I'd been lucky. Everyone wants to think they could do what Jim Lyford did that night. There'd have been no way to save us both. But the accident haunted him, too. How could it not?

My brain was spinning with it. My hands were fixed and rigid on the wheel as the bridge came into sight. My adrenaline was burning off as I stopped at the dip; the reach wasn't more than ten yards, but panic had taken over and made a wall—I couldn't get past it to propel the car forward. I turned into the curve, off-road, edging closer to the bank. My body seemed to find my brain's messages on a delay—stop, brake, cut the engine, unfasten my seat belt.

Exposure therapy, Lissa had said.

Yes, I was in shock. Rolling in it, powerless to it. My entire body was shaking as I forced myself to get out of the car and walk to the bank on rubber legs. The water was partitioned off with rope and multiple nailed warning signs, the letters in Day-Glo yellow—even if you couldn't read, you'd know not to take another step.

If I made it out along the lip all the way to the drop, I probably could get myself onto the other side.

My jacket was too light for the weather; I was goose-pimpled under my clothes, and mud oozed and squelched beneath my boots. When I'd reached the drop-off point, I pushed down the rough rope and hauled myself, one leg and then the other, over into what felt like a fresh darkness. Water slapped at my boots as I walked the bank. Everything was so much closer to me now.

No clicks.

I caught the final hours and wound back through them.

We'd been planning Valentine's Day for a couple of weeks. It was so hard to find time together, with all of his school and work commitments. But somehow, we'd been delivered this pocket of freedom. And I knew that Aunt Gail would be cool about me showing up with a guest—because Aunt Gail was cool about everything. But I didn't want to tell her too much in advance, just in case she slipped it to Mom and Dad. Who were typically less mellow about these things.

But there was nothing to let me think that everything wouldn't work out. Earlier that day, I'd packed, driven into the city, found meter parking, and stayed in the car, waiting for Anthony to finish class. I'd brought homework, knowing that he'd bring work, too. Even this weekend, he'd find ways to cram in some extra studying. But he'd also wanted to make it special, too. For us. Valentine's Day was the six-week anniversary of when we'd met for the very first time, on New Year's Eve, out on the fire escape of Areacode.

When I looked up, in the gathering twilight, I could see him perfectly, and I watched him walk in that way that was also a bit of a saunter, as he swung out of the front door and saw me, then crossed the middle of the street. Anthony would never *not* cross a busy street. He lived in the city as if it were his alone. It's what gave him the nerve to tag, even if his street art had made him a target for the cops, whom he dodged the way Road Runner consistently beat Coyote. With a wink, though, as if it were all a game.

That evening, I watched him with a full and beating heart. His messy, just-out-of-the-shower hair. The raindrops making a pattern on his shabby olive jacket that he wore open, always, whatever the weather. I could see that beneath it he was wearing a favorite T-shirt he and Hatch had silk-screened together last year for Day of the Dead. I'd never been big on clothes with skulls and crossbones. Those grinning dancing skeletons on Anthony's chest had unnerved me.

Had I felt it even then, a chill of foreboding? But I'd said nothing, as he'd swung into the passenger seat, and then leaned over and kissed me. Anthony's kiss, so unlike anything else I'd ever known.

As if my lips had no other purpose but to meet his.

We stopped for gas, for coffee. The rain had strengthened as we hit the usual Friday traffic. We hadn't reached the Henry Hudson Parkway before Aunt Gail's text had chimed: Sushi or pizza? Or pizza with sushi?

Anthony had read me the text. "What should I write back?" His fingertip hovered. "Dinner with a plus one?"

"No, no. Not yet. I don't want to throw her off. You'll need to charm her with your real-live awesome."

"Easy."

We'd laughed. We were laughing at everything, that evening. Hours rolling out like a red carpet in front of us. That weekend, for once, we had all the time in the world. Anticipation had made us bold. At the next red light, I'd leaned over and kissed him full on the mouth until the light changed and the cars behind us started to honk, and we laughed at that, too.

Why was I walking so far out? I was freezing, it was impossible to see out here. I was so far from my car. And yet I plunged on in a blind stumble farther and farther into nothing—and what was I looking for? The air sharpened my breath. I shouldn't have come, my lungs weren't strong, my corpse-stiff bones were wrapped in a wet cardboard of useless muscles, but still I plowed ahead—listening to the sound of wet sand sucking beneath my boots—and when I saw it, I wondered if I'd been guided here all along.

The moon was shining just enough to direct me to the dull flash of silver, and it might have been anything—but I knew it was only one object, empty and buoyant because we'd finished the coffee, with a plan to stop somewhere for a refill once we'd made it outside the city.

"*You live on coffee.*"

"*Coffee and you.*"

270

Flung from the car to wash up on the bank and lodge here, caught in the long sea grasses all these months, the water lapping at it, anchoring it, a message in a bottle, a message that was mine alone.

When I pulled it from the mud, I used my sweater to rub at it until I could see the initials R.G.O. Though I knew, of course—but only then did I let my knees buckle, because I no longer worked; some deep, animal part of my brain wasn't allowing me to operate myself, to find the strength to get control, to get myself back to the safety of the car, to drive away from all this. For a while I stayed slumped and heavy in the grass, until my hands reached into my jacket pocket, fumbling for my phone. It was too dark to see—I punched the numbers mostly blind.

The oldest number that I knew. My breath rasped thin and shallow.

One, two, three rings.

Please, please, please answer.

And when I finally heard a voice on the other end, I couldn't even find the words to speak.

31

Real Time

Rachel's house was modern, dark, and sterile—a contrast to the people who lived there. I couldn't even remember the last time I'd been in the Smarts' living room, with its lacquered black furniture and either dove-gray or dove-white fabric tones. Not the most comfortable place to straggle inside, shivering and sniffling and dribbling water.

Not that the Smarts minded. They moved around me like a herd of giraffes, long and quiet, soulful and dark-eyed. Rachel gathered pillows as her mother brought me random offerings from their nearly empty fridge—takeout Chinese sticky rice, some gingersnaps—and her dad attended to the remote control, finally settling on classical guitar.

Rachel had grabbed me a pile of blankets from the closet, and I was bundled up in most of them. She'd also taken a blanket for herself, and now she sat opposite me in a wingback armchair with her legs drawn up, staring at me like when she'd played the caterpillar in *Alice in Wonderland*, back in fifth grade and atop a papier-mâché mushroom.

"So you know," she said quietly. "I want the real story of why you were out there. Just as soon as the 'rents vamoose."

In answer, I burrowed tighter in my blankets. Was I really ready to tell? The shower I'd taken on my arrival had made me sleepy. I'd already called to tell my parents I'd be staying over at Rachel's tonight. Now I just wanted to sleep.

Rachel's house smelled like pine. It had already been decorated for both Christmas and Hanukkah, even though Thanksgiving wasn't for another week—but her mom must have had some free time in her breakneck career. And when Julia Smart had time, things got done.

"Ember, honey," she said now, "Rachel's dad and I are going up, but I've got the spare room ready for whenever you want to head off to bed." She stood over me, long and knobby-boned as Rachel, only with silver streaks through her hair and bifocals perched on the edge of her nose. "You look like you could use a good night's rest."

"Yes," I agreed. "In a few minutes."

Rachel planted another gingersnap in her mouth. "Mom, I will totally take care of Emb, but right now we want privacy, hint hint."

"All right, all right," her mom said as she handed Rachel a napkin. "And I'm not lecturing, Ember, but I do think you should report to your doctor about this episode." She lifted her palms. "Just one ole mom's opinion."

"I will," I promised.

She nodded and left, closing the door purposefully behind her. Rachel exhaled long, as if her mother's very presence had been keeping her breath locked in her body. She refurled her bean-sprout limbs into the armchair. "All's clear."

My eyes filled with tears. They'd been hiding so long, and I was so ready to let them spill. "I went back to Bowditch Bridge."

"That I know. That Mom and Dad and I witnessed when we came to get you, when we found you there shaking and soaking wet like a rescue dog. The question is—why the hell?"

I didn't want to say it. Out loud meant forever. I wanted the clicker.

Don't click. No more clicks.

"Ember, what's going on in there? I'm so shut out from what-ever you're thinking! Bottom line! So just tell me, please. Tell me."

Once I told her, I wouldn't be able to get him back. He would be gone. I knew that without doubt. But of course he already was gone. I pushed the truth past my last barricade of resistance. "I knew him. Anthony Travolo. I knew him, and I loved him, and he died, and I made him up again inside my head so that I could get back to him."

"Okay. Now say that in English." Rachel's eyes were owlish on me. "Here's where I make a lame dishrag joke, and I can't. I think I understand what you're saying . . . but how did you do it? And why?"

"Maybe so that I could let go of him on my terms. I could only give him up a little bit at a time. It was easy to believe in it. It was like my brain found a way to loop back. And he was a graffiti tag artist, so he'd marked everywhere we'd ever been together—from the Central Park subway stop to the Cobble Hill Cinema. I'd saved things, too. A matchbook that I found in my coat. A sketch Anthony'd made me that I kept in my jewelry box. And there was a voice mail message from the night before our first date to Coney Island, where I could tell that he was serious about me, that he was going to figure it out, find ways for us to be together, even though there were about a million other things going on in his life. I'd archived the message—so sometimes I'd play it as if it were about to happen all over again. And do you remember the time I left you that voice mail, when I called the cab on Halloween?"

"You said you'd met someone, that night. So . . ." Rachel frowned. "Was there even anybody else in that cab?"

"No, not on Halloween. But on New Year's Eve, yes. Anthony and I had left Areacode together." *Waffles, waffles,* I'd giggled into Lissa's voice mail on New Year's Eve. The joke being that I'd found something surprising and better. I'd found Anthony.

"You were living out memories like they were happening in real time," said Rachel. "It seems like a horrible thing to do to yourself. Because wasn't it like losing him all over again?"

"I don't know. It was always so amazing to be in it, to immerse myself in it. And that New Year's Eve—it's indelible, it stands out from everything. He followed me out onto the fire escape. He kissed me at midnight, right as the fireworks went off."

Rachel was using the long fingers of one hand to crack the

knuckles of the other. Her mood had clouded over. "Look, Embie, I've got to say this—I knew you were seeing somebody, before the accident. I knew there was a guy, someone important, someone time-consuming—and I should have told you. Especially after, I had to wonder if Anthony and you had been close. But you never mentioned him, so I couldn't shake you up like that. I wanted to protect you, to keep you moving forward. Not stuck in some tortured nightmare."

"So you *did* know Anthony?" I struggled to sit up higher.

"No! I never met him, ever. But sometimes you'd ask me to cover for you, like when your Mom called. I knew somebody was taking up all of your time. The thing was, after the accident, you had so much to deal with when you came home. And this guy, Anthony, he hadn't been part of anything—of your old life, with me, or with Holden, or anybody. He was your secret door prize, and you weren't sharing. So I made a deal with myself. I'd bring it up if you brought it up." Rachel looked miserable. "And now you've brought it up. Going back to the bridge—it shook some-thing loose, didn't it?"

I nodded. "I remember it now."

"Even our fight?"

"Even our fight." It was coming back to me. A horrible drag-out right upstairs in Rachel's room that had left both of us in tears and pitched in a grudge match.

"And I said stupid things, of course. I was mad that you'd retreated from me. So I said things like, 'I hope your taste in guys isn't as crappy as that jacket.' Jokes that Claude remembers and holds me to, of course. I meant to be hurtful. I blamed the new guy for stealing you from Holden. I blamed your new art-house and club crowd. And then, three days after that fight, you almost died." Rachel put her hands over her face. "And all I could think was I'd never been able to tell you I was sorry."

"Rachel, stop. Really. It was such a long time ago. I'm sure I was awful, too. I wish I could remember precisely all the stupid petty things I said, so that I could apologize for them."

But she wasn't listening to me. She was shaking her head, lost in her recollection. "You can't believe how bad I felt, standing by your hospital bed, you looking like that, your eyes all pulpy and bruised—you were so far away from us all. I was watching those drugs pumping into your veins, and I just kept praying please, please, please God let her be okay. Let her wake up so that she can forgive me."

"You were there for me that night, and at Addington, and you're here for me tonight," I reminded her. "I called you knowing you'd show up."

"Ember, I'm so sorry I never got a chance to meet him!" she blurted.

"Oh." That startled me. I nodded. "Me too."

"But now I want you to tell me everything," Rachel continued, her eyes starry with emotion. "I'm not kidding. Tell me all about how it felt when you first saw Anthony. Start with that night. I want to hear every single detail, Ember." She tucked the blanket so that it covered my feet, making sure I was comfortable, and in my gratitude, I could feel the burden of everything that had been unspoken between us start to dissolve, as Rachel sat rapt, waiting.

She was here for me now, and I wanted to tell her all of it. I could feel the whole entire story contained within me, pressing for release, ready to become real in my voice and in her listening.

"Technically, it was his brother, Hatch, who I met first," I began. "He'd gotten a job to hand out flyers that Anthony had designed, for this New Year's Eve party at a new club in Bushwick. I was walking down the street—I'd just bought my boots, and I was feeling really good. I felt like anything could happen."

"And then," said Rachel with a little smile, "something did."

32

I Think I Know a Place

I stopped by El Cielo right after school. It wasn't open for dinner yet, but Hatch was already there and working on setup, as I knew he would be, rolling silverware and refilling the containers of ketchup, hot sauce, and red-pepper flakes.

"You want coffee?"

"Sure."

He had to brew it first. I sat at the front bar and watched him shake out a filter and scoop six cups of grounds into the industrial-strength coffeemaker, one of those machines sturdy enough to withstand a hundred novice waiters and waitresses. Hatch had

had a growth spurt this year, and he looked so much like his big brother that it was hard to take my eyes away. Isabella would be coming in soon, and so would the prep cooks and waitstaff. We had about half an hour in private.

Once the coffee had brewed, Hatch poured my mug. One sugar and a splash of whole milk. He'd absorbed that detail about me, just as he'd learned anything else about me that could be discerned through the power of observation. Hatch was a sensitive kid that way; there was a special wattage in him that burned like a flashlight, trained on others.

We'd met back when I'd first come into the restaurant, early last January. I wasn't supposed to be there, obviously. And Anthony had warned me not to act like Hatch and I knew each other too well.

"My aunt will already be suspicious of you," Anthony had told me. "And my little brother has a crush on you. So consider yourself double-warned."

"Oh, save it," I'd answered. "Families love me."

After the party at Areacode, I'd tracked Anthony down. I'd had his matchbook, with an address that I was sure would lead me in the right direction. It's why he had given it to me, before he'd followed me out onto the fire escape. So even when he hadn't called me, I'd known how to reach him. He'd admitted it, later. That although he'd taken my number, he'd left it up to me to make the first move.

I'd come in and sat in the back bar. I'd watched for Anthony's signal, and then we'd sneaked downstairs to the cold-storage room where we could talk without interruption.

But I'd met Hatch that night, too. To love Anthony was to create space for his baby brother. We hung out first on New Year's

Eve, at the St. George dormitory, with the reverberation of Area-code's DJ beat matches and mash-ups still thudding in my ears, we'd watched Bela Lugosi movies with Hatch until 4 a.m., when Anthony had walked me home.

Another time was a few weeks later, in freezing Cobble Hill Park, where the whole gang, led by Alice de Souza, had painted that amazing mural. Hatch and I'd watched from the bench, as Alice, Maisie, Anthony (though he was "Kai" that night; he was always Kai on guerrilla-art nights), his friend Antz, and a few others had created a summer forest of trees.

We'd clapped and hooted as he'd tagged the bottom—that *K* for *Kai* that was also a sideways *A* for *Anthony*.

"I'm getting addicted to coffee," I admitted to Hatch now. "Funny thing was I never used to drink it before." I'd slipped the flask from my backpack and set it on the bar. He saw it, and I knew it was too much to acknowledge it. He took it in silence, quickly, without looking at me, and he disappeared downstairs—to lock it in his employee locker, I bet. When he returned, some minutes later, his eyes were red. I knew better than to explain how I'd found it. It was his now, that was what mattered.

He slid onto the barstool next to me, a boy who was beginning to act in so many ways like a man. "Sometimes I stay in his dorm room," he confessed, almost tonelessly, staring ahead. "I've got the key card. It's still activated."

"Even after a year?"

Hatch nodded. "They kept it empty. I'm sure that'll change come spring."

My heart quickened. Anthony's room had been a study in intensity, a still-life whirlwind of mess and inspiration. If only I could go there. Just to sit on the edge of his bed, to pore through his papers, his books, his prints, the vellum and watercolor and charcoal sketches rolled up on shelves and stacked in orange crates.

"I want to see it, Hatch. Just for a night. If you'll let me, please. I want to see his room again."

Hatch seemed unsurprised at this request. He reached into his back pocket for his wallet and pulled from it a plastic card with a magnetized stripe on one side.

I slipped it into my jacket. "Thank you."

"The journal's in the top drawer of his desk. You know what it looks like." Hatch shrugged. "It's yours, anyway. I read it once—but it wasn't for me. Everything that's in that notebook is about you."

I nodded. Yes, I wanted that journal. The journal that Anthony had cracked open and started writing the night we met. He'd never let me see, not once. But I knew that this evening I'd go to his room, and I'd spend the night reading everything in that notebook once, twice, three times over.

And when I became too sleepy to read, I'd curl up on the empty bed, and I'd tuck his notebook under my cheek, and I'd fall asleep with all of his outsized, kind, funny, strange, wild thoughts burning up my brain. In my dreamworld, I would feel him take me in his arms again and unwrap me, his body heavy on mine, his hands cupping my face, kissing me just as he had that last weekend, the weekend I'd stayed with him in the dorm before Valentine's Day.

"It's so noisy tonight."

"Dorm life." His breath in my ear had sent warmth from my neck down my spine. *"How it always is. Thursday means the start of the weekend. I got used to it this semester. But it's making you uncom-*

fortable, so let's just go to sleep." He made a curve of his body that mine fit perfectly inside.

He was right. It was hard to feel intimate when it sounded like a house party in every other room.

And then, my idea. "*Listen, I think I know a place we can go next weekend. Upstate.*"

"*I don't care what we do. Long as I'm around you.*" Pushing his nose into the hollow of my neck. Whispering. "*Ever since I met you, I've been nonstop. Ideas for one painting, then for another—it's totally crazy.*"

"*Ha. Does that make me your muse?*"

In the darkness, I sensed his mind circling the thought in earnest, though he didn't answer. "*Talk to me more about this getaway.*" His arm closing me in.

"*My dad's sister, my aunt Gail. She lives up in Mount Kisco. I know she'd like to meet you. If you can get the time off, I'll drive us.*"

"*She'd be cool with that? With . . . us?*"

"*No doubt. She'll love you.*"

"*How do you know?*"

"*Because I love you.*"

That night, everything had seemed so perfectly, effortlessly possible.

"*Next weekend, then.*"

"*Only thing is it's supposed to snow maybe.*"

"*What's a little snow? Makes it more romantic, right?*"

And I would feel his body again, heavy over mine. I would feel him slip away from me into sleep. And then I would close my eyes, willing myself into my unconsciousness, to disappear first before he disappeared again.

Epilogue

I see it as soon as I enter the gallery. It's hanging at the opposite end of the room. Which means that when they moved it out of that apartment, they noticed the K sprayed bold and directly onto the dining room wallpaper. That must have shocked them. It makes me smile.

Familiar and yet foreign; at first I'm afraid to approach. It has been almost three years since Anthony painted it. I can fit into the shape of that girl, but I know that I am changed. He only knew me as a girl who turned to face in a new direction. But now I am the girl who actually left.

It's crowded. Hatch is here, and Lucia's uncle Carlos, who is the curator of the show, and Lucia herself, who ended up staying in the States, where she's attending Hunter College. And Maisie—and others, so many others. It's a bump and jostle. I'm only off work and home for a few of these end-of-summer days, and still I feel a bit jet-lagged. Also maybe a little self-conscious in my California casual, my jeans faded and my T-shirt simple and loose. No sleek fashion getup for me.

"Those jeans! You hold on to clothing the way other people keep pets," Rachel joked when she came over last night with some of the old gang, including Sadie and Perrin and Holden—with Cass—for my tasting-menu Folly. It was an ambitious medley of everything I'd learned this past semester in culinary school, with a few dishes straight out of The Reef, the restaurant in Long Beach where I've been working all summer.

I knew I'd feel off-kilter, mixing in with this sleek arty world. But I never would have missed this night.

"Hey, you!" Alice raises her hand from across the room. Alice de Souza is why the gallery space is packed, although the show itself is stand-alone provocative—Lucia's uncle has an eye for art that goes beyond just-another-rich-dude-collector. There's a lot to look at on the walls. But Alice is the main draw. She's become even more famous in these years since I first met her, when she was just a wild-card member of Kai's street-artist pack, another bandit with a spray can and a chin-set view of her big place in the world.

Alice is legit; she's graduated past It-girl into purposeful, complex work. I read all about her in a glossy magazine piece in a San Bernardino hair salon while I was getting a trim; her likes and dislikes and her goals and what she ate for lunch. She'd seemed as far away as Mars.

But Alice is worthy of her hype. She's eye-catchingly cool,

too, as she strides toward me, knowing that every eye is on her—some trying not to stare, others completely unapologetic. "I'm so glad you could make it." And then she cuffs the side of my ear with a kiss. It is a kiss-kiss sort of night, and we're all playing our parts.

"Me too."

"Ready?"

"Yep."

"Good, then come on. Come see it, Ember." Her hand, an artist's hand, is large and brown and fine-boned. My hand, a chef's apprentice hand, is nicked and burned and well protected in hers.

We are immediately sidetracked, of course. By Lucia's uncle Carlos, who greets me with the manic energy befitting the host of a highly successful party. This is officially a hot venue; it will be written up, photos are being snapped, paintings will be sold.

But not that painting. Never that painting that has given Anthony Travolo this moment of fame—the online posts, the tribute pages. Carlos himself promised in his email message, inviting me to the event, that the painting never would be sold. Its worth, he said, was personally incalculable "as a memory of that fine young man."

I know that part of my presence here is sensationalism. I'm the crucial bit of the story that is whispered—*she must feel so awful, so guilty, he would have been a big star, maybe.* My role in the tragedy is still, in moments, almost too crushing to bear. Too much story. And it makes me glad that I don't live here anymore, and likely never will again.

Alice is navigating me through rubberneckers and well-wishers and bloggers, gallerinas and critics, collectors and scenesters. She's done this a hundred times before. But ever since I contacted her about Anthony's painting—along with the taped photo he'd printed from our day in Coney Island, plus the sketches he'd left in his notebook—she has become proprietorial of his art, of me, of our meaning. I'm grateful.

Anthony's art is raw, mostly potential. Even my untrained eye sees that. He's trying to find me in those freezing January dunes. But my shyness of his prying camera phone, my desire to be beautiful for him, my heady joy in our brand-new romance—he found all of it.

I stare at the painting and I find that girl, and I see all the things that lit me up. The palette of thick dream-dappled colors, my cold bright cheeks, the peek through my fingers—shy, but I couldn't resist seeing and being seen by him.

"It's about love," murmurs Alice at my shoulder.

"Yes," I agree. I can taste again the salt in the wind. I can feel my fingers splayed against my face. The oily chop of the brush, my half-closed eyes.

He has captured our light exactly, that stark and glowing afternoon. I never wanted it to end. On oil and canvas, forever, *Ember was here*. Even if cell by cell and day by day, I am aging past that moment when Anthony laid bare everything he knew about me.

In this painting, he has found our eternity.

Lucia, who has approached noiselessly to stand at my side, breaks my trance. "Uncle Carlos is taking the piece to Italy next week," she says. "It will be part of a group show in Florence, and then another in Rome."

"Oh. That's cool." Anthony, who had not even owned a passport, who would have wanted almost more than anything to be at home in the world. How he would have loved that.

They leave me with the portrait, and I am alone with it until I feel him.

I turn, shading my vision. The sun is behind him so that he is all shadow, a crisp cutout of darkness backlit by the window. I hear his voice in my ear again, that night in the Tribeca apartment, when he brought me to the dining room and showed me his painting of me for the first time—*"Look. Look at you. You're my best work, the best that's in me."*

I never saw him again after the night I went back to the bridge. I never wanted to. I'd found some peace in my grief, and in many ways I've traveled far from that hour. To build a new life, to become another Ember; I'd had to.

He raises his hand.

Tentatively, I raise mine. As I watch him, I let his image burn through me, and then I close my eyes and let the impression, as if on the slow beat of a hawk's wing, take flight.

"Ember." Hatch has bounded over. He is taller than I, finally, and filled out—there is substance to him. A junior this year; next year he will be the same age as I was when I met Anthony. And then a year older. And so it goes.

"What's up?" I don't need to look to know that Anthony is gone.

I give Hatch my full attention.

He smiles his brother's smile. "A few of us are heading out for dinner at this Moroccan joint in Bensonhurst. Supposed to be great. If you want to join up?"

"Fez."

"Yeah. That's it. How'd you know?" He looks surprised. "You ever been?"

"No," I say. "Not yet."

Acknowledgments

I would like to thank everyone who has encouraged and assisted me with this book. Special thanks to my first readers—Mackenzie Brady, Meredith Kaffel, Charlotte Sheedy, and Courtney Sheinmel—who believed so fiercely in the manuscript from its earliest days. I am always indebted to team Knopf/Random House: Stephen Brown, Lauren Donovan, Sarah Hokanson, Adrienne Waintraub, and particularly my editor, Nancy Hinkel, who brings such grace and insight to every moment of our process. A big thanks to my husband, Erich Mauff, for ever respecting my "room of one's own," even as we expanded our family and doubled our chaos this year. And finally, I am especially indebted to my brother Robert Watson for speaking with such candor about his own neurological trauma and recovery after the nearly fatal car accident of his youth. I never could have told Ember's story without knowing the reality of Robert's survival, as well as the strength it took for him to get there.

ADELE GRIFFIN is the author of *Tighter* and *All You Never Wanted*. She lives with her family in Brooklyn, New York. Find her on the Web at adelegriffin.com.